HURT ME SWEETLY

A DARK ALLIANCE NOVEL

KIRA JAMES

THE DARK ALLIANCE SERIES

Crave Me Roughly (prequel novella)
Embrace Me Darkly
Torture Me Gently
Tempt Me Deadly
Crush Me Tenderly (prequel)
Hold Me Wickedly
Claim Me Sinfully
Hurt Me Sweetly

For exclusive content and updates,
visit www.kirajamesauthor.com to sign up for
Kira's Elite Reader Group!

COPYRIGHT

Hurt Me Sweetly © 2023 by Kira James

ISBN:
Digital - 978-1-953572-76-9
Print - 978-1-953572-77-6

Cover Design by T.M. Franklin
Images by depositphotos.com©vencav ©Funniefarm5 @connect
@photocosma @EBFoto

Published by Martini & Olive Books
V-2023-3-27P

HURT ME SWEETLY

A DARK ALLIANCE NOVEL

KIRA JAMES

For exclusive content and updates,
visit KiraJamesAuthor.com
to join the Elite Readers Group!

CHAPTER
ONE

"Your turn, Kevin!" Stu yelled, rubbing his fist, his knuckles red from having just pounded the shit out of Jordan Lowe's nose and jaw. "Go for the nose. Come on, Kev, nail the fucker!"

Kevin Whalton cringed; Stu's shouts were making him even more nervous than he already was. He glanced around the darkened alley, half-hoping there'd be someone else in the shadows behind the locked-up laundromat. *Nobody.*

"Fucking hell, Kevin. *Now.*"

He jumped, scared as a rabbit, but he did what his friend demanded. He tightened his fingers into a fist, lashed out, and watched as his knuckles smashed into their victim's nose.

No—not a victim. He had to remember that. Had to remember who was the dangerous one here. Because if everything Wes and Stu had told him was true, Jordan Lowe could never be a victim.

With a snap, Jordan's head slammed back, making a sick crunching sound as it impacted the brick wall. He howled—literally howled. A low, pained keening that bounced off the wall and filled the dark space around them.

Kevin glanced back at Stu, who was miming punching movements and shouting, "Hell, yeah! That's the way! Get in another—come on, man, show the freak what you've got."

Wes stood a couple of yards from Jordan, his mouth pulled into a tight smile. "You fucked with the wrong people, puppy dog. We know what you are, and we are so going to take you down." He swiveled his head to look at Kevin. "Another. Get in another."

Kevin hesitated, a little sick to his stomach. Less than an hour before, they'd all been having drinks at a bar a few blocks down. Everything had seemed perfectly normal then. Hell, Wes and Stu actually knew Jordan pretty well; they'd been hanging with him for weeks. But tonight they'd pulled Kevin aside to tell him that they didn't trust Jordan. That they were certain he was a mole. And that Kevin was going to want to see the shit that went down.

Then they'd put something in the guy's drink. And when Kevin had asked Stu why, Stu had just grinned and said that if they didn't dose his drink, Jordan would be able to rip all their fucking heads off.

At the time, Kevin had believed it, because why the hell would Stu lie about what Jordan was? About what he could do?

Now, though...

Well, now Jordan looked whipped. Like he couldn't beat up a six-year-old girl, much less three college sophomores.

"Goddammit, Kevin. Are you a fucking pussy or what? Hit the mongrel bastard! Hit him!"

"Do it!" Wes added, and their voices bolstered him. Made his muscles tighten and his pulse quicken. "Goddammit, do it now—do it and I swear to God the unholy fuckwad will show you that everything we've told you is true!"

That did it. Kevin lashed out, his right fist connecting hard with Jordan's temple even as his left jabbed into the kid's gut. Jordan went down, doubling over as he clutched at his stomach. Then he looked up, and Kevin stumbled backward.

Holy fuck—Jordan's eyes were yellow.

Yellow and wild and full of hate and anger.

Kevin shivered, not sure what he was seeing. Not sure what to believe. He'd gotten in with Wes and Stu and the rest of them because they'd told him what was out there —and that they needed his help to stop it. To stop *them*. But until tonight it had all been theory and conjecture and folks making speeches about what they knew and what they believed.

Until tonight Kevin had never actually seen one of them. Hell, he hadn't even been sure if he believed in monsters or if he just wanted to get on Wes and Stu's good side.

But he believed now. Fuck, yeah, he did.

"Don't fight it, pup," Wes said, giving Jordan a kick. "We wanna see. Don't we, Stu? Don't we, Kevin?"

"Shit, yeah," Stu said, bouncing like a boxer itching for a fight. He pulled out a knife, the blade glinting in the dim light from the alley's street lamps. "Scared, fucker? It's pure silver. That's gonna hurt." He lunged forward, the blade aimed at Jordan's stomach, but at the last second, Jordan thrust his arm up, moving fast considering how battered he was, and knocked the knife to the ground.

Quicker than Kevin could see, Jordan had Stu pinned on the ground. "Think you're clever?" he rasped, his body bent over Stu's. "How clever will you be when I rip your head off with my goddamned teeth?"

Jordan's skin started to ripple, and Kevin could see his bones shifting beneath his skin. A loud roaring filled Kevin's head, and his knees started to give out—fuckin' A, he was about to faint.

"Kev! Kevin!"

Wes's voice pulled him back, and he blinked, groggy.

"Get Stu's knife, man! Now!" As Wes spoke, he was lunging toward Jordan with his own knife out. Kevin couldn't move; he couldn't do anything but stare at the creature in front of him.

Holy shit. Holy fuck.

They'd told him what would happen, what the kid was. But telling and seeing were two different things. And seeing was fucking terrifying.

"Now, goddammit, or Stu's dead!"

Jordan was clutching Stu's head in his hand, and he slammed it against the asphalt with a sickening thud. The noise spurred Kevin to action, and he darted sideways for Stu's lost knife, then rushed forward, leading with the point of the blade. He felt the resistance as the tip hit Jordan's skin, then the give as it slid into the muscle, the full force of Kevin's weight pushing it right to the hilt, right to the bone.

On the other side of the creature, Wes was jabbing, too, his mouth moving, his words a mishmash of unintelligible curses with only a few words like *silver* and *fucking* and *werewolf* coming out clear.

Another roar echoed—only this one wasn't inside of Kevin's head. It was coming from Jordan, who'd reared back, arms flailing as he knocked aside their knives and climbed to his feet. Kevin braced himself, certain he would need to do battle with this, this *thing*. But then Jordan turned and loped off down the alley, leaving Stu curled up in a ball and moaning on the pavement.

"Catch him!" Wes cried, pulling out a gun and firing it

so close to Kevin's head that for a moment he thought he was deaf. He wasn't, though, and Wes's shouts pushed through the cotton that now seemed to fill his ears.

"Goddammit, I missed the fucker! Catch him! Run! Shit, we have to catch him. If he gets away, we're dead. We're totally fucking dead."

He was dead.

No other possible outcome. No other way for this to end.

He'd been stupid. Lazy and reckless, and somehow they'd found him out.

And now Jordan was dead, or he would be soon enough.

Except he couldn't die—not like this. Not without letting someone know how bad it was. How close they were. And how dangerous.

His legs pumped as he moved down the alley, the weakness unfamiliar after so many years of pure, glorious strength. He'd known about the dangers of silver, of course. What werewolf didn't? But he'd been arrogant and foolish enough to believe they'd never get him with it. To believe they'd never find out about him. That he'd be smart. That he'd be safe.

He'd been an idiot, and soon he'd be a dead one.

Not once in his wildest dreams had he imagined that they would lace his drink with colloidal silver. But they had, and he'd drunk it down, and it had ripped his advantage away from him right then and there, weakening his muscles and making his mind fuzzy and confused.

Once he figured out what they had done to him, he

managed to get away, pushing through the thick Friday night crowd to the kitchen, then out the back door through the alley. He'd run aimlessly in the dark, just wanting to put distance between him and his tormentors. He'd thought he'd lost them, had even leaned against a Dumpster to take a deep, self-satisfied breath.

And then they'd arrived with their taunts and their jeers and, most dangerous of all, their knives forged of silver.

He'd fought, but he'd been weak. Extraordinarily weak. That he'd managed to get away at all was a miracle. That they were following was a curse.

Right now he had only one thing to be thankful for—that Wes's silver bullet had only nicked his heart. If it had pierced it, he'd already be dead, and all his warnings would be lost.

They still might be if he didn't hurry. But he was weak. So damn weak.

He heard the footsteps pounding behind him and realized that he'd slowed his pace. *Go.* He had to get somewhere safe. Had to find a Shadower.

For three months, he'd been deep undercover, trying to find out what the humans were up to. About four weeks ago, he'd managed to wrangle an introduction to Wes, and that had gotten him closer, because the frat boy human was poised to go far within the organization.

Jordan had spent this last month watching and learning and trying to get closer. Close enough to gain trust, to learn what they were up to. The humans who wanted him—and all the Shadowers—dead and gone. If he couldn't tell someone, then all that time would be for nothing, and he couldn't let it be for nothing. Because then... because then...

His head was fuzzy, his thoughts crashing into each other. The silver.

Had to hurry. Had to move.

With concentration like he'd never known before, Jordan forced his heart to beat harder, his blood to surge stronger. Forced his legs to go.

Something fast whipped by him, brushing his sleeve, and when he realized that one of his tormentors had thrown a knife, a new burst of fear fueled his speed. He didn't know why they hadn't used the gun—wait, yes he did. There were people, and a gunshot would draw attention.

He peered around him and realized that although he was still racing down the alley that ran parallel to the street, there were people up ahead. They were mingling at the intersection of the alley and the sidewalk of a perpendicular street. The sound of laughter coupled with the scent of alcohol wafted toward him, and Jordan almost cried out in joy. Without even trying, he'd stumbled upon another bar, upon people. Dear God, he needed people.

To his left, a door burst open, a yawing metal mouth against a pockmarked face of brick. The stench of fried food and flowing alcohol wafted out. He'd found the back door to the bar where all the people were gathered.

His forehead creased in concentration as he tried to figure out what to do. Thinking was so hard, and his thoughts were all jumbled. Go in. Go in and get lost in the crowd. Yes. Yes, that was what he should do.

He shifted, then stumbled toward the door, pushing inside past a couple who were emerging, a tangle of arms and legs and lips. He sniffed—human. He pushed off the wave of disappointment. The odds that he'd randomly find a Shadower bar had been thin. But this would do. He just needed bodies. Just needed to hide.

Hallway. Dark. Flooded with the scent of sweat and lust. To his left and right were restrooms. Ahead, flashing lights and pounding music. He headed into the light, his hand steadying him against the wall. Other humans passed him, coming from the direction he was heading. Their eyes cut to him, then cut away, their faces twisted with fear and repulsion.

He was changing.

His own pain, his own fear—it was pushing the change even as the silver kept the wolf from fully bursting free. His bones were bulging, his face deforming. The humans would be no help to him—he could tell that much from the terror on their faces.

He needed to think, dammit, but his head was too full of cotton. Had to find a Shadower. Had to do it soon.

They were coming. Of that he was certain. They'd find him, and they'd kill him.

He'd always thought that despair would be a cold, frenetic thing, but now he knew that it was warm and languid. A quiet acceptance. A slow descent into the thick sludge of acquiescence.

Just before the hallway opened onto the main dance floor, another hall intersected, veering off to the left. He turned, ignoring the sign that said the area was for employees only. It was quieter here, and he realized he could think better now that he wasn't walking straight into those damned pulsing lights. Ahead, he heard voices. If he could get to them, just get to them, then maybe—

His knees buckled, and he grabbed at the wall for balance. But the walls were spinning, the silver in his blood working its way into his brain. He closed his eyes and sagged to the ground, hoping to stop the horrible, gut-wrenching rocking.

Bile rose in his throat, and he sucked in air through his nose, but the nausea kept building.

"Hey—hey, mister? You okay?"

Slowly, he peeled open his eyes and looked up at the three women staring down at him. No, not three. Just one, but she was blurry around the edges, coming in and out of focus. He sniffed. Another human.

"I'm—" He didn't finish the sentence. For that matter, he wasn't sure the words had even left his lips. But the girl had knelt down, her face full of concern. And when she did, he saw the mark on the wall behind her. An elaborate S painted in gold and bisected by a silver arrow.

They were here!

"I'm going to call nine-one-one," the girl said, pulling out a cell phone.

"No." He croaked out the word, then thrust out his hand to grab hers. "Don't."

Her eyes went wide, and he followed her gaze. The bones of his hand were elongating, pushing against his skin. And thick tufts of fur were sprouting.

"What are—?"

"Go," he snarled. "Get the hell out of here."

She didn't argue, just took a step back, then turned and ran down the hall, back toward the noise and the lights.

He threw himself against the wall, fingers scraping for the notch that had to be there. Please, please let it be there. He had to get in—had to get safe—before his human tormentors found him. Surely they were in the club now. Surely they were tracking him. Surely they'd meet the woman and she'd point, horrified, down the hallway. And then they'd come with their guns and their knives and they'd—

There.

His fingernails found the crevice between the wall panels. A subtle click, and then one of the panels swung open. He fell into the dark space, kicking the hidden doorway shut behind him.

But he could go no farther. He'd reached safety, and in doing so had sapped his meager supply of strength.

In front of him, a beautiful pale face loomed. Vampire. He could smell the blood along with the revulsion. There was no love between the weren and the vamps, but they would unite against their enemies. They had to, Jordan thought. Because if they didn't they would all surely die.

With effort, he opened his mouth, lips parting just enough to make a sound. He saw the vampire's eyes narrow, long lashes dark against ivory cheekbones.

Help.

He tried to force the word out, but it wouldn't come. How could it when there could be no help now?

"You shouldn't be here. This isn't a place for you."

He tried again to form words, but he was too far gone, his life slipping away. No. No, no, no.

Conjuring strength he didn't know he possessed, he struggled to force out three little words. Three words that he hoped would save them all.

"Get," he said, then sucked in a breath and tried again. "Get the percipient."

And then, with a gasp, Jordan Lowe laid back his head, and died.

TWO

A thin sheen of sweat covered him, and Ryan Doyle kicked the cotton sheet off. The ancient, window-mounted air conditioner belched out cool air, and he closed his eyes, letting the chill soothe his heated skin as much as his feverish thoughts. He'd come here—with this woman—with the intention of clearing his head. Of letting the case—and the images of the kidnapped human girls—disappear under the surface for an hour with the hope that the distance would bring clarity. Because right now he was at a goddamned dead end, and if he didn't figure something out—

No—back it down. Back it the fuck down.

That wretched, violent anger was rising inside him. The compulsion to lash out, to explode, to rail against the filthy vampire that had flaunted the darkness inside him by taking those girls.

That anger's pure. Just let go. Let it out. They're probably dead, so the fury is totally justified. Hell, it's human. Feel it— just fucking feel it.

He clenched his fists, fighting the temptation to give in. He wasn't going there. Justified or not, he couldn't let it explode. For centuries now, he'd managed to keep it under control. He had a temper—hell yes, he did. But snapping at a uniform who wasn't doing his job was a far cry from the blood-red fury that boiled inside of him, ready to explode the moment he relaxed. Each day Doyle battled it down, and each day's battle was a little bit easier than the last. That was progress, and he wasn't going to toss it away. If he did, he might never find his way back to the man he'd worked so damn hard to become.

Beside him, the woman shifted and rolled over. A moment later, her naked breasts pressed against his back, her lips on his shoulder. "Stay the night," she said. "You might as well. It's almost sunrise anyway." Her hand slid over his waist, fingers dancing down bare skin until she found his cock and stroked it slow and easy. "And I can think of a lot of ways to welcome the morning."

He closed his eyes, allowing himself a brief moment to enjoy the sensation. Then he sat up, the movement of his body forcing her hand away.

"What's wrong?"

"Nothing," he said. He stood, started looking around for his pants. He wouldn't stay. He never stayed.

"Nothing?" Her voice grated with annoyance. He heard the brush of skin against cloth as she shifted back on the bed. "Shit." The word was little more than a breath.

He closed his eyes for a moment, just long enough to gather himself. Then he turned to her, saw her body, warm and fresh on the sheets, and knew that no matter what else he might be, right then—as far as this woman was concerned—he was being an asshole.

"You knew what I was when you invited me home with you."

She laughed, and the sound was not attractive. "God-damn cop," she said.

"Yes."

Her eyes narrowed. "Why are you smiling?"

"Am I? I guess it's because you know me so well." He moved to sit on the edge of the bed, then drew the sheet up to cover her. He rested his palm on the flat of her stomach and looked into her guileless eyes. She didn't know what he truly was, and even after all these years, it still amazed him that he could pull off the illusion.

Slowly, he pressed a kiss to her forehead. "Thank you."

She eyed him suspiciously. "For what?"

For believing I'm human. For proving I can keep up the charade. "For last night."

Her expression relaxed and she smiled softly as she reached for his hand, her fingers twining with his. "Like I said. Come back to bed."

He'd be lying if he didn't admit it was tempting, but long ago he'd promised himself not to go there. He'd had a few relationships with his own kind—with the Shadowers. If a week or two of dinners and sex could be considered a relationship. But with humans? With them he wouldn't even stay through the night.

"You're going to say no," she said. "I see it on your face." She eased up onto her knees, the sheet falling away. "Let me try to persuade you otherwise."

"Brenda—" he said, recalling the name that had been pinned to her uniform.

"No, no," she said. "You don't want—"

But he didn't hear what he didn't want, because the sharp chirp of his phone interrupted. He tugged it from his pants pocket, saw Tucker's name on the display, and answered. "Yo."

"It's Rhys," his partner said. "I just got a call from the office in Victorville. I think we've got him."

Doyle felt his pulse increase as he got the details, told

Tucker he'd meet him in five, then snapped the phone shut.

"You really do have to go," Brenda pouted.

"I do," he said, and this time he meant it. "Because you're right. I'm a cop. And I've got a job to do."

"Dead," Officer Gomez said, his voice carrying across the parking lot as Doyle crossed toward him, his long strides kicking up the dust that seemed to blanket all of Victorville. "All of them."

"Shit." Beside him, Doyle's partner Severin Tucker shoved his hands into his pockets. Then, as if something inside him had popped, Tucker kicked a rock and sent it rocketing across the lot. "Goddammit all to fucking hell."

Doyle seconded the emotion, but he didn't give in to it. He was too on edge; the anger that all their scrambling to find the missing girls had been for nothing hovered too close to the surface. Let it go, and he couldn't guarantee that he could pull it back.

He met Gomez in front of the entrance to the shabby, abandoned motel. The place sat about five miles outside of town on an old highway that had been made redundant by a new freeway. It had been empty for decades; and the only building within sight was an equally desolate gas station.

The intense summer sun beat down upon them, filling the air with the strangely sharp odor of melting tar and baking dust. A tumbleweed rolled by. A ghost town, Doyle thought, and cursed the monster who'd brought more death to this place.

"Time of death?" Doyle demanded. "Come on, Officer, I need information."

Gomez swallowed, the only betrayal of his youth. "Not sure, sir. Four hours, at least. But maybe longer. Could be eight. We—we expected the medical examiner to arrive with you."

"We?" Tucker asked.

"My partner and I. He's inside. With the bodies."

"Just the two of you?"

Gomez nodded. "Victorville's a small post, sirs, and since you both arrived so quickly..."

"Not quick enough if they've been dead for four hours," Doyle said.

"Maybe eight," Tucker reminded Doyle.

"Fuck." One hour and Doyle had a chance. Maybe even four. But eight? If it had been eight hours, the bodies would be useless to him. "You told Los Angeles dispatch you had a bead on Rhys," Doyle said, referring to the vampire he had been hunting nonstop for the last three days, ever since the body of Cecilia Winfrey had been discovered in the attic of a recently listed Venice Beach cottage.

The description of the injuries in the real estate agent's frantic call to 911 had been tagged by Division 6 dispatch, and Doyle had arrived even before the human police. He'd taken one glance at the girl—bloodless skin, ripped-up neck—and knew immediately that his trip to Venice hadn't been a waste of time. A vampire had killed the girl, and the case was well within the jurisdiction of the Preternatural Enforcement Commission, an ancient organization that investigated, prosecuted, and meted out punishment for crimes performed by vampires, werewolves, demons, jinns, and all the other Shadowers.

Tucker had wasted no time. A human with the rather rare but extremely useful gift of mind control, he'd worked his mojo on the gathering crowd, and soon the local cops were on their way back to the station and the real estate agent was headed to her next listing, completely clueless that anything untoward had happened at the beach property.

After that, the case had belonged to the PEC. More specifically, to Doyle and Tucker, and they'd immediately gone to work. Cecilia was dead, but she still had a story to tell, and Doyle had crouched beside her, his hand pressed to her forehead. As a percipient para-demon, he'd seen Cecilia's fear. Had experienced the horrors of her last hours when Joaquin Rhys had bled and tortured her—and not just by causing her pain. No, he had added insult to injury by describing in intricate detail exactly what he was going to do to ten of her college friends. And he'd recited each girl's name and address just so that she could have no doubt of his sincerity.

Most vamps fought against that kind of depravity. They used willpower and rituals to help bind and suppress the *Azag Mahru,* the serpent-like malevolence that was released in the transition from human to vampire. Lose the battle, and they became rogue, giving in to their bloodlust and losing their humanity in the process.

As a para-demon, Doyle had always had that dark force living within him, throbbing and needy beneath the surface. Unlike a vampire, he couldn't call upon any rituals to help him battle it down. Despite his human mother and his human appearance, he wasn't human and never had been. He had to fight the seething, bubbling rage inside of him solely through the force of his own will.

The effort cost him, and dearly, but the constant battle made him stronger. It also ensured that he had no patience for vamps who didn't at least try to control their serpent. They were vile. Lazy. And the ones like Rhys, who were evil even without the serpent? Those he hated beyond all reason.

Those, he'd made it his mission to fight.

"So where the fuck is Rhys?" Doyle's voice cracked with irritation. He was tired and hungry, but it wasn't the kind of hunger that a quick stop at the golden arches could solve. He'd planned to feed after leaving Brenda, but there'd been no time. Not with the girls missing. Not when there'd been a chance to save them.

That chance was gone now. All that work, all that worry, and still Rhys had won.

"I don't know, sir," Gomez said, stumbling over his words. "We thought—when we found the girls—we assumed. But he's not here. We've searched, and there's not a sign. Nothing at all."

From the moment he'd caught sight of Gomez's face, Doyle had expected that answer. But that didn't stop the sudden surge of rage inside of him. It threatened to burst free, and when it did, he hoped the lowlife vampire who'd murdered these humans would be there to suffer the onslaught of his wrath.

"And all the vics are in there? All ten?"

"Ten? No, sir. There're only six girls."

Doyle glanced at Tucker, who frowned. "You're sure?" Rhys's promise to Cecilia had been crystal clear—ten girls. And all ten of the girls he'd named had in fact been abducted.

An eleventh girl had been killed and left behind. Her boyfriend had found her on the floor of the apartment she shared with one of the missing girls, her head bashed in from a hard landing against the brick hearth.

The poor girl hadn't died immediately, though, and her suffering had gone on for hours. The weight of her pain had sat heavily with Doyle when he went into her head. Had she died immediately, he would have been running blind. Because she'd suffered, he'd gained a lead. A reference to the desert. A place to hole up. A lot of rambling, mixed-up words that Rhys had crooned to his terrified abductee, which the dying girl had overheard. Jumbled because of the injured girl's pain and fear, but still enough for Doyle to work with.

He'd recited the words to a tech team back at Division 6 headquarters in Los Angeles, who'd gone to work running combinations of the words through a computer, trying to generate possible locations from them.

While the program ran, Doyle had gone out to clear his head and feed, an excursion that had landed him in Brenda's bed. Before he'd had a chance to take his leave of her and move on to Orlando's—where he could slake his unique appetite—the techs had hit upon the Desert Rose Motel in Victorville. Gomez had been dispatched, and Tucker and Doyle had arrived only minutes later, traveling from Los Angeles to Victorville by wormhole. It beat fighting the traffic on LA's highways, but it was a damned unpleasant way to travel, and it drained the shit out of Doyle. Yet another reason he was teetering on the edge now.

"Four still missing," Tucker said. "Shit."

Doyle sucked in a noisy breath, then exhaled on a curse. "Let me see the girls."

Gomez nodded, then turned and led the way inside. Doyle and Tucker followed him past the reception counter and into the dank little office. It looked like a set for a 1950s television show, right down to the plastic covering on the teal blue sofa. In the corner, Gomez's partner spoke into a radio. He nodded at Doyle and Tucker but otherwise didn't acknowledge them.

"There," Gomez said, pointing to a filing cabinet that had been pulled back from the wall. "It was like that when we got here. Like he wanted us to find his nest."

This time, Doyle went first, with Tucker and Gomez bringing up the rear. The filing cabinet, it turned out, was attached to a hinge, turning it into a makeshift door. When opened, it revealed a hole in the plaster that led to a short tunnel, which ended abruptly in a gaping pit.

Tucker edged up beside Doyle and peered down into the dark, then grunted in frustration. After a second, he dropped a coin into the void. They didn't hear it land.

Tucker looked at Doyle. "How far down?"

"Only about ten feet," Doyle said. Unlike his human partner, he had preternaturally keen vision.

"Shoulda heard it land, then," Tucker said.

"The body was soft," Doyle said. The dime had landed on the breast of a young girl who was positioned directly beneath the hole. Doyle had the feeling Rhys had done that intentionally, positioning the girl so that it was almost impossible for her would-be rescuers to avoid landing on her already abused body.

"They're all down there," Gomez said.

Doyle didn't bother answering. Carefully, he lowered himself through the hole in the floor. He swung his legs out a bit so that he wouldn't fall straight down. As it was, he still stumbled when he landed, and he had to steady himself on the body of another girl. That sick fuck Rhys had stacked them all around.

A moment later, Tucker and Gomez joined him.

"He sucked 'em all dry," Gomez said. "Every single one of them."

Tucker fished a flashlight out of his pocket. He turned it on, cast it around, then whistled. "Doyle, partner, we've got a problem."

Doyle followed Tucker's gaze, then immediately rounded on Gomez. "Are you fucking crazy?" He pointed to the four tunnels that led away from the hub where they were standing. "We're goddamned sitting ducks."

Gomez stumbled backward. "It's okay. We—we went down all the tunnels. They all circle back here. All but one. It opens up into one of the rooms in the back of the motel. But he's not there, either."

That fury rose up again—and again Doyle battled it back down. Gomez was young. Inexperienced. But he'd just made a potentially fatal mistake.

He looked up at Tucker. "Let's get these girls up. It's too dangerous down here." If Gomez and his quiet partner had already checked the halls, they were probably safe. But Doyle wasn't in the mood to take chances.

"Already ahead of you." Tucker stood and nodded at the officer. "What special tricks you got, Gomez?"

"Huh?"

"Forget it. Leap like a superhero and drop us down a ladder or something so that we can lift the girls out."

Gomez—who Doyle guessed was some species of shapeshifter—literally leaped to the task, and soon they had one of the girls laid out in the main office. Doyle knelt beside her, then turned to look at Tucker.

"Not worth it," Tucker said. "Too much time. You're just going to drain yourself more."

"He might have said something in front of her. Some hint of where his other hidey-hole is."

Tucker's face was tight, but after a moment he nodded. "If it's only been four hours you might still see something." Tucker was Hollywood handsome, but right now his face was creased with frustration. "We're running out of leads, and Rhys has a taste for this now."

That was damn sure. Ten girls they knew of, but Doyle was certain the body count would rise.

Doyle pressed his fingers to her forehead. Nothing.

Damn it, they needed some luck.

As a percipient, he knew that he was an asset to the PEC. If he arrived at a crime scene in time, he could reach into a victim's mind and withdraw their last moments—what they saw, what they felt. His gift was rare—there were only a handful of percipient demons across the globe—but incredibly useful. The gift had defined his life ever since he had discovered it, realizing that he could use this power that was tied to his demon half as a tool to help the weak. The victims. The humans.

And maybe, by helping undo even a little of the harm done to them by a Shadower, he could shed some of the foulness with which he'd been marked at birth.

Determined, he pressed his palm hard against the cold forehead and tried again. *Come on, come on.* He recalled the list of names that Rhys had rattled off to Cecilia, along with the photos they'd pulled of the identified girls. This one, he remembered, was named Alicia.

Come on, Alicia. Help me out here. Let me in. Let me see.

His body shook from the effort of pushing past his exhaustion. His powers weakened when he didn't feed, but if he could just push harder. If he could just catch even the slightest whisper of the memories that lingered after death.

Silvery wisps seemed to dance in front of him like fingers of fog. He stretched out with his mind, trying to catch the threads and pull them closer. They slipped from his grasp, easing off into the dark veil of the beyond.

A hand closed on his shoulder, and he jumped.

"Back it off," Tucker said. "You're pushing too hard."

"Is it too hard if I find the son-of-a-bitch?" His voice was harsher than he'd intended, but Tucker didn't even flinch.

"Wear yourself down and you won't make it back," Tucker said. "Unless you're willing to feed on the street."

Doyle flinched. In Los Angeles, he could go to Orlando's, a soul-trading club where at least he had some level of dignity. If he fed on the street, he was nothing more than a monster.

Tucker knew damn well how Doyle felt about feeding. And if Tucker was pushing, Doyle knew that his exhaustion must not only be showing, it must be spilling out of his skin. Didn't matter, though. There wasn't time to feed. Wasn't time for anything except to push it down and press on. "We're running out of options."

"Doyle." Tucker's voice was firm, but kind. "It's been too long."

"There was something," Doyle said. "A remnant, but too faint to catch. Maybe one of the others survived longer. Even half an hour more of life might do it."

"You're going to slide under."

Doyle ignored his partner, turning his focus to Gomez. "Bring up the rest."

"Dammit, Doyle. I don't want you looking at me like I'm a Happy Meal."

"I said I'm fine," Doyle snapped, the words coming out with rare fury.

"The hell you are."

The tight wire of Doyle's temper snapped. "I don't feed off friends, and I don't need a fucking babysitter."

"No?"

Doyle's fists clenched, and he battled the urge to take a shot at Tucker's too-perfect nose. Shit.

Back it down. Back it the fuck down.

He drew in a breath. Tucker was right—he was ripped up. Getting close to the point where he'd have no choice but to feed. Cross that line and he might not make it back to Los Angeles. Too far gone and it wouldn't just be the vamps who were hurting humans.

But damn it all, he couldn't walk away now. Not when they were so close. Not when Rhys was killing so many, so fast, and girls were still missing.

"I have to do this," he whispered, so low he doubted that Tucker's human ears could hear him. As usual, his partner surprised him.

"Fuck," Tucker said, then sighed. "If it gets bad—if I think you're going over—I'll do what I have to do."

Doyle nodded, and as soon as Gomez brought the second girl up, he bent over, pressed his hand against her cold skin, and let himself slide in. Nothing. He checked all of the girls, the result was still the same—a big load of nothing, only now Doyle was so weak he could barely stand. "Just give me a minute," he said, giving up and sinking back down on the filthy linoleum floor.

In front of him, Tucker stood shaking his head.

"I had to try," Doyle said.

"I know. What now?"

It was a good question. With effort, Doyle forced himself to his feet, determined to focus. Cobwebs seemed to fill his head, and he rubbed his temples, trying to banish them. "Rhys had a reason for coming here," he finally said. "This motel."

"It's remote. Abandoned."

"A lot of motels are. And office buildings. Apartments. Why this one?"

"Might be random," Tucker said.

"Random doesn't do us any good. Besides, he's a methodical son-of-a-bitch."

"So we pull the strings," Tucker said. "See if we can find a connection. Something that ties this place to Rhys." He frowned. "Pretty thin."

"Maybe. But it's all we've got. Start with the property owner. Maybe we'll get lucky."

Apparently the stars were aligned in their favor, because within five minutes, the research team back at Division 6 pinged Doyle's smartphone with the motel's tax records. Doyle took one look at the file and whistled.

Tucker was at his side in an instant, peering over his shoulder.

"Creevey. Well, color me intrigued."

The motel was owned by one Horace Creevey, a human who happened to be the father of one of the vilest human serial killers currently biding his time on death row. Kyle Creevey had kidnapped and tortured almost two dozen girls, and bragged about it. Not only that, but he swore that he'd done the deed to impress the vampires who were going to make him immortal.

It was a ridiculous ploy that the press had assumed was part of a pitch for an insanity plea. The PEC had thought differently and had kept an eye on Kyle, but the case was within the human system's jurisdiction, and as no rogue vamps had made any obvious attempts to contact Kyle, the case was filed once he was locked up.

"Maybe all his talk about knowing vampires was true," Doyle said.

"The property's owned by his dad, and Dad wasn't exactly supportive of his son during the trial."

"But it's a connection," Doyle said tightly. "And right now it's the only one we've got."

THREE

"Glad you came back, sugar-snatch." Kyle Creevey, gorgeous enough to have made the cover of People magazine with the headline Too Pretty to Be Evil?, pressed his lips up to the visitor window at the federal penitentiary in Lompoc, California, giving Andrea Tarrant a rather disgusting view of his tongue and artificially whitened teeth. He smacked his lips, and when he looked hard at her she could see the evil behind those startling blue eyes. "Guess you missed me, huh?"

Andy didn't even blink. Once he had completely grossed her out—okay, he still completely grossed her out—but after spending five months covering the investigation and trial, there wasn't a lot about Creevey that surprised her anymore. In fact, the only thing that had surprised her was the call she'd received that morning from the prison's visitor coordinator telling her that Creevey wanted to see her.

Now she was sitting nose to nose with him, separated only by a glass barrier. His voice was muted, softened by the cheap speaker embedded in the cubicle wall. All around her, she could hear the buzz of the other prisoners' conversations. There were eight of them in the room today. Four men behind glass, four women talking in soft voices. Of all the women, she was the only one who wasn't in tears, the only one who wasn't pressing her hand against the glass and wishing it would dissolve so she could touch the man beyond. God, just the idea repulsed her.

"You asked me here, Kyle," she said, knowing how much the convicted kidnapper and murderer hated being called by his first name. "Why don't you tell me why?"

"You sayin' there has to be a reason? Maybe I just like seeing your purty face." He spoke with an affected accent, calling on his dirt-poor Mississippi roots in favor of the fine speech patterns he'd perfected at Pepperdine and the affectation of class and breeding that had become his trademark. The spit and polish that had drawn women toward him like a spider drew in a fly. Kyle Creevey was an actor, through and through, and his stage had been all of Southern California. He'd played the part of the heartless sociopath, and twenty-three women had been sucked into his theatrics, believing that the smoke and mirrors were reality.

"Like seeing me? I doubt that." She narrowed her eyes and leaned forward, knowing she was intentionally baiting him. "I think it's more of a compulsion. I think you liked talking to me because you couldn't figure me out. Couldn't understand how there was a woman who didn't fall for your shit. I think you still can't believe it."

Andy kept her eyes on his face as she leaned back. She was only slightly exaggerating. Surely there were other women in Southern California who'd seen something vile in this man. Women who were alive because, after meeting him in a bar, they'd turned around and walked in the other direction, some sixth sense letting them know that the blond man with the patrician face wasn't going to sweep them off their feet. At least not the way they were anticipating.

But considering his body count, there weren't too many of those women. Most fell to his charms, then fell dead into his arms.

Andy had never been tested—not in that way. But she'd been the first reporter to interview him after the police talked to him in connection with the disappearance of Melissa Jane Roth. At the time, nobody had considered Creevey a suspect. He'd been a regular at the Back Street's Wednesday night happy hour, and he'd been seen chatting with Melissa on one or two occasions. He'd been cooperative and polite with the police and with Andy. Happy to help, he'd said. Anything to find out what happened to poor, pretty Melissa.

The police had believed him. Andy had believed him, too, but she hadn't liked him. He'd turned on the charm, and although she couldn't put her finger on what it was about Kyle Creevey that bothered her, she'd walked away from their interview feeling stained. She wasn't surprised when he was arrested for the kidnapping and dismemberment death of Janeen Rusch, but she was annoyed with herself for not trusting her intuition. Especially when Melissa's case was reopened and the LAPD's investigation zeroed in on Creevey as the prime suspect.

"Didn't fall for me?" Creevey repeated. "Sweetheart, don't flatter yourself. Maybe I didn't shove my tongue into your honeypot, but you came for me just the same." He licked his lips, and Andy shivered. "I called, and you came, your pen poised over your paper, looking all professional and serious, but underneath it all you were creaming your panties, knowing I could give you what no other man could—one hell of a fucking good story."

"And you know what, Kyle? I did get the story. I used

you to get a cover story in one of the country's most prestigious newsmagazines, and that story's still paying off for me. And what did you get? A nice warm cot on death row." She smiled sweetly. "Don't play games with me, Creevey. We've known each other too long."

He tossed his head back and snorted with laughter. "You got me there, buttercup. And you're right. We've known each other too long—too intimately—to play foolish games."

"So you're going to tell me why you asked me here today? Because flattery or not, I don't believe it was to compliment my ass."

"I called you here because of that story you're so damn proud of. I read it, you know."

"Did you? And were you astounded by my insight? Blown away by my perceptive prose?"

"Mighty arrogant take you had there, missy. Calling me evil. Strong word."

"True word."

The corner of his mouth rose just a little. "Maybe so, girl. Maybe so. But that don't mean you got the rest of the story right."

"No?" She forced herself not to cross her arms over her chest. She could hold her own against Kyle Creevey, but he still creeped her out. Especially when he slid into that bumpkin routine of his—the bad grammar, the lip smacking. Somehow the knowledge that he could shift on a dime and be not only proper but downright classy made him all the more creepy.

She'd thought when the story printed that would be the end of it. And even though the story really had bumped her career to the next level, she was still happy to be done with him. The call from the visitor coordinator had sent a hot wire of dread shooting through her, and she'd almost declined. But ambition won out, and so here she was. He'd reached out and reeled her in, just as he had with his victims, leaving her with self-loathing almost as strong as her determination to ferret out whatever new story he might be sitting on. "All right," she finally said. "So tell me."

He tilted his head back and laughed. "Could set my watch by you, girl. You don't want to need me, but you do. You owe me, babycakes. If it weren't for me—if it weren't for all those purty dead girls—you'd be serving coffee at Starbucks, and you damn well know it."

"You're the one who asked me here. You want to tell me, then tell me. Otherwise, it's a lovely Saturday, and I've got better things to do than look into your ugly face."

"Now don't be mean, sugar. I'm your golden goose. More important, as fond as I am of seeing my picture plastered all over the media, you turned your spotlight on the wrong guy."

"The wrong guy?" She shoved her chair back and started to stand. "Nice talking to you, Kyle. But if you called me down here to feed me some bullshit about how you've been wronged and the jury convicted the wrong man, then let me be the first to tell you to go screw yourself. I'm outta here."

He barked out a laugh. "You wouldn't be the first to tell me that—and that's not what I'm gonna say. I killed 'em. Oh, yeah, I slit their pretty throats and watched them die. But you weren't listening earlier, sugar plum. The question is how? How did I get away with it for so very, very long?"

An accomplice. Of course—he had an accomplice. And that meant that she had a scoop. She worked to keep the excitement out of her voice. "The how doesn't much matter now, Kylie. You're in for life, asshole, and considering you're on death row, life isn't going to be too long."

"Ouch. You got a mean streak in you, don't you sweet

cheeks? But that's okay. You play it cool. I know you're curious. I can see it in your eyes. Those strange, fuck-me eyes."

Andy flinched, then bit the inside of her cheek to keep from spitting out a retort. She did have unusual eyes, and their oddity—the pale color, the slightly oval irises—had always been something she liked. It made her different. Special. But she had no desire to be special to Creevey.

"You called me here to tell me," she snapped. "So get on with it."

"Oooh. Touched a nerve." He held up a hand to keep her from pushing out of her chair. "Calm down, I'm talking. The truth is, it's all about friends. The right kind of friends." He smiled, wide and easy, and leaned back in his chair. "Did you know that vampire blood makes you stronger?"

She couldn't help groaning as she scooted her chair backward. She thought about the other story that she was currently working on—an investigative piece about a group of locals who really believed in vampires. Had everybody in the world gone loony? "Sorry, Kyle. I didn't realize that you dragged me here just to waste my time."

He thrust forward and slammed his hands against the glass so hard she jumped. "Goddammit, girlie, you listen to me."

She sucked in air, gathering her courage. "The cops didn't believe your bullshit story, and neither do I. What? You think you can wrangle an insanity plea now? It's too damn late."

His face turned a mottled red, and she could see that he was trying to control his breathing.

She knew she shouldn't bait him, but she just couldn't help it. She leaned forward, her voice all low and sweet. "So you had a vampire's help, Kyle? So what? Didn't do you much good. Maybe your bloodsucking friends got pissed that you told the world about them, because they sure as hell haven't done their little vampy thing and pulled you off death row." She sat back. "Now, you want to tell me something real, or do you want to keep talking about your bullshit fantasies? I'm not twelve, Kyle, and I don't believe in monsters."

That wasn't entirely true. She believed in good, and she believed in evil. And she knew perfectly well that monsters existed—she was looking right at one.

Kyle said nothing, but the anger seemed to flow off of him in waves, so thick it could probably have knocked her over.

She felt the comforting weight of the necklace that had once belonged to her mother. She wore the delicate gold cross always, and now it was tucked beneath her blouse, the metal cool against her skin. She resisted the urge to brush it with her fingertips, and stood up instead. "I'd say it was a pleasure seeing you again, but my daddy taught me not to lie. You're old news, Kyle, and I don't have a reason in the world to be talking to you now." She watched his face carefully—he'd called her here for some reason, and not this vampire bullshit. The question was, had her bluff worked? She had no doubt that this was about exposing an accomplice. Would he break down and tell her without the ridiculous games?

And then she saw it, a tiny flicker in his confidence. A slight dimming of the smugness in his eyes.

Oh, yeah, Andy. You've got him now.

Confident, she took a step toward the door. Sure enough, he called out, stopping her. She paused before turning to face him, making sure her glee didn't show on her face.

"Sit," he said.

"Why the hell should I?"

"You want a name? I'll give you a name."

"Playtime's over," she said. "You show signs of bull-shitting me, and I'm out of here. I've got laundry that's more interesting than listening to you." She was pushing it, but he had to believe she'd really walk away.

"He took me under his wing. He helped me. Introduced me to others just like him. And he made promises. Glorious promises."

"Are you saying you killed because he promised you something?"

"I'm not saying anything like that. Not yet." But his voice was reverent, and he looked sincere. Of course it could all be an act. Still, Andy was willing to take the chance.

"Have you got a name?" she asked.

"Rhys," Creevey said. "But don't go looking for him."

Behind them, the door to the visiting area clicked open. Probably another woman here to see one of the prisoners. Andy ignored it. "He wouldn't like me?" she asked.

Creevey's smile was pure evil. "He'd like you too much."

"Tell me his full name," she said, but before Creevey could answer, the guard shouldered around her, squeezing into her field of vision. "Dammit, we're not done." She gave him her most businesslike glare. "I have unlimited time today—it's already been cleared with the warden."

"Sorry, miss," the young guard said. "But these gentlemen—"

"Agents," a deeper voice cut in, and Andy swiveled to see who was speaking. The voice came from a man she recognized. A lean man with sharp eyes that belied the exhaustion in his face. The weariness didn't diminish his rugged good looks, though. She'd spent a summer in Oklahoma with her father when she was a teenager, and the agent who spoke had the wind-sculpted face of a cowboy combined with an almost arrogant self-confidence.

He took a step forward, wearing his rumpled suit with the same air of authority as a politician in perfectly pressed linen. He reminded her of the Marlboro Man, earthy and sexy all at the same time.

He commanded the room, made it his own only seconds after entering, and she knew right then that if she butted heads with him, she was going to lose.

"I'm—"

"Agent Doyle," she said. "You're with Homeland."

His eyes narrowed, as if he was trying to place her.

"Reporter," she said with a shrug. "I've seen you a couple of times at crime scenes. Andrea Tarrant."

He nodded slowly, something in his eyes suggesting that he recognized her. He didn't say as much, though. Instead, he waved at his companion. "This is Agent Tucker."

Andy nodded. Tucker was also attractive, but much more polished. Tucker was the kind of guy that casting agents drooled over and women fantasized about having in their beds. But Andy barely noticed him. She was too intent on Doyle. There was just something about him that sang to her, like one of those geometric puzzles where the pieces were all so different, but they fit together perfectly.

Andy, however, wasn't there to solve a puzzle. "This is my time, agents. If you'll just wait outside, I'll be happy to share him when I'm done."

"No can do. Official business. We'll have to ask you to leave."

"Excuse me? This is my interview, dammit. First Amendment ring any bells? Freedom of the press?"

He looked right at her, held her gaze for a moment, then shifted his attention to the guard. "I need him in an interview room now. No glass barrier. And I want him transferred as soon as the paperwork goes through. You understand?"

"Transferred where?" Andy asked. "Are you commuting his sentence? On what authority?"

"Homeland Security. Just like you said." Beside her, the guard stepped closer and took her elbow. A hint of a smile touched Agent Doyle's mouth. "And now, Ms. Tarrant, I really have to insist that you leave."

As a guard guided Creevey into the bowels of the prison, the woman shoved past Doyle, her disturbingly familiar eyes piercing him with anger and disappointment, and sending a jolt of regret coiling through him.

Those eyes. Jesus. He'd noticed her before at crime scenes, of course, but he'd never gotten such a good look at her eyes. They were just like Kathryn's. That pale blue, so faint it seemed like little more than wisps of fog. The flecks of gold in the irises, unremarkable until the light caught them just right, and then they sparkled like jewels.

"Who's Kathryn?"

Doyle's head snapped up to meet his partner's eyes. "What?"

"I knew you weren't up to this. You're zoning on me, man. The way you get when you need to feed. Only this time you said a name. You said—"

"Kathryn." He turned away from Tucker, not wanting his partner to see his expression. Kathryn, his love. Kathryn, so fragile and pure. Kathryn, who had been dead for centuries, her beautiful body perishing in the fire that took so many that night. The fire that had started because of him. Him, and Lucius Dragos, a goddamned vampire he'd once called friend.

"So?" Tucker persisted. "Who is she?"

"Nobody," Doyle lied, deliberately shedding the memory like a snake sheds its skin. He shifted his gaze back toward the glass barrier. Behind it, Creevey's chair now sat empty. "Let's go. They must have him set up in interview by now. We don't want to keep our little friend waiting."

As they moved down the hall, Doyle let Tucker lead the way as he hung back, breathing slow, trying to work past his exhaustion and gain the control he needed to do his job. His skin felt alive, as if a thousand small creatures were crawling just under the surface. Not creatures. *Him.* What he was inside just bursting to get out.

Half-human and half-demon, the child Doyle used to be had learned early how to keep his demon side buried. His bastard of a demon father had raped his mother, and she'd kept the baby only because she believed that God was testing her, and that he'd entrusted her with the mission of pushing the demon out of Doyle. Every night, she honored that mission by bruising his bottom with an elm switch, telling him to focus on the pain, because it would drive the evil out. And if he couldn't rein it in, then beheading would surely do the trick.

So, yeah, he'd learned control, and he'd easily passed for human as a young boy.

But then he'd turned twelve, and the hunger had begun. The raw craving, not for food, but for souls. A vile appetite that he'd inherited from his father and that even his mother's switch couldn't beat out of him, though she'd tried her damnedest.

He'd fought as he always had, wanting to be the perfect human child his mother had always wanted, because then maybe she'd love him, and he would love her, and the black, bilious hatred that had grown between them would fade away. But there was no way he could fight that hard. He'd lost in the end, and he'd learned the true, horrible nature of what he was.

With effort, he stifled a shiver, forcing the memories down. He didn't want to go there. He'd learned; he'd changed. For centuries he'd been controlling the hunger; he wasn't weak like some Shadowers. He could hang on for a few more hours. He had to, because the lives of the still-missing girls depended on it.

Tucker had paused at the door to the interview room, and now he watched critically as Doyle approached.

"I'm fine."

"You're not," Tucker said, but he pulled open the door. "After this, you feed."

Silently, Doyle shoved past his partner into the room. He knew Tucker was only watching his back, just as partners were supposed to do. He also knew that this itchy, gnawing urge to bite his friend's head off was because of the hunger. But that didn't make it any easier.

Since there was no glass barrier in the interview room, Creevey was secured to the sturdy steel table with handcuffs and leg irons. Unnecessary precautions, Doyle thought. Creevey was vicious, but only human, and Doyle had a para-demon's strength. But neither Creevey nor the men who ran the penitentiary knew that, and rules had to be followed.

"Caught Homeland's attention, did I? Guess I should feel pretty flattered."

"Homeland? Creevey, you don't know the half of it. You've stirred up quite a lot of shit." Doyle slid into a chair as he shot a sideways glance toward Tucker. "Are we recording?"

"That's a negative. This is off the record."

Creevey's face hardened. "The fuck it is. You want me to talk, you get me my lawyer. I know my rights."

"Rights? Kyle, my boy, you haven't got shit. Not with us. Not in this room. And I'll tell you a little secret—we're not really with Homeland Security."

"No? Then what the hell are you doing here?" Creevey's face didn't change, but Doyle heard the hint of fear creep into his voice. Even on death row, Creevey wasn't used to not being the one in charge.

"Got a few questions for you, Kyle. And I don't have time to dick around."

"That a fact?" The human leaned back, his smug expression grating on Doyle's already tight nerves.

Doyle leaned in, slow and dangerous. He caught the rotten scent of Creevey's tattered soul and felt the hunger rumble through him once more. "Careful, Creevey. I eat shitbags like you for breakfast."

For a moment, Creevey's face suggested that he knew exactly what Doyle was saying. Then he blinked, and the swagger returned. "You came to see me, remember? Guess that means we're on Creevey time now."

Slowly, Doyle settled back into his chair. "Tell me about Rhys. Tell me where he'd go to hole up."

Creevey's knuckles whitened as his hands tightened against the edges of the table. "Who the fuck is Rhys?"

"Wrong answer, you sanctimonious shit. The FBI may not have believed your story about how you were trying to impress your vampire friends, but I'm more open-minded. Because I know something the FBI doesn't. I know that vampires are real. But guess what, Kyle," Doyle added, lowering his voice as he stood and eased around the table. He got right behind the sick fuck and leaned in close, his voice dropping even further to whisper, "I'm the guy that even the vampires are afraid of. So tell me where he is. Because if you don't, I can promise you'll regret it."

Creevey turned his head slowly, his mouth curving into a sneer. "I think you're full of shit. But even if I didn't, there's not a damn thing I could tell you, seeing as I don't know what the fuck you're talking about."

"There are lives on the line, asshole. Rhys dumped his victims at a property your family owns. And you spent half your trial telling folks that you were in nice and cozy with some bad-ass vampires."

Something dark and cunning flashed in Creevey's eyes. "That was just talk. I don't really believe that shit."

"Oh, I think you do. And if we had all day, I think I could convince you to tell me exactly what you believe, not to mention what and who you know. But we don't have all day."

Creevey leaned back, once again smug. "Brother, in case you didn't notice, I've got all the time in the world. Least until they shove the needle in my arm. And once they do that, I'll be no help to you at all."

"Can't argue with that," Doyle said, and Creevey barked out a smug laugh that would have had Doyle fighting the urge to punch him in the face if it weren't for the fact that Doyle already had this well in hand. "Fortunately, I'm not here to play your games."

"No? Well, that's a downright shame, ain't it? Because I'm in the mood to play."

Doyle glanced sideways at Tucker. "I'm tired of talking to this fuck. Your turn to have a chat with our friend."

"My pleasure," Tucker said. Then he leaned forward and said, in that casual way that Doyle so admired, "We're going to talk about Rhys, Creevey. We're going to talk about where he might have taken the rest of those girls."

FOUR

The Club Rouge had been around since the 1920s, and the enterprising human who founded it had been one of the few who knew about the existence of vampires. Much like other club owners who had established back rooms that served bathtub gin, he had set up a private room. Only the clientele at the Club Rouge didn't indulge in alcohol; they were served blood. Fresh from the humans who clamored to be admitted to the exclusive back section, little knowing that their memories would be wiped and their veins opened.

The humans weren't permanently damaged—that would raise too many questions—but they were sent on their way thrilled to have gotten a little peek in the back, and upset that they'd been too damn drunk to remember the details.

Millicent Teal had been working as a waitress at the club for years, and she was perfectly content with the status quo. And part of that status quo was that while a few select and tasty humans were allowed in the back, admission to werens was absolutely forbidden, and any fur-back who wandered in learned that lesson the hard way.

This one, however, was beyond learning any lessons. The shitbag had wandered in already battered and bloody. And then he'd been rude enough to die right in front of the damn ladies' room.

"He said to call the precipice," Joleen said. "What's a precipice?"

"Who cares?" Millicent said.

"Someone messed him up really bad." Joleen knelt down beside the dead weren. "Isn't that like a cliff? Don't you jump off a precipice?"

Millicent toed the body, frowning as her Jimmy Choo impacted the weren's chest. "He did jump off," she said. "Right into the deep end if he came in here."

"Maybe he meant the PEC? Precipice," Joleen said slowly, as if tasting the word on her tongue. "PEC," she murmured, equally slowly. She shrugged. "They don't really sound alike, but maybe?"

Millicent tossed her hair. "Even if it's not what he wanted, it's what he's getting. I'd just as soon have Tony dump him out back with the trash, but I guess we have to report it." Millicent was proud of the fact that the owners —a vampire couple that had purchased the place twenty years before—trusted her enough to let her be acting manager on the nights when they weren't around. Unfortunately, that meant that she couldn't always do what she wanted to do. Because even though the Club Rouge was very, very, very anti-weren, it wasn't cool to be too public about that. Which meant that if a weren died on the premises, they needed to be all concerned and good citizen-y.

"I'll go make the call," Joleen said, and hurried away, her heels clicking on the laminate floor.

Left alone with the body, Millicent cursed softly. The

last thing the club needed was for the PEC to start poking around. Feeding from a licensed faunt might be legal, but none of the human snacks invited into the back of the Club Rouge were licensed. After all, where was the thrill if the human actually wanted a little stick and suck?

And now this idiot weren may have gone and ruined everything. "Fucker," she said, giving him another soft kick. "If you've screwed this up for us, you're gonna be so glad you're dead."

Damn but she hated werewolves.

"And that's it?" Tucker asked. "You can't think of any other place where Rhys might hole up?" He leaned back in his chair, just as casual as you please, like him and that shitbag Creevey were two guys having a drink around the kitchen table. It was, thought Doyle, a beautiful sight. More than that, it was the reason he could so easily forget that his partner was human. Technically, Tucker scored a ten in that regard. But for more practical purposes, he was as much a Shadower as Doyle was.

"That's it, brother," Creevey said. "Those are the only places I know about." Tucker had started the conversation by leaning in close, all smiles and penetrating eyes. He'd told Creevey he needed his help and thanked him for being so eager to give it. And then he'd told Creevey to list every possible place where Rhys could have taken the girls. Like a puppy trying to please its master, Creevey had eagerly rattled off three possible properties, including one in Culver City that he'd inherited upon his father's death. It had fallen into bankruptcy after Creevey's arrest. Although Doyle was sending teams to each location, that was the one he was putting his money on.

"You're sure? No others you're sitting on?" Tucker asked, as Doyle surreptitiously finished sending messages on his smartphone to PEC headquarters in Los Angeles.

"Come on, man," Creevey said. "You know I wouldn't yank your chain. We're buds, right?"

"That we are," Tucker said, scooting back the chair and standing. He turned to Doyle. "You got agents en route?"

"Hell, yeah. But Culver City is mine. We go by wormhole. I want to be there when the team arrives."

At the table, Creevey was blinking slowly, his frat boy face contorting as he shook free of the whammy that Tucker had zapped him with. "What the hell—?"

"Sorry to pick your brain and run," Doyle said, rapping on the door to signal the guard, each knock reverberating in his aching head. He gritted his teeth against the pain, then pulled his lips back and aimed a grossly exaggerated smile at Creevey. "But you should know we appreciate your enthusiastic cooperation."

The door opened and they slipped out as Creevey's numb brain finally figured out the score. He howled in frustration, but the heavy door slammed shut behind them, cutting the sound off as effectively as steel shears through ribbon.

"Hold on a second," Tucker said, taking Doyle's elbow and trying to tug him to a stop. Doyle yanked his arm free and kept on going, pushing through the air that seemed to be getting thick with sticky threads, like walking through a field of cotton candy.

"Dammit, Doyle," Tucker said, this time parking himself directly in Doyle's path. "We came here by wormhole and it just about ripped you up. Your skin still looks gray, and I bet if I poked you in the chest, you'd topple over. There's no way in hell we're going by wormhole again."

Doyle wrenched his arm free and sucked in air through his teeth, then forced it out through his nose, concentrating on letting the breathing calm him. On tamping down the rising urge to tell his partner to fuck off or, worse, to lash out and hurt him.

"Don't mess with me," he said. "Not now."

Tucker straightened his shoulders. "Then don't you fuck with me."

There wasn't time for this shit. "Do what you want," Doyle said. "I'm going." He thrust out his hand, palm parallel with the wall in front of them. He focused all his energy—his anger, his frustration, and his desperation to find those girls while they still had lives to save—on pulling the power of time and space around him. It was a quick means of travel, allowing him to cross even the globe in mere seconds. Unfortunately, the wormhole was composed of energy—and it demanded energy in return.

Tucker was right; considering the state he was in, traveling this way was a risk. But goddammit, this was what he was—a cursed and wretched demon who had to steal bits of soul just to stay alive. Pathetic and horrible and vile, so if he could use one of his so-called demonic gifts to maybe save an innocent life, then he was damn sure going to do it.

"Now," he cried, commanding the air. The vortex burst open, a swirling maelstrom of energy surrounding a dark tunnel that twisted and curved toward a terrifying void.

Each time he entered a wormhole, Doyle wondered if it would be the last. Because if he conjured it wrong, there was no telling where he might end up. Deep inside the earth, lost in the vacuum of space, far down in the depths of hell. The latter he deserved. The others, he sometimes longed for.

Not today. Today, he had a job to do, and without looking back at his partner, he threw himself into the void, aware only of the rushing sound of swirling energy and then, yes, the undeniable presence of his partner beside him.

"You're an idiot," he snapped, as the wormhole spit them out onto the Culver City pavement.

"I wouldn't dream of denying it." Tucker stood up and dusted himself off, managing to look all pressed and proper. Doyle, of course, looked as rumpled as always.

Doyle pushed aside the temptation to yell at his partner some more. For one thing, it wouldn't do any good. More important, underneath the curling, poisonous tentacles of his hunger hid the knowledge that Tucker had thrust himself into the void as much for friendship as for the case. Even lost as Doyle was in his need to find and stop Rhys—even as snared as he was in the claws of the hunger—Doyle couldn't discount that.

"There," he said, pointing to the shabby structure's entrance. "We'll station agents there and at the back exit. But we go in through Rhys's entrance."

"And where's that?"

Doyle flashed a feral smile. "That's what we need to find out."

FIVE

The eight-man Recon and Capture team arrived only moments after Doyle and Tucker, and Doyle pressed forward, forcing his limbs to move and demanding that his voice bark out commands. He was hungry—so damn hungry—and yet he couldn't afford to show it. In front of him, a RAC lieutenant, a Jinn named Cort who'd recently transferred from Chicago, stood rigidly at attention.

"Rhys has had access to this location for a while. If he's on site, he'll most likely be dug in, and he's damn sure going to be dangerous. He'll have the place tricked out, and the girls tucked away. First order of business is access. Find me an entrance that's not through one of the doors to the building. Second order of business is to find the girls. Do not—I repeat, do not—allow anyone on your team to breach the building until we're confident of the target location. Get them out, then we concentrate on Rhys. I want the bastard, but not at the risk of those girls' lives."

"We believe there are four potential victims?"

"Don't assume," Doyle said. "But yeah, that's our intelligence."

"On it."

"Wait," Doyle called out. Cort paused and looked back over his shoulder. "He'll have cut tunnels."

"Already on it, sir."

Doyle caught Tucker's eye, saw the glint of approval there.

"What's your plan for finding the victims?" Doyle continued.

"Assuming Rhys is on the premises, he won't be emerging during the daylight."

"There's not much daylight left," Doyle pointed out.

"Another reason we have to move fast," Cort said. At Doyle's nod of approval, he continued. "We can't locate him with heat-seeking equipment because, well, as a vampire—"

"There's no heat," Doyle finished. "Go on."

"So we search for the females. Find them and go in—a risk because Rhys will be trapped inside and undoubtedly dangerous. But we'll blast the place with hematite dust first."

It was a solid plan, and Doyle said as much. The mineral hematite was anathema to vampires. Like Superman's kryptonite, it weakened the fang gang, sapping their strength and stripping them of their ability to transform into animal or mist.

"The team's already putting the equipment in place." Across the parking lot, Doyle saw the other RAC members setting equipment up at the ventilation system.

"Odds are he knows we're here," Tucker said.

"Agreed," Cort said. "He'll undoubtedly assume our first priority is to get to his victims."

"And he's right," Doyle said.

"How do you expect him to react?" Cort asked,

training that firm, military stare on Doyle. "Will he seek to conceal himself? Hole up so that he can engage when we locate him? Will he attempt to harm the females before we can get to them?"

"He's a survivor," Doyle said. He clenched his fists tight at his sides, the pain of his nails cutting into his palms helping him stave off the waves of hunger. "There will always be other girls. Other fights. He'll hole up and hide if he has to. Pride isn't something he's worried about." He paused. "But that doesn't mean he'll give up easy. The place will be rigged. You guys ready for that?"

"Hell yes we are." The voice came from behind Doyle, and he turned to face a hulking werewolf, his smooth black skin marred by a fresh red scar. "Agent Doyle. It's been awhile."

"Rand," Doyle said, with a curt nod. "Been rough-housing?"

Rand grinned. "You know me."

Doyle did, and the weren was a hell of a warrior. The last time they'd seen each other had been at Orlando's. Rand's wife, Lissa, was the succubus who owned the club. The fact that Rand was aware of how often Doyle needed to feed—of the very nature of what he fed on—didn't make him warm to the weren. "Status?"

"We've located Rhys's entry point," Rand said.

Beside him, Cort tapped his earpiece, then caught Doyle's attention. "And we've found a heat signature."

"Only one?" Tucker asked, echoing Doyle's thoughts.

"I'm afraid so."

"I'm taking the team in now." Rand lifted his hand, signaling to the other six men on the team.

"I'm a part of that team," Doyle said, keeping pace as Rand strode toward the entrance Rhys had concealed in the closet of one of the building's moldy, abandoned rooms. As they walked, Doyle checked his weapons, confirming that he had a full load of wooden bullets, along with a Taser that shot hematite wire.

"This is going to push you over the edge," Tucker said from beside him.

Doyle ignored him.

In front of them, Rand paused, his eyes searching Doyle's face. "Call Lissa," he said to Tucker. "She'll have a room waiting for him when this is over."

Crimson fury burst out of him, and even though Doyle knew it was the hunger, he couldn't pull it back. He was in Rand's face in a second, hands on his collar, nose pressed right up to the wolfish bastard. "Stay the fuck out of my business, weren."

"Stay out of my face, demon," Rand retorted. "I'm in command of this mission. You want to go into these tunnels with us? Or should I send you to Orlando's now?"

For two long seconds, they faced off. Then—dammit—Doyle caved. "Make the call," he said to Tucker. "And you, get moving," he added to Rand. "But let's be clear. You may be in charge of this operation, but I'm in charge of the case. You countermand my orders and you'll spend the rest of your time at the PEC pushing papers. We clear?"

"You interested in saving that girl?" Rand asked.

"Damn straight."

"Then I won't have a reason to countermand, will I?" He signaled to the team, and the first two men dropped through the entrance. The next four followed, with Doyle, Rand, and Cort bringing up the rear. Because the target was a vampire, the RAC team consisted entirely of non-vamps, which made the use of hematite practical, albeit unpleasant for the team, all of whom wore masks to filter the dust and make breathing easier.

Doyle descended beneath the building then pulled his own mask off. The air was thick with particles, but he'd rather breathe them in than continue wearing the claustrophobic mask. Instinctively, he turned to check on Tucker, only to remember that his partner wasn't with him. On most missions, Tucker had Doyle's back, but he'd recently received orders not to engage in combat situations. Presumably, the powers that be were trying to protect his persuasive abilities by keeping him safe. But what they wanted those powers for remained a mystery.

Rand dropped down beside him and signaled for the group to move forward. Moving slowly, they inched their way through the earthen tunnels that Rhys had clearly crafted with care. Cort edged to the front of the group, his attention focused on the monitor that was strapped to his arm. The tunnel broke into a Y, and he signaled for half the team to veer left and the other—including Doyle—to veer right.

"The vic?" Doyle mouthed. Cort nodded and tapped the monitor, indicating that they were heading toward the heat signature as Rand led the rest of the team in the other direction, hopefully toward Rhys.

The tunnel sloped sharply downward, and they struggled to keep their footing. Once again the tunnel split into a Y, and this time Doyle and Cort continued together to the right while their two companions veered left.

A little bit farther. Slowly, slowly.

And then there it was—an opening in the side that led to a cavernous room. The girl's prison.

She looked up, startled, as they stepped inside, weapons drawn and senses on hyperalert. Cort took the left, Doyle the right, and Doyle had to admit he was impressed with the way his temporary partner handled the room.

"Don't!" the girl cried, but it wasn't until Cort set his foot down that Doyle understood. He'd crossed an imaginary line—and in doing so, had triggered one of Rhys's traps.

The trip to the cavern had been uneventful, and they'd gotten sloppy. But now fire sprung up inside of the room —two raging walls of flame that blocked both the entrance and their path to the girl.

"Shit," Cort snapped, whipping around to look for Rhys, who, of course, wasn't there. He pulled out his radio. "We found the girl, but we got fire," he said. "Tell Leon to get his ass over here. An eater," he added for Doyle's sake after he signed off, indicating that Leon was a jinn that consumed fire for nourishment.

But Doyle was barely listening. He was staring past the flames at the terrified girl beyond.

Staring ... and remembering.

CHAPTER

SIX

Fire.

It was an inferno, and it was raging through the chateau. Raw fear surged through Doyle as he clawed through the smoke, trying to find her. Trying desperately to save his Kathryn.

The impressive mansion had been built in 1649 by Kathryn's great-great-grandfather using stone from nearby quarries just outside of Paris. The walls would withstand the flames, Doyle knew, but the humans within them would not. Already, the tapestries that seemed to cover every wall were crawling with flames, the crackle and hiss sounding like vile laughter. The delicate chairs burned, arms red and writhing, as if urging a victim to sit. Sit, and be consumed.

He raced into the mirrored ballroom, hoping to find her there. But when he burst through the doors, Kathryn wasn't there, and the doors to the garden were still firmly shut.

Backtracking, he pushed into the depths of the chateau, then stumbled as he tripped over something. No.

Someone. Desperate, he sank to his knees, blinking to clear his vision. *Rhiana*. Kathryn's maid. But where was the lady herself?

Doyle started to rise, frantic to find his love, but he dropped back down hard onto the hot marble floor. He had to try to help the girl...

But there was no help to be had. She was dead, taken by the smoke.

Cold terror curled through him as he imagined Lucius finding Kathryn this way—sprawled on the floor, dead.

Where the hell was she? And where the hell was Lucius?

He started to stand, then realized that Rhiana would never have willingly left her mistress. It was a risk, and it would take time—precious seconds that were ticking away—but the chateau was too big to search randomly. He needed a goal, some clue to where Kathryn was. And if Rhiana could provide that...

He placed his hand on the girl's forehead. Hurry. Hurry.

And then he was in. Feeling Rhiana's terror. Looking through her eyes at Kathryn's beautiful face, distorted in horror as she looked at—what?

Frustrated, Doyle silently urged Rhiana to turn. To look at what her mistress saw. But the dead girl didn't cooperate. Instead, she ran, following Kathryn as she fled through the door and into the hallways that wound deep into the bowels of the house.

A moment later, the girl was on her own, having lost sight of Kathryn in the thick fog. And then there she was again—Kathryn DuLac—and Rhiana's joy mirrored Doyle's own. The girl stumbled toward her mistress, lungs burning, head fuzzy from the smoke, so thick in this narrow hallway. Then a cold wave of disappointment cut through her—cutting through Doyle at the same time, so intense it would have brought him to his knees had he not already been kneeling by the girl.

It wasn't Kathryn. Her portrait, yes, but not the woman herself.

Rhiana's memories flooded through him—the day Kathryn had stood for that life-sized portrait. Tightening the stays of Kathryn's dress. Brushing her long, golden locks into curls that danced flirtatiously around her shoulders, bared by her daring gown.

An image. A vision. A ghost.

The girl stumbled and fell, the impact of knees against tile sending pain through Doyle. She gasped, and Doyle's lungs burned as she took in the scalding hot air. She'd reached the end—the smoke and her fear clutching at her, weakening her. Without Kathryn, she didn't want to go on. Doyle knew how she felt, and it took all of his own strength to break the bond with the dead girl. To fight the sweet lure of death.

But he couldn't let go. Not if there was even the slightest chance that she was still alive, trapped and frightened.

And so he wrenched free of Rhiana's grasp and pushed forward once again. More bodies littered the way. These he essentially ignored, glancing down only long enough to confirm that Kathryn was not among them. There was no help for these fallen; he was certain they were as dead as Rhiana.

A sudden scream startled him, the sound thick in the unwieldy air. He put on a burst of speed and rushed toward it, wondering again where Lucius was. A new fear stabbed through him. He'd been traveling with Lucius on and off for the last two centuries, and the vampire had become one of his closest friends. They'd come here so that Doyle could introduce Luke to Kathryn. So that he could draw on his friend's strength when he finally revealed his true nature to the human woman he'd come to love so desperately.

But though he worried for Luke's safety, that concern barely registered against the icy fingers of his fear for Kathryn as he pushed his legs to move harder and faster toward the dwindling sound of the scream. There was no discerning the voice, and yet he somehow knew it was her. In pain, perhaps. Afraid, most definitely. But at least she was alive, and as his feet pounded against the floor, he kept repeating the word like a mantra. *Alive.* His love still lived, and he was going to her.

He found her upstairs, her back pressed against a wall, her eyes fixed on a window that was barred to her by a wall of flames. Flames licked the doorway, too, making it impassable for her.

For her, yes, but not for him.

Without thinking of how she would react, he thrust his hand forward and down, calling upon his innate power over the elements. Exhaustion and fear worked against his powers, but he managed to clear enough of a path through the fire to let him pass, and he scooted through, the cotton of his shirt and breeches getting singed in the process.

Her eyes widened as he moved unharmed through the flames. "Darling—how?"

"Later." He moved toward her.

"It was him!" she cried, her voice raw from the smoke. "By the Virgin, I couldn't trust what my own eyes showed me."

Around them, the air shimmered from the building heat. Kathryn did not seem to notice. "I'm being punished. God has smited me for sinful thoughts."

"You have not sinned."

"I let you touch me. And I—I wished for you to touch me as a husband, even without the bond of matrimony."

"There was no sin," he said firmly. "I love you, Kathryn."

She didn't seem to hear. "And now brimstone rains down upon us and demons have entered my home." Her beautiful eyes burned wild. "I did this—I brought it upon us. I brought the fire to dispel the minions of Lucifer himself. I set fire to the curtains, and then I ran, but it spread so quickly, and I got lost in the smoke."

His mind was reeling. "You? But why? What did you see? No, later. Tell me later. We have to get safe." Behind him, the flames in the doorway had flared up again, and he turned toward them, his free hand outthrust once more. Nothing happened.

A vile curse sprang from his lips, and he felt a sudden rush of horror. He was, quite simply, exhausted. He'd stayed in Rhiana's mind for far too long. And he'd breathed the smoke in deeply, weakening his human shell. He'd pushed aside the flames, a gift, yes, but one that extracted a price. And now that he'd found his love, he had no energy left to save her.

No.

It couldn't end this way. Not with Kathryn in his arms.

With fresh determination, he called upon his power once again. He felt it rise within him, bubbling up and curling into a hard ball before shooting out through his fingertips. The power thrust him back a step, and he stumbled, grasping at Kathryn to steady himself.

"It worked!" he cried joyfully as the flames descended. "Come, Kathryn, hurry!" He turned to look at her face. Her eyes were wide and horrified, her mouth forming a little O.

"You, too?" she cried, her voice full of fear and horror.

"No, Kathryn, no." But even as he spoke, he knew that he could not convince her. Because he could see his reflection in a mirror on the far wall. His eyes were orange, his skin dappled. He looked like the minions she so feared. He looked like he reigned in hell, and she'd seen him command dominion over the flames.

"Kathryn," he said, taking hold of her arm, ready to pull her out of the room. First he'd save her, then he'd convince her. All that mattered was getting her out. Everything else could come later.

She jerked hard and twisted herself free from his grasp.

Then, before he could take even one step, she tumbled backward into the flames, the hem of her gown catching immediately.

"Kathryn!"

He reached for her, but she recoiled, her eyes darting to and fro as she sought an escape. For a moment, her eyes met his, and he saw the horror that filled them. Then she turned toward the open window, the glass having already shattered from the rising heat.

Her movement thrust him into action and he forced the flames down. It was the wrong thing to do. Fresh fear flooded her face, and as he stepped toward her, she threw herself out of the open window, leaping into the arms of death. He didn't hesitate—he leaped out of the window too, fear and love bolstering his powers. He commanded the air to cushion both of their falls, but it was too late for her, and she landed in a charred, burned heap on the ground.

He came down with a thump beside her, his body twisting to cradle hers as something inside of him broke. With an anguished cry, he pressed his palm against her forehead, desperate to see what she'd seen, and yet terrified of what he might learn. At first there was nothing, and he feared he was too weak, his gift fading as his hunger grew. But then he caught the tail of an image. Then another and another. Vague outlines, patterns and shadows that meant nothing and then, like a mirage in the desert, it all came together to form a picture. A terrible, horrible picture. And, seeing it, Doyle understood.

Because in his love's mind, he saw fangs. And blood.

He saw Lucius Dragos feeding upon a housemaid.

Lucius, who had lost control of his serpent, and in the losing had killed Kathryn as surely as if he'd sunk his fangs into her neck.

The memory flashed through Doyle's mind in an instant, bringing fresh grief and fresh anger.

He pushed both aside, then froze, careful not to move and inadvertently spring another trap. He had to be careful. To concentrate on this moment. On getting this girl out alive.

Cort rushed forward—Doyle tried to stop him, but the agent was too quick. He was obviously intent on leaping over the flames, and he ignored Doyle and the girl, who was screaming that it was a trap.

A split second later, a thin blade burst from the side of the cavern, swooping down in an executioner's arc—taking Cort's head right off at the neck.

The girl shrieked, the sound filling the room like breaking glass. Doyle ignored her, because now there was a new problem—the blade had emerged from a slab of stone that doubled as a doorway. Rhys burst from it at a run, heading toward the girl, who had the self-presence to clamp her mouth shut and run in the opposite direction. But that was no help. She was still caught behind the wall of fire—and Rhys was in the fiery trap with her. Doyle pulled his gun and fired, emptying the magazine, but the wooden bullets burned up before reaching their target. The hematite Taser would be no use, either. Not from this side of the barrier.

There was only one solution, and he didn't know if he had the strength for it. Even if he made it, he'd be drained by the time he reached Rhys, and the vampire would be able to take him out as easily as squashing a bug.

The girl stared at him through the flames, her eyes wide, her expression terrified. Her blond hair was wild around her face, and he knew that he couldn't abandon her. No matter how low their odds, he had to at least try.

With effort, he gathered his remaining strength, calling upon his control over the elements, which swirled like a storm around him, gaining power. He drew it in, letting it build, then thrust the power back out toward the flames, demanding their obedience.

It worked—but only barely.

The fire seemed to leap off the ground, leaving a gap of heated, shimmering air between the floor and the base of the flames. Doyle threw himself to the ground, momentum sliding him under the flames and into the enclosure with Rhys and the girl.

It happened fast, and considering Rhys's almost comically surprised expression, the vampire hadn't expected his trap to be breached. Doyle took advantage of his surprise, rolling onto his back and pulling out the Taser. Now that he was beyond the flaming wall, the hematite threads it ejected wouldn't disintegrate. He fired, but Rhys moved with exceptional speed, managing to evade the danger.

Worse, Rhys was heading toward the girl, and there

was no time to reload the Taser and recharge its firing mechanism. That meant that Doyle was unarmed, and he was no match for Rhys in hand-to-hand combat—not on a good day, and certainly not when he hadn't fed.

There was no time to consider his options—no time to think about the danger he'd be putting the girl in if he drained himself to the point that his body overruled his brain and simply took what it needed. He drew upon his power once again, letting it surge through him before he sent it spinning out into the world, this time even stronger than before, fueled as it was by desperation.

At first, nothing happened. Then the fire seemed to spring to life like dancers in a wild ballet. Spinning and shifting and twirling, it burst into the void between Rhys and the girl. The vampire hissed with displeasure, then turned to face Doyle, who had compelled the flames to encircle the vampire. The makeshift prison held him, but weakness was hitting Doyle hard.

He stumbled, trying to hold on to the flames—trying to maintain the circle around Rhys.

He wished that Tucker was there—with his gift, he could have influenced Rhys, especially weakened as he was by the hematite. Tucker could have told the vampire to leap into the flames or, at the very least, stand still long enough to be captured.

He wasn't there now, though, so there was no point in wishful thinking.

Exhaustion flooded Doyle, but he kept his eyes firmly on his quarry. Saw the look of dark intensity in Rhys's eyes.

Waiting. Biding his time.

He couldn't risk the fire—it was potentially fatal for vampires. And he couldn't transform into mist and rise over the flames or call upon his strength to leap over them. The hematite dust had taken care of that.

But he could wait.

And Doyle knew that the vampire's simple plan would work because he had to concentrate on holding the flames, and he was so tired. His eyes so heavy.

The flames sputtered, and Doyle shuddered, struggling to hold on. There was nothing left in him, though, and as he faltered, the flames fell away and Rhys lunged. It was all over, and despair surged through Doyle.

Then Rhys froze, thin strands of hematite descending around him. Capturing him and holding him tight mere inches from the girl.

Confused, Doyle managed to shift his position, and he saw Rand in the doorway, a ferocious expression on his face.

In front of him, the girl cried out, the sound a mixture of terror and joy. She fell to the ground, then pushed herself up, half-running and half-crawling to Doyle. She wanted his comfort—he could see that much in her eyes.

He shifted, turning away from her. Fighting the urge to go to her. To clutch her close and murmur warm platitudes—and then rip the soul from her slender body.

It would come to that, he knew. He could feel it—the need, the hunger—rising in him, and he dug his fingers into the hard, packed dirt of the cavern floor, ripping his nails and slicing his fingertips as he fought against that horrible, vile reality.

In his peripheral vision, he saw Rand glance at him then rush forward and gather the girl himself. At the same time, the team moved in to secure Rhys in binders, ensuring he couldn't escape.

"Thank you," the girl murmured, her words muffled against Rand's chest. "Oh, God, thank you all. Thank you all for coming." For a moment, she only sobbed. Then she seemed to collect herself. She pushed back from the werewolf, her eyes searching his face. "He wasn't—he wasn't human," she said, her tone full of shocked wonder. She shifted to look at Doyle. "He wasn't human," she repeated.

Doyle met her eyes and tried to meld himself to the ground, fighting the urge to lunge and feed. "No," he finally said, the word coming out half gasp, half growl. "No, he wasn't human at all."

"You should eat more," Andrew Tarrant said, setting a metal tin of Danish butter cookies down in front of his daughter. "That was probably my biggest failing as a parent—not making sure you ate better. You get all involved and then you forget to eat and then you get too thin."

Andy didn't want a cookie, but she took one anyway, just to please her father. She'd been named after him, and in a way that gave them a special bond. Not that they'd needed a name to bond them; they'd been bonded in tragedy when Andy was only eleven years old. That was the year her mother had been mugged and beaten and stabbed.

She'd fought hard for days—Andy could still remember the astringent smell of her hospital room—but the blade's jagged edge had done too much damage. Andy's mother had pulled her close and told her that she loved her, would always love her. Then she'd pressed something into Andy's hand—the gold chain with the beautiful cross. "Wear it," her mother said. "Wear it and both God and I will be watching over you."

She'd put the necklace on then and there, liking the way it made her feel closer to her mom, yet hating what it meant. Because even at eleven, Andy understood what was coming. One of her dad's parishioners took her into the hallway and sat beside her patting her hand, telling her over and over how the whole congregation was praying for Gretchen Tarrant to rise above this horrible evil that had been done to her, and if she didn't pull through it was a sign that God wanted her home with him. Andy had reached up and rubbed the cross between her thumb and forefinger as if it were a wishing rock from a dime store. She'd nodded, silent, and pretended the parishioner's words had made the hurt better. Of course, they hadn't. The cross, though ... that she'd clung to, fiercely wishing for something she knew wasn't going to come true.

She'd sat there, listening to her companion drone on, until her father emerged hours later, his face pale, his eyes red. He said nothing, just took Andy into his arms, and she'd cried and cried, trying to find comfort in the normal, familiar smell of mint and tobacco that permeated her father's shirt.

The memory was still with her, as strong as ever. But while she'd always miss her mother, the pain had faded. The necklace had become her talisman, but whether she was looking to her mom or to God, she could never truly say.

"You had no failings as a father," she said after she swallowed the bite of cookie.

"You're very kind."

"But if you did..." She trailed off mischievously.

"Ah, and here it comes. The other shoe dropping."

"If you did, it wouldn't be that you didn't encourage me to eat, it would be that you encouraged me to eat cookies." She lifted the buttery flower, one petal now gone. "Not one of the basic food groups, Dad."

He tsked. "I kept meaning to take a nutrition class when I was in school, but they didn't offer one at the seminary. But I'm serious, sweetheart. I worry about you."

She leaned back against the couch and then tucked her feet under her. Her coffee was in arm's reach on the side table, and now she grabbed it, cupping the mug in her hands to warm her up. In the summer her father always kept the thermostat on sixty-eight. She'd carried a blanket around throughout her childhood, not for security but for basic warmth.

"So what are you worrying about today? And don't tell me this," she added, nodding at the cookies. "If you weren't worried about me eating pizza for breakfast at age twelve, I don't believe it's keeping you up at nights now that I'm twenty-six."

For a moment he didn't answer, just sat in his own chair and sipped his coffee. Then he put his cup down on the crocheted coaster Gretchen had made more than twenty years ago. "I don't think you should have gone back."

Andy focused on the cookie, pretending she didn't understand. "Back?"

"To see him. That monster." He shuddered. "You walked through my door, and I swear I felt cold. Like you'd brought back a piece of the devil himself."

She smiled at him fondly. "I'm not one of your parishioners, Daddy. The theatrics don't work on me."

"I'm not being theatrical. There's evil in the world, sweetheart. You know how I feel about you brushing up against it."

"We've been over this a hundred times. The opportunity to write about Creevey was too good to pass up." That wasn't entirely true. When she'd pitched the original article to the LA Times legal editor, she hadn't realized how big the case would become. How much attention it would garner because of Creevey's pretty-boy looks and his ridiculous claims that he had connections to vampires. And it wasn't until she was already deep in the thick of it that the prosecutors had added more counts, revealing to the public that Creevey was being charged with multiple brutal murders.

She'd sought the story out not because she'd known it would make her career, but because she'd wanted a window into the mind of a man who could so willingly torture and kill a woman. She wanted to understand.

That, however, wasn't something she could tell her father. She told herself it was because she feared dredging up the memory of her mother and opening her father's old wounds, but that wasn't true either. The truth was that she wanted to understand how someone could do that—could so brutally take a life—and the only way she could do that was to look evil in the face.

But she couldn't bring herself to tell her father that she wanted to peer that far into the dark.

"I don't want you to think I disapprove of your work, baby. What you're doing is good. You're shining light on things that have no business hiding in shadows. And the coverage you provided of that monster's trial has paid off in your career. That article was a good investment of time."

"I know it was." She'd already been approached by a publisher. If she could pitch an equally compelling piece, she just might be able to spin her newfound fame into a book deal. Heady stuff, if she could pull it off. That, of course, was the trick.

"But at the same time," her father continued, "I don't know that it's a good idea going back to that watering hole. Now that you're established, maybe you should focus on something ... cleaner."

"You don't want me writing a follow-up."

Her father shook his head. "No, but that's only part of it."

"Daddy?" His expression was dark, so unlike his usually jovial persona, and it worried her.

"You've been mingling with evil, Andrea. You've been seeking it out. And sometimes, when you look in dark corners, you find things that are better left hidden."

She realized that she'd lifted her hand to her neck and was idly toying with the cross. She pulled her hand away. "You're talking like there're monsters out there. Real ones, not just dangerous men like Creevey."

"As surely as there are angels, there are devils, too. And I don't want my daughter butting heads with them."

She shook her head, not sure if he was speaking in metaphors. Her mother had always teased that another world existed alongside their own, but the world Gretchen had told her daughter about consisted of fairies and pixies living on flower petals. Gretchen hadn't really believed it, of that Andy was certain. And she'd never before had the impression that her dad thought anything otherworldly existed on earth; that was the realm of heaven and hell, after all. A reason to be good and guard your soul, maybe, but nothing was going to jump out of your closet at night if you didn't.

"Honestly, Daddy, you've thrown me for a little bit of a loop here. I mean, you're not serious, are you? The boogeyman?"

For a second, she thought he was going to tell her that's exactly what he meant. Then he shook his head and gave her that half smile. "There's evil inside that man, Andy. I used to think there's good inside everyone, but it's not true. Some folks are born evil and some take it in like wine. And those that do, well, they'll always try and spread their evil ministry."

"I'm not turning to the dark side, Daddy. The Force is strong within me."

"I'm not joking."

She sat back, chagrined. "I know you're not, but I'm okay. Really I am. I'm stronger than you think."

He moved from his chair to sit beside her, then took her hand, the way he had when she was little. "I know how strong you are. Without your strength I would have collapsed after the Lord took your mother. But sometimes strength isn't enough. Remember, even if you fight against evil, it's fighting, too. And it's strong." He sighed. "We all have to fight in our own way. Just remember, with everything I do, my first goal is to protect you."

She thought about the latest story she was working on —one that could potentially be big enough for a book— and wondered how her dad would feel about it. A fanatical group whose members believed that supernatural creatures walked among humans—the kind that would make Creevey look like a kitten. It wasn't a story he'd like her to be on, but it also wasn't one she could give up.

She hated keeping secrets from her dad, but she didn't want him to worry. And, yeah, she didn't want to have to justify herself.

"When you were writing articles about the film industry, I didn't worry," he continued. "But this—"

"I couldn't handle being shuttled through any more press junkets." She'd spent a year as a staff reporter for an LA-based entertainment rag. She'd gone from press event to press event, just one in the crowd covering nothing of substance. She'd been bored out of her mind, and she wasn't about to go back to it. "But I'll ask around," she lied. "Maybe there's a meatier story out there. Maybe I can write about some Hollywood hunk's secret love child. I'm sure that's never been done before."

To his credit, her father laughed, then hugged her. "Just be careful. Even if he is behind bars, he still scares me."

"Me, too," she said, meaning it. It was that fear that had driven her to the story, made her want to understand what made Creevey tick. Because if she understood him then—then what? Then she could avoid it? Then she could bring her mother back?

She didn't know, and she supposed it didn't matter. It was what she wanted to do, and it was a hell of a lot more interesting than covering the premiere of Friday the 13th Part Eighty-Three.

"Speaking of Hollywood," he said, "why don't you stay for a movie. Something fun. How about *The Music Man?*"

She rolled her eyes. "How about *Die Hard?*"

"Deal."

"Great. I'll make the popcorn—oh!" She flashed an apologetic smile. "I can't. I signed up to help at the teen center tonight."

Though her father's ministry didn't advertise its involvement, it sponsored a recreation center for teens in Santa Monica. The idea was to give kids a safe place to hang out, and since the goal was to attract as many of them as possible, the religious component wasn't flaunted. Andy didn't get too involved with her father's church-related activities, but the Pacific Teen Center was something she felt strongly about. She volunteered as much as she could, spending time with the kids, letting them know that she was there if they wanted to talk about anything at all.

"I'll take a rain check," her dad said. "Be sure to give Kevin a call tonight, though. He's called twice looking for you."

"Here? Why?"

"Said you weren't answering your phone. Sounded a little hyper, but considering how your cousin usually acts, I wasn't too concerned. Everything okay with you two?"

"Of course," she said, but worry crept into her voice. "I had to turn my phone off in the prison. I forgot all about it." She pulled it out and looked at the display. He'd called, but he hadn't left a message.

Though she was six years older, she and Kevin had been as close as siblings growing up. That alone would have been enough to cause her concern on his behalf, but add in the fact that he was the one who had introduced her to the Dark Warriors—and that he'd recently told her that two of his college buddies had promised to show him something that would blow his mind—and she was definitely feeling anxious.

"Girl trouble?" Andrew asked, almost hopefully.

"That would be a good thing?"

"At least one of the kids in this family would be dating," he said, pointedly.

"I could say the same for you," she said archly. "Half the women in the congregation have their eye on you."

"And I have my eye on the flock."

"You should date, Daddy. I worry."

"As do I. And not about Kevin."

"I'm looking. I'm just extraordinarily picky. The man I end up with has a lot to live up to. A girl idolizes her dad, you know."

"Now you're just trying to flatter me."

"Is it working?"

"It is," he said, then laughed. He waved his hand toward the door. "Go on, now. Have fun at the Center. And let me know what's up with your cousin."

"Night, Daddy." She hurried toward the door, wishing she hadn't missed Kevin's calls. And hoping that it really was something as simple as a college romance gone bad.

When she'd first found the Pacific Teen Center, CeeCee Jane Gantz had thought it was pretty lame. And she sure as hell didn't think it had anything to offer her.

Maybe if she'd found it a few months earlier, back when she was still human—a sixteen-year-old runaway trying to stay alive in Los Angeles. Maybe then it would have been cool.

But she didn't have to worry about that staying alive thing anymore. And she wasn't alone anymore, either. She had Luke and Sara, the two vampires who'd adopted her. And she had her mentor Serge whenever she needed to talk to someone. And she even had Serge's wife, Katherine, when she wanted to hit the malls and do some shopping.

She wasn't alone.

Except sometimes she still felt lonely.

In a couple of hundred years, she'd only look sixteen. But right now, she still really was sixteen. And nobody she was hanging out with was even close to her age. Katherine and Sara each beat her by more than a decade. And Sergius and Luke had a couple of millennia on her. They didn't listen to Lady Gaga, they had no clue what TikTok was, and not a single one of them wanted to watch any of the Star Wars spin-offs.

It was on one of those lonely days that she'd finally wandered into the Center.

She knew it was run by some church group, and CeeCee was a long way from religious. But the place didn't flaunt it. Instead, it was all about the snacks and the air hockey, the library corner, and the television room. The adults who volunteered there mostly stayed out of the kids' way, and so the place had the vibe of a giant living room. Or the common area of a frat house.

Most of the kids who came were at risk—meaning they were dancing around gangland stuff or girls who'd gotten pregnant or the freako kids who didn't quite fit in. CeeCee was part of that latter group.

At first, she didn't talk much. Just hung out and read books. Maybe played some hoops in the lot behind the building. After all, it wasn't like she was going to plunk down next to someone and start oversharing about how she drank blood and was going to live forever.

But still...

For some reason, she kept coming back. If she wanted to go all psychoanalytical on herself, she'd say it was because she was still clinging to her old, human life. And, yeah, that was probably a lot of it.

But part of it was because the adult volunteers were pretty cool. Like Andy, who tended to hang out in the library section and would always ask CeeCee what she liked to read. She never pried or wanted to get all analytical or find deep meaning in CeeCee's book choices. Instead, she'd make book recommendations for things she thought CeeCee would like. She'd even play basketball and air hockey, and she wasn't half-bad.

CeeCee didn't tell Luke and Sara about the place at first. She didn't know why—they'd been so kind to her, maybe she was afraid they'd think she was ungrateful? Or that they weren't enough? Whatever the reason, she'd come here during the day, because she was still young and the sun didn't bother her. She'd tell them she was walking on the beach, and leave it at that.

Then one day Luke's car showed up outside, all black

and tinted windows. And when the sun went down, he got out of the car and came inside. He'd stood by the door until she'd noticed him, and then she'd shuffled toward him, certain he was going to rip her a new one, because that's what her asshole of a stepfather would have done.

Instead, he told her that they worried when they couldn't find her, and that they'd appreciate it if she'd just call or text them when she came here. They'd even come and pick her up so she didn't have to walk, or Sara would walk with her since she could still tolerate the sun, too.

In fact, it turned out that Sara even knew Andy. Because Sara used to be an Assistant District Attorney, back when she was human, and she gave a lot of press conferences. And Andy was a reporter, which was seriously cool.

Honestly, the whole situation with her new guardians was pretty cool.

And Luke's approval couldn't have come at a better time, because the truth was, she enjoyed spending time at the Center. And not just because the public library had donated a new stash of books.

No, she was all about the center now because Kurt Wiley had started coming there after school.

Kurt Wiley. He was tall and gorgeous and he played basketball like a pro. But he wasn't just a mindless jock. He read tons of books. And once or twice, CeeCee had seen him playing chess with the younger kids, so that meant he was a nice guy, too. And he was funny. He'd spoken to her a couple of times—offhand comments when they happened to be together in the television room or the library. Nothing deep or meaningful, but that could come eventually, right?

Except, it couldn't.

Because what would be the point? Even if she got the nerve up to go talk to him—even if she managed to articulate a real sentence instead of some shy grunting—in the end, she was going to be sixteen forever, and in the blink of an eye, he'd be twenty, thirty, forty. And, sure, maybe that wasn't such a big deal. Katherine was human and Serge was head-over-heels happy with her, and she with him. But Katherine knew the truth. She'd known before they fell in love that Serge was a vampire.

Kurt didn't even know CeeCee existed. Not that she was looking to get all relationship-y. But even just dating was, well, stupid. So he'd take her out for dinner. But that would be a big lie, wouldn't it? Because what she'd really be hungry for was blood.

Or he'd hold her protectively if they passed some scary gangbangers on the Venice Beach biking path. But he'd never know that she could kick the shit out of them.

And it wasn't like she could tell him. She wasn't living in some angsty vampire series with really, really pretty people. This was real life where most humans either didn't believe in vamps at all—or they were terrified of the mere idea.

Which meant that CeeCee came to the Center and she watched Kurt from the sidelines and she pined, just like a human girl too scared to talk to a cute guy.

And she wondered why the hell she bothered at all.

EIGHT

Doyle pressed his cheek against the car's window, wishing the coolness could bring him back to life. He was so far gone he could barely move. And they were still blocks away from Orlando's.

"I'm not going to say I told you so," Tucker said.

"I got the girl, didn't I?" Doyle's voice sounded groggy, his words slurred as if he were drunk.

"You did great, partner. In an hour you'll be good as new."

Doyle nodded. Or he thought he did. He wasn't entirely sure.

The sharp ring of his phone cut through the mush in his head like a knife. He fumbled for it, managed to close his fingers around it, and pressed the button for the speaker.

"Agent Doyle? Ryan?"

Shit. He knew that voice. That was Luke's voice.

"What is it, Dragos?" Tucker said.

"We need Doyle at the Club Rouge. Dead weren. We need him there now."

"Can't do it. He's wiped. Completely wiped. I'm taking him to Orlando's."

"Forget Orlando's," Luke said. "Consider this a direct order." As the Assistant Chairman of the Alliance and lieutenant governor of the Los Angeles territory, Luke was well within his rights to issue orders to PEC agents, even though that reality pissed Doyle off mightily. "We need into this guy's head."

"Then get another percipient, because Doyle's useless at the moment. He doesn't feed, he doesn't see. You know that as well as I do."

"You know damn well that Doyle's the only one on the continent," Luke said. "And he's going to want to see this guy."

At that, Doyle lifted his head, the effort costing him. "Who?"

"Jordan Lowe."

"Who the hell is Jordan Lowe?" Tucker asked, but Doyle didn't answer. Just motioned for his partner to turn the car around.

"Go."

Tucker cursed under his breath, but he turned. "He's not going to be any good to you," he told Luke.

"I'll have a source waiting."

Doyle shuddered. Out of the corner of his eye, he saw Tucker watching him, waiting for him to protest. His partner knew how much Doyle hated feeding directly off humans. At Orlando's, the succubi on staff extracted the souls that were sold by willing donors, then stored them in special receptacles. Those who needed them for nourishment could either lay with one of the girls or obtain the soul through a less personal mechanical process. That was what Doyle always opted for. He was still sucking down part of someone's soul, but somehow it seemed more palatable that way.

"Who's Lowe?" Tucker asked.

"Informant," Doyle said. He had to force the word out.

"You don't have a CI working right now."

"One of my first." He pressed his fingertips against his head to ward off the pounding. "Haven't talked with the kid in years."

"That explains why you didn't argue with Luke. Pretty sure I've never seen you not argue with Luke."

"Hurry. Someone killed him. I want to know who."

They arrived in less than five minutes to find the building cleared out and the humans' memories altered. True to his word, Luke had a source waiting—a succubus whom Doyle had met before on one of his trips to Orlando's. He cut a glance at Luke. He'd been afraid that he'd be forced to feed from a homeless person or a streetwalker. Though feeding from humans was illegal for vampires, certain concessions existed in the law for species that required souls to live. Doyle, however, didn't stoop so low. Not unless he was desperate.

Today, he would have been desperate enough, and despite the constantly pounding thrum of anger he felt for Luke, he had to acknowledge that for this, at least, he was grateful.

"Hello, Ryan," the succubus said, reaching for his hand. "There wasn't time to bring a device with me. I hope I'll do." Doyle was relieved that she had dark eyes. He didn't want to think of Kathryn. Of her pale eyes.

Or of the reporter whose eyes had so startled him. Was that only a few hours ago? It seemed like days.

"Hurry," Luke said. His expression was taut, and he seemed more imposing than usual. "He's been dead for hours. Apparently the folks in the club didn't move partic-ularly fast."

"Fucking vampires," Doyle said, looking defiantly at Luke, because he didn't want to be grateful to his old friend for anything. But Luke refused to be baited. He simply inclined his head and repeated, "Hurry."

The woman took Doyle's hand. Normally such things were done in private, but she pulled herself in close, pressing her body against his, and her soft mouth to his lips. That was all it took. Even if he'd wanted to resist, he couldn't, not with his hunger this high, and the moment their lips met, his parted, and he breathed in the warm, sweet ambrosia of soul.

He could feel it curling through him, warming him in the same way that good liquor spread through a man. The same way that the pleasure of pure passion built up in the moments before release.

He groaned, and in his mind, he saw her. Those eyes peering at him. Those lips, smiling. So close he couldn't see her face, but he ached for what he'd done to her. For how he'd failed her. Then the image shifted, coming more fully into view. Not Kathryn. *Her.* The reporter who'd been interviewing Creevey.

Startled, he broke off from the succubus, pushing her away.

"Did you get enough?"

"It'll do." He took only a moment to gather himself, and then he was all business. He looked down, frowning at Jordan's body sprawled on the ground. The lights were on, and the shabby condition of the place was obvious. "What was he doing in a vamp bar, anyway?" Doyle asked.

"Later. We've already wasted too much time."

Doyle nodded, then bent down beside the young weren who'd worked closely with him so many years ago. It wasn't right that he'd died like this, and Doyle was determined to find out who'd done him in. "Help me out, Jordan," he said. "Show me what you know."

But it had been too long.

He got in, yes. Sucked into the dark. Into the pain and the fear. He could tell that Jordan had tried to organize his thoughts before he died; that he'd wanted to leave Doyle a message. He heard Jordan's voice—Get the percipient—and then he felt the cold hand of death sweep the boy away.

And then Doyle was left in the void, alone with a few lingering images. Three faces. Young men. And names. Wes. Kevin. Stu. And another name, this one without a face. Paul. And fear, shock, and urgency.

"Danger," he said, as the vision snapped shut and he was thrust out of Jordan's mind. "Danger from the humans. And bad. I don't know what, but it's bad." He looked up at Luke. "The only reason I got that much is because he tried to leave a message for me in his mind."

"What message?"

"I don't know. Too much time's passed. All I got were names. Emotions." Doyle told him the specifics, and Luke's face hardened. "I think the faces I saw belonged to the men who killed him. But who's the other one? Who's Paul?"

"Their leader," Luke said. "One of them, anyway."

"Their leader? Whose leader? What are we dealing with here?"

"A group of humans," Luke said, and the genuine concern in his voice made Doyle frown. Doyle knew how dangerous humans could be—his mother was a prime example—but most Shadowers considered humans to be pretty innocuous.

"What group?" Doyle asked. "You have intelligence?"

"Some. Jordan was our man inside. They call themselves the Dark Warriors. And while they started out as little more than a nuisance, we have reason to believe they're becoming a serious threat."

Doyle exhaled and looked down at his informant, dead on the floor. "I guess you could say that."

"No," Luke said. "You don't understand. If what we fear is correct, Jordan's death is nothing but the beginning."

Andy pressed a damp cloth against the fifteen-year-old boy's nose, trying to stop the bleeding. Usually things were calmer at the Teen Center, but sometimes the basketball court turned into a war zone.

"I'm sorry, Miss Tarrant."

"Andy. Come on, Jerry, how many times do I have to tell you to call me Andy?"

The kid shrugged, and she laughed.

"I'm not your teacher, your principal, or your mom. I'm not going to lecture you. Do you think I don't get how hard it is for you to control your temper?"

"David baited me," he said. "All that crap about my mother? Like it's any of his business what she does for a living. He's—"

"You're right. It's none of his business. But sometimes you just have to rein it in."

The kid snorted. "Not that easy."

"I know. I'm proud of you. You didn't pummel him."

"Yeah, and look what I've got to show for it."

She gently pulled the cloth away. "I think it's stopped, but keep pressure on it for a few more minutes, okay? Seriously, I'm proud of you. A few months ago, I bet someone would have walked off that court with a couple of broken bones."

He shrugged and said nothing, but she had the feeling

he was pleased with the praise. She hoped so. She'd like to know she was making a difference.

After a few moments he headed out of the kitchen area. She lingered behind to check her cellphone, which had just buzzed to signal an incoming text.

Kevin.

Finally! She'd called and texted him more than once over the last hour. His message didn't say what was up, but it did say he'd meet her at the Center. Good. She had no idea why he'd been so persistent about trying to reach her and yet so reluctant about leaving a message. But she supposed she'd know soon. Considering that this was Kevin, the reason could be either grave or ridiculous; there really was no sense speculating.

She tucked her phone back into her pocket, then pulled a generic soda—the only kind that was covered by the Center's budget—from the ancient fridge. She popped the top and leaned on the counter, looking out over the pass-through bar at the kids who were mingling around. She knew most of them—could even guess what they were thinking. Alicia was studying in the corner, determined to ace her next test. Jerry was strutting around, trying to look cool despite his swollen and bloody nose. Seventeen-year-old Kurt had just finished up a game of chess with eleven-year-old Martin, and he was being a good sport about the fact that the genius kid had whipped him in only eight moves.

And then there was CeeCee. Quiet CeeCee who spent most of her time on the couch reading—and when her eyes weren't on a book, they were focused on Kurt.

She was looking at him now.

Andy tried to figure out how long the girl had been watching the handsome young teen. At least a couple of weeks. Probably going on a month now. And although Andy spent a great deal of her spare time at the Center, she'd never seen the two of them have an actual conversation despite the fact that CeeCee was obviously seriously crushing on the boy.

Most days, CeeCee would come in and read and watch Kurt until the time her guardian came for her. He was a huge man with a scar on his right cheek, and he always arrived in a car with darkly tinted windows. Andy had asked CeeCee if the man was her father, and the girl had hesitated. "I think of him that way, but technically he's my guardian."

Andy didn't know anyone who had a guardian rather than a parent or stepparent. "What do you call him?"

"His name," CeeCee had said, as if it were the most absurd question ever. "Luke Dragos."

The sun had recently set, signaling the time when Luke usually picked the girl up. But he wasn't here tonight. Andy wandered over and sat down next to her. "No ride tonight?"

"Luke texted that he has to work. I can walk home, though. It's not far."

Andy nodded. "You know you all fill out forms when you join the Center."

CeeCee looked at her sideways. "Yeah? So?"

"Kurt doesn't live far, either. Maybe you two could walk home together."

CeeCee's throat moved so dramatically that it was all Andy could do not to laugh.

"Or not," she said.

"Don't talk so loud!" CeeCee's voice came out as a blasting stage whisper that undoubtedly carried farther than Andy's normal speaking voice.

"He's outside on the court," Andy said. "Martin whooped him on the chessboard again, so he's taking it out on the hoops. Why don't you go watch? I bet he'd like a cheerleader."

"I don't think so."

"Why not?"

The girl only shrugged.

"Everyone's shy at sixteen, CeeCee. But if you like him…"

"It's not that."

"No?" Andy waited, giving CeeCee a chance to rethink that whole "shy" thing. She'd noticed how the girl tended to keep to herself. That had to be the reason, and if it was, Andy was happy to step in and play matchmaker. "Cee-Cee?" she prompted when the girl stayed silent. "Do you want me to say something to him?"

"God, no!"

She looked so mortified that Andy had to laugh. "Not that you like him. Just that you look bored. Maybe he'd ask you to play chess."

"And then what?"

"And then he'd realize what a cool kid you are and ask you to play chess again. Then he'd offer to walk you home, and maybe take you to a movie."

CeeCee almost smiled. "That sounds nice. Really normal."

"So…?"

"I don't think so."

Andy sat back, examining the girl's face, trying to get into her teenage head. "All right. I give up. Do you want to tell me why?"

"Because there's no point. We're too different."

"Different isn't necessarily bad."

CeeCee shrugged.

"Lots of people are different. That doesn't mean they can't be friends. Or more."

"Look, I appreciate it. I mean, I really like you. Of all the adults here, you're definitely the coolest."

"Thanks."

"But you just don't get it. It wouldn't work. It couldn't work."

"If it's important to you," Andy said, "you can make it work."

"Nothing personal, Andy, but that's pretty naïve." The girl stood up. "It sucks, but that's just the way it is. And I need to learn to deal with that."

"CeeCee—"

But the girl just waved and headed out the back door. Andy was debating what to do next when she heard Kevin calling her name. She turned and saw her cousin waving at her from across the room.

She glanced in CeeCee's direction one more time, but she didn't try to follow her. She didn't understand what the trouble was, but she knew that CeeCee wasn't going to talk about it right now. Andy would give her space and try again later.

"What's been going on with you?" she asked as she crossed the room toward her cousin in long strides. "Why didn't you just leave me a message? Why all the cryptic stuff?"

He took her arm and pulled her into one of the small rooms that opened off of the main area. They'd been intended as study halls, but the kids rarely used them, choosing instead to crack open their books in the open area if they felt inclined to study.

Kevin shut the door. Then he locked it.

"Oh my God, Andy, you won't believe it. You absolutely won't believe it." He paced behind the big Formica table, shifting directions so quickly he was making Andy's head spin. If she'd met him on the street, she would have assumed he was high on coke. As it was, she knew that this was just Kevin.

"FUBAR," he said. "You know what that is, right? The

situation is completely FUBAR. Fucked Up Beyond All Recognition."

"Thanks for the translation, I'm familiar with the term."

"But FUBAR in a good way. Or, a freaky way. Oh, shit, Andy, it was wild."

"Are you going to tell me what happened, or do I have to guess?"

"Guess—no, you'd never guess. Oh, shit, Andy. I saw one. Hell, I helped kill one."

"Kill one?" She leaned forward, her skin prickly with concern. "One what?"

"A werewolf."

"Oh my God, Kevin. Are you telling me you killed somebody?" She realized that she was clutching the back of one of the plastic chairs, and her fingers were tight and sore from pressing so hard. "Did you call the police? A lawyer?"

"You're not listening to me. I didn't kill someone. I killed something. And actually, I only fought him. And then he ran and we lost him." He frowned. "Maybe he's not dead." The frown deepened. "If he's not dead, he'll probably come after me. Oh my God, Andy. I need some wolfsbane and a lot of silver knives."

Andy's head was spinning, which wasn't unusual when she talked with Kevin, but this conversation was worse than normal. At least it was starting to sound like he hadn't actually killed someone. But something bad had happened, and she wanted to get every last detail. "Start over, and this time start at the beginning. And go slow, Kevin, okay? As a personal favor, slow it down to about a hundred miles per hour."

"Very funny," he said, but he complied. "You remember Wes and Stu? You met them at that first meet-up."

She nodded. Kevin had found out about a group of guys in his class at Cal State Northridge who were knee-deep in a meet-up group that centered around the members' shared belief that vampires and werewolves and the like lived among us.

That, of course, wasn't a fact worthy of her reporting skills. Los Angeles was a crazy town, after all—but then Wes and Stu had befriended Kevin and he'd learned that the meet-up group was a sort of testing ground. There was, in fact, a more powerful group—a secret group. It went by the name of the Dark Warriors, and apparently it included at least one local politician, though Kevin didn't know who.

That was a story. Possibly only National Enquirer worthy, but it had the potential to be huge. After all, no one wanted a nut-job running the country.

It wasn't a story Andy was willing to pass up, and she got Kevin to bring her in on the meet-up. Without a Wes and Stu of her own, though, she was pretty much stuck there, spending Saturday afternoons sipping cappuccinos with the same guys who thought that the science in Star Trek was real and that vampires really did sparkle and tended to congregate in the Pacific Northwest. In other words, even though she knew a story was just over the mountain, she didn't have a sherpa to get her there.

"So you're telling me that Wes and Stu dragged you into a fight with a werewolf? Come on, Kevin. You know it had to be some sort of fraternity prank. Some guy in heavy makeup working with Wes and Stu to make you look like a fool."

"No. No, you weren't there. It was real. I mean, it was down-and-dirty real."

She opened her mouth to argue, then decided that it wouldn't get her anywhere. She needed to hear the whole story first, so she just nodded. "Okay. Tell me what happened. But start at the beginning."

"Right. Right, okay, so it turns out that Wes and Stu have been hanging with the Dark Warriors' leader. That guy I told you about. Paul Vassalo."

"Really?" That could be a way into the story. "How did they manage to get in close like that?"

He waved his hand. "That's not the point. But apparently they met this guy, Jordan, and they started feeling each other out, talking. And they hit it off, and Jordan starts hinting that he wants to do more. So they think they'll introduce him to Paul. But turns out that things didn't add up."

"What things?"

"I don't know." Kevin's voice took on a whiny tone. "They didn't tell me. Can I please just finish the story?"

"Sorry. Go on."

"So we go out with the guy. And we have drinks and stuff, and he seems pretty normal, but then he starts to change." His eyes cut away from her as he said that last part.

"Starts to change? What does that mean?"

"Haven't you been listening? It means he was a were-wolf. And I saw it. With my own eyes."

"I—" She closed her mouth, not sure what to say.

"You don't believe me. Uncle Andrew would. And Aunt Gretchen would have, too."

"Kev—"

"She would," he said. "I remember her stories."

"Yeah, stories. About pixies and fairies. Not exactly the same thing."

"She used to say there was dark stuff, too. I remember. One time right before she died we were sitting on the back porch watching fireflies, and she started talking about how you couldn't tell if someone was bad just by looking at them."

Andy felt herself relax and she realized that for just a minute she'd wondered if he was right, if her mother had actually believed in werewolves and the like. But she remembered that night. "She was speaking metaphorically, Kevin. Just like in Daddy's sermons."

Kevin shook his head. "She wasn't," he said petulantly. "But that's not even the point. I'm not talking about when we were kids, I'm talking about last night."

She wanted to argue more about her mother—wanted to set the record straight. But Kevin was agitated and right now it was her cousin she had to worry about, not her memories.

"Look," she said gently. "I believe you that something happened last night." She just wasn't sure what, except that she was sure it wasn't a werewolf.

"Hell, yes, something happened. Fur. And this weird shifting in his bones. That's what happened. And the silver. It really messed him up."

"Silver?"

"They laced his drink with colloidal silver. And, well, there were knives."

"Jesus, Kevin. You stabbed somebody?"

"Why are you not listening? I told you that at the beginning. And the whole point is that He. Was. A. Werewolf."

"Even if I believed that—and I'm not saying I do—from what you've told me, he was hanging out and having drinks with you until your friends laced his drink and got him messed up. Then they chased him and hurt him and maybe even killed him. That sum it up?"

Kevin dropped down into a chair opposite hers looking absolutely miserable. "I didn't know what they were going to do, I swear. And the rest of it's absolutely true. He wasn't human, Andy."

Her mind was whirring at a million miles an hour, and some deep, pathetic, embarrassing part of her actually wanted to believe him. Because wouldn't that be the most amazing story?

And maybe the tooth fairy drove a Harley.

"Were you smoking anything?"

"God no!" he said. "Dammit, I thought you'd believe me. I thought you'd help."

"I am going to help. Even if this kid was a werewolf—" She forced her voice to stay firm and serious. "Even if he was, you need to find out what happened to him. I mean, come on, Kevin, if you really did kill someone, you need to turn yourself in. Turn yourself in and cut a deal. Tell them about Wes and Stu."

He looked positively horrified at the thought. "But maybe he didn't really die. There was a lot of blood, sure, but werewolves can survive a lot of trauma."

"How on earth would you know that?" Her voice rose with impatience and she tamped her temper down. Was she really arguing about how much abuse a werewolf could survive?

He bit his lower lip. "If he didn't die, he's gonna come after me, Andy. I'm sure of it."

"Hang on." She rummaged in her purse for her phone, determined to put an end to this. "Give me an address. Now."

He did, telling her the name of the bar they'd started at and the club where they'd ended up. Someplace called the Club Rouge. She called one of her sources at the LAPD. A dead kid ought to be easy enough to confirm, but after fifteen minutes on the phone, all she knew was that nothing out of the ordinary had been reported in the area.

Confused, she ended the call, sat back, and looked at

her cousin. "Nothing. No one in the area reported being attacked or even called in a report of strange activity. Are you sure you gave me the right address?"

Slowly, Kevin nodded.

"Seems pretty strange that he didn't call the cops if you three got into it with him."

"A werewolf isn't going to call the cops."

"Kevin..."

"If he's alive, he's gonna kill me," he said, running his hands through his hair. "He's gonna rip my head off."

Andy wasn't at all sure what was going on, but at least it didn't sound like Kevin had really harmed anyone. He truly believed the kid was a werewolf, and although she'd like to think that it was all a silly prank organized by Wes and Stu, she didn't really believe it. They'd all ganged up on some guy. Some guy they really believed changed into a wolf during the full moon.

And she had to assume that the rest of the Dark Warriors believed the same thing. Not only believed it, but were acting on it. Chasing after shadows, maybe, but that didn't make it less of a story. It just made it more of a freak show.

"You have to get me in with these people, Kevin."

He looked at her, confused. "But you're already in."

"Oh, please. You have me going to meet-ups with guys who just want to meet Sarah Michelle Gellar. It's nothing."

"But—"

"Kevin, this story is huge." She started to tell him about how the world needed to know about an organized group of violent whackjobs, then realized that her cousin counted himself as one of them. She backpedaled quickly. "Think about it, Kevin. If there are werewolves, the world needs to know."

"I don't think they'd like it. Having a reporter on the inside, I mean."

"They don't need to like it because they don't need to know." Years ago, when she wrote her first entertainment piece, she'd decided to write under a pen name so that she wouldn't get hit up for free movie tickets or introductions to celebrities. As it turned out, she didn't get many of those perks anyway, but she still liked the anonymity, and when she started to write darker investigative pieces—like the article she did on a local pedophile and her coverage of Creevey's trial—she'd kept the pen name. Now only her closest friends and family knew that Andrea Tarrant was the reporter Allison Stahl. Even Creevey himself thought her name was Allison.

His teeth dragged over his bottom lip. "Don't make me, Andy."

"This is what I do, Kev. And like it or not, you brought me a potentially great story."

He sighed. "You're not gonna write bad stuff about them, are you?"

"I'll write the story as it is," she said vaguely.

Kevin was frowning. "Maybe you should write a story. You should praise the Warriors as heroes. That was scary stuff last night, Andy. I mean, seriously scary."

"I know. You must have been terrified." She chose her words carefully. "But, Kevin, even if the kid you chased really was a werewolf, he sure didn't sound all powerful. I mean, three college kids brought him down with knives and a drugged drink. That doesn't sound too heroic to me."

She could tell by his expression that she'd pushed too far. "I'm sorry, Kev. Really. And I want to understand. Help me in, Kevin. Help me see the story the way you do."

He shook his head. "I'm not up there. I haven't even met Paul."

"I bet you will, though," she said. "After what happened last night, I bet he'll want to talk to you." She tried not to look too eager. "When he does, will you think about helping me? Kevin, it's the story of a lifetime. And I swear, they'll never know I'm a reporter."

Kevin stood up, his teeth raking over his lower lip. She shifted on the chair, sitting on her fingers so that she wouldn't fidget.

"Kev?"

Finally, he nodded, and her entire body went limp with relief.

"I don't know what I can do," he said. "But I'll try."

NINE

"You wanna tell me what the hell is going on?" Doyle demanded, his hackles rising. They were at PEC headquarters now, a subterranean series of floors hidden beneath the Los Angeles County Criminal Justice Building. Ten of them were settled around a huge conference table. Luke, of course, though he didn't technically work for the PEC, sat across the table from Doyle. His wife, Advocate Sara Constantine Dragos, who was another vampire, sat next to him. Doyle liked Sara, though he didn't understand what a smart girl like Constantine saw in Dragos. Rand was there, too, along with Tucker and a few of the support staff—some vamps and jinns and weren—that Doyle didn't know as well.

At the head of the table sat Nikko Leviathan, the head of the violent crimes division.

"What was Jordan into? Who are the Dark Warriors, what are they up to, and how can I make them pay for killing my CI?"

Leviathan and Luke exchanged a quick glance, then Luke nodded. Leviathan lifted a finger, and the lights dimmed. An image popped up on the projection screen. A lean, muscular man with a rugged, sunbaked face and a broad forehead below a receding hairline. He looked like he had a stick up his ass, and Doyle was certain the guy had to be part of the human military.

"Paul Vassalo," Leviathan said.

"Marine?" Doyle asked.

"Former SEAL team leader. Been retired for over a decade now. Came to our attention about seven months ago."

"Seven months?" Tucker asked. "Does this have anything to do with that incident in Australia?"

"Australia?" Doyle asked.

"Remember? A group of humans bombed a bar in Sydney. Possibly a random terrorist attack, but the inside scoop was that the humans knew the bar was frequented by vampires."

"Right. I remember. But Division Two never brought in any suspects."

"Because there were none," Leviathan said. "But at about that time, Paul flew from Australia to California. And a week or so later—"

"Two werens were killed in Griffith Park," Doyle finished. "Silver bullets."

"That's right."

"And Paul was behind it?" Tucker asked.

"At the time, we didn't know. Jordan confirmed it."

"How?" Doyle asked.

"We began to hear rumors of cells. Humans who know about Shadowers. Or about vampires and werewolves, anyway. There are more who believe the stories than who know the actual truth. That works to our advantage."

"There've been stories for centuries," Doyle said. "How is this different?"

"The attacks, for one," Leviathan said. "Australia and

Griffith Park weren't the only incidents. There have been several across the globe."

Doyle frowned. "Why haven't I heard about it?"

"The PEC has chosen to keep the incidents confidential. They've been revealed to Shadowers—including our own agents—only on a need-to-know basis."

"Why?"

Luke aimed a hard stare at him. "Come on, Ryan. You know why."

Doyle bristled. "It's not as bad as all that."

"It's getting bad," Sara put in. "I don't spend much time with humans anymore, but I'm in a position to hear things on both sides. More humans believe. And more Shadowers disdain humans. Or," she added, correcting herself, "if not more, then the ones who think humans are beneath us are becoming a much more vocal group."

"And if the attacks by the humans were made public, the PEC is afraid that those human-hating Shadowers would retaliate?" Doyle said.

"In a word, yes." Leviathan stood. At the same time, the lights came up.

"Is Paul Vassalo really such a threat?" he asked, although he already knew the answer. He'd seen Jordan's fear. And Doyle knew that Jordan hadn't been the kind to overreact.

"It's our belief he's not yet an international player. But he wants to be. He sees himself as leading the charge."

"His military background has made him organized," Rand added. "So far, all the human attacks on Shadowers have been limited in scope. Small clubs. Personal attacks like the werens in the park."

Luke took up the thread. "With the exception of those werens, we don't have any proof that the violence was organized. But based on what Jordan learned, we can assume that at least forty percent of the attacks across the globe were in fact the acts of human terrorists against Shadowers. The cells are only loosely organized, though."

Doyle considered that. "And you think Paul wants to step up as the big man in charge who can pull the cells together and increase the number of attacks?"

"That sums it up nicely," Leviathan said.

"So how do I get assigned to this case? It's because of this Paul asshole that Jordan's dead. Whatever I can do to make life miserable for him, I'm in."

"Glad to hear it," Luke said. "We need you on the inside."

Not what Doyle had been expecting to hear. "What? Undercover? I haven't been undercover in ages." He aimed his thumb at Rand. "Why not him? Or Sergius?" he added, referring to another vampire—a friend of Luke's who'd recently joined the PEC as an undercover agent.

"Serge is on assignment in London, and it wouldn't be prudent to pull him out. As for Rand—"

"I'd do it in a heartbeat," Rand said. "I've had a few beers with Jordan. A good man, and he didn't deserve to die that way." He hitched a thumb toward Luke and Leviathan. "But these two said no."

"You're the best man for the job," Luke told Doyle. "Like you said, you're motivated. More than that, though, you're half-human. They've already spotted a weren in their midst, so we don't want to risk sending in another. And vamps are out of the question. Daylight."

"Send in a young fang-banger. They're not sensitive to the sun."

Luke smirked. "Not enough experience, and you know it."

"You're telling me that Jordan was our only man inside this organization?"

"One of three, actually," Leviathan said. "Keep in mind that on a local scale, it's a small group. They recruit from local meet-up groups, Comic-Con, that sort of thing. Paul's inner circle pays attention, gets a feel for whether someone has the right sensibility. If so, he brings them in. Jordan was the only one who got tagged. The other two were ignored. We had to reassign them."

"Screw that," Doyle said. "I was in Jordan's head. We don't have time for me to go running around at Comic-Con. The boy was freaked. Something big is in the works. We need to move in, and fast."

He glanced sideways at Tucker. "Shit, just let my partner here get close and have a little chat with Paul. Get Paul to spill his plans. For that matter, get him to change his plans. Have Tucker take him to his happy place."

"Don't think we haven't considered it," Leviathan said, an answer that confirmed for Doyle just how serious this was. Using influence over humans was standard operating procedure to keep gathering crowds or local law enforcement from remembering an active Division 6 crime scene. But the use of influence in other situations—such as to change the way a human acted or thought—was officially sanctioned only in the most dire of circum-stances.

"But?" Doyle pressed.

"Jordan confirmed what we feared—Paul isn't suscep-tible to influence. We're not sure if he trained himself to withstand it or is naturally immune. Besides, our ultimate goal is to stop whatever Paul has planned. To do that, we need a better sense of how he's organized. Does he have a second in command? How many men does he have working for him? Where are they based and how orga-nized are they? In other words, we need answers. Answers and evidence sufficient to support prosecution."

Doyle shifted his attention to Sara. "Can we do that? Prosecute humans?"

"It's not done often, but we can. As you know, the PEC

doesn't have jurisdiction over a human who decides to become a vampire hunter or a werewolf slayer. That lack of jurisdiction stems from the long-standing presumption that if the human is setting out to, for example, stake a vampire, it's probably because that vampire has caused him or his family harm. And the PEC will look the other way."

"Law of the jungle instead of civilized law?" Tucker asked.

"Something like that," Sara agreed.

"But?" Doyle pressed.

"But in a situation where humans are organizing to seek out and attack Shadowers—especially if they're targeting Shadowers who've done them no harm—the humans are stepping over that jurisdictional line and into PEC territory. We'll have to make sure the evidence is solid and sparkling, but there are grounds for prosecution."

"So let's nail the bastards."

"Evidence," she repeated. "We need lots of it. And we need someone to gather it." She looked firmly at him. "We need you, Doyle."

He hesitated only briefly. "I'll do it. But I need to know what I'm walking into. Did Jordan compromise the operation? Are they going to see me coming?"

"We don't think so," Luke said. "But we can't be sure."

Doyle nodded slowly; it was the answer he'd expected. "But you still haven't addressed the biggest problem. Time. We don't have time for me to climb the ladder. Considering how freaked Jordan was, I'd say we're lucky if we have a week."

Leviathan grimaced. "Hopefully we have longer than that. But your point is well taken. Fortunately," he added with a thin smile, "we've come up with a way to get you in." Once again, the lights dimmed and an image flashed onto the screen. "Meet Assistant District Attorney Travis Sullivan. His office is several floors above ours. It's quite possible you've passed each other in the lobby."

"I recognize him," Doyle said. "Hasn't he been making noises about running for the State Senate?"

"That's the one. And he's well placed to succeed. Not only does he come from a political family, but he made a splash when he prosecuted Kyle Creevey. That case was a career maker and it got his name out to the voters."

"I don't know him well," Sara said. "But we crossed paths when I worked upstairs as an ADA. He's ambitious. I'd bet my salary that he wins the senate race. He's just the kind of man that Vassalo would want in his pocket."

"And is there a connection between him and Vassalo?" Doyle asked. "Or are we just speculating?"

Leviathan's smile was thin. "We've learned that he's hovering around the fringes of the Dark Warriors."

"The fringes?"

"We don't have the details, of course," Luke said. "According to Jordan's reports, Paul seemed to be courting Sullivan. But Jordan wasn't in a position to get any more specific than that. We intend to use Sullivan as your gateway to an introduction to Paul."

Doyle leaned back in his chair and snorted. "Do we? How?"

Leviathan and Luke both turned to pointedly stare at Tucker.

"I'm up for the job," Tucker said. "But what if he's not susceptible? You said Paul may have trained himself to avoid influence. What if he's been training his friends, too?"

"Actually, that's exactly what we think he's doing," Luke said. "And that may be why Sullivan is still only on the fringes of the group. We've done a few test runs and he's still susceptible, but the operator can't go deep."

"So we can tell him to trust Doyle, invite him for coffee, drinks, whatever," Tucker said. "But we can't have him forget he's ever seen Doyle?"

"Exactly."

"Too bad you can't go deep enough to make him forget that I supposedly work for Homeland Security," Doyle said. "That's going to be a stumbling block."

"I'm not so sure," Leviathan said. "I think it could actually work to our benefit."

"That I'm in law enforcement?" Doyle asked.

"That you're like him. Don't forget, he's a prosecutor. You two are simpatico, or so he'll think."

"Two like-minded men looking for a type of justice that the system isn't providing," Luke added. "He'll believe it. With Tucker there to enforce the idea, I think we can be confident of that."

Doyle nodded. "Fair enough." He faced Luke. "Are we certain he doesn't know about Division Six?"

"As certain as we can be," Luke said.

Sara leaned forward. "We're confident. I asked Porter myself," she said, referring to Alexander Porter, the District Attorney, and the only person in the DA's office who was aware of the existence of Division 6. "Unless Sullivan's keeping it a secret, he doesn't know anything more than I did back when I was an ADA."

"And what exactly did you know?" Tucker asked.

"That Division Six was a special division of Homeland Security. I assumed it focused on covert work. But believe me, until I saw the PEC floors myself, I had no idea what —or who—shared the building with me."

"So whatever he believes about Shadowers, it's not because he works here and has been rubbing shoulders with us," Tucker said.

Doyle considered everything they'd said and had to agree that they'd plugged the biggest holes. It still wasn't a foolproof plan, but he sure as hell didn't have a better suggestion.

Of course, Travis was only part of the problem. "Even if I manage to get in tight with Travis, Paul is likely to be more careful. And we already know we can't use influence on him."

"A fair point," Leviathan said. "But once you do earn his trust, he'll undoubtedly find you indispensable for your position within Homeland. But you'll need to work fast."

"Earn his trust?" Doyle repeated with a tight grin. "Got any ideas?"

"Not a one," Leviathan admitted. "But we will. And the first step is for you to get in good with Sullivan. Everything else depends on that."

"Fine," Doyle said. "How do I do that?"

Sara pushed back her chair and stood. "Just follow me."

"Analysts have been combing through surveillance footage of the lobby since Jordan reported Sullivan's involvement," Sara said as they rode up in the elevator from the secret sub-basement level. "At five he takes a walk to the end of the block, grabs a coffee, and comes back before putting in a few more hours at the office." She eyed Doyle and Tucker. "You ready?"

"A little more warning before diving into the op would have been nice," Doyle said. "But yeah. I'm good to go. You?"

"Hell yes," Tucker said as the elevator doors slid open.

"There he is," Sara said as they stepped into the

cavernous lobby. Her head cocked slightly to the left, and Doyle saw that Sullivan had just emerged from the elevator next to theirs. He had a politician's smile, and as Doyle watched, Travis shook hands with no fewer than five colleagues, working the after-work crowd like he was at a political rally.

"Here we go," Sara said. Then, louder, "Travis!" He glanced over, then held out his arms in a gesture of surprise and greeting.

"Sara Constantine—look at you! I heard you were transferred to Division Six. Congratulations."

"Thanks," she said. "But it's nothing like what you've been up to. I followed the Creevey trial. Amazing work. He's an absolute monster."

Sullivan's face clouded. "He is indeed. Honestly, it's never easy seeking the death penalty, but with Creevey I had no hesitations."

"I wouldn't have, either," Doyle said.

"Oh, I'm so sorry." Sara gestured to Doyle and Tucker. "Agent Doyle, Agent Tucker, this is Travis Sullivan, one of our assistant district attorneys."

They shared greetings, and then Sara glanced at her watch. "Great running into you, but I've got to get to a meeting." She glanced at Doyle and Tucker. "Agents? You coming back to the office?"

"Gonna grab a coffee," Doyle said. "Shame the snack bar only has dreck."

"I'm heading to the Coffee Bean if you'd like to join me," Travis said. Of course, Doyle and Tucker agreed.

"So how long have we been doing this?" Doyle asked Travis a few minutes later as the barista handed their coffees over. They moved to the nearby table that Tucker had snagged and sat down.

"This?" Travis frowned, clearly confused.

"Three months," Tucker said, putting on the whammy. "You two have been grabbing coffee together on and off for three months."

"That's right," Travis said. "We've been getting coffee together for three months. I've enjoyed our breaks."

"Good to be with someone who understands the way you think," Tucker said. "Who knows what you do." He leaned in, lowering his voice. "Who knows about the vampires and the werewolves and the other creatures."

"Hard to do what we do, isn't it?" Travis said. "We put away criminals, but it only makes a dent. The real danger is hiding in the dark, and there's nobody out there fighting against that evil."

"Nobody?" Doyle said.

"You know you can trust him," Tucker said. "You've trusted him for weeks."

Travis looked between the two men. "That's right. I have."

"It's time you let me in," Doyle said. "You know how I think. You know what I want."

"To eradicate evil," Travis said.

"Hell, yeah," Doyle said. He leaned back and lifted his coffee, secure in the fact that at least for the moment he wasn't telling a lie. "Hell, yeah."

Twice Kevin picked up the phone to call Wes, and twice he put it down again. He wasn't sure what he'd say to the guy. Just like he wasn't sure what to think about the fact that Andy's cop friend didn't know about any dead or injured kid at the Club Rouge. Or a dead werewolf for that matter.

But Kevin knew what he'd seen, even if Andy thought he was nuts.

Did she?

He couldn't tell. He'd known her his whole life, and yet she always kept a part of herself shut off. It would bug him except that he'd gotten used to it. And he knew she was smart. So maybe it wasn't that she didn't believe him. Maybe she just needed to see it for herself. Like doing labs in school or dissecting a frog or something.

God.

He plopped down on the sofa. What he really wanted was a beer. He was tired and ripped and he was supposed to be in class right now, but the last thing he wanted to do was think about class. He didn't even know what he was doing half the time, and the other half he felt lost and in over his head.

He hadn't been like that in high school. Then, he'd been popular. He'd fit in. But college had thrown him for a loop. That was, he realized, why he'd been so happy when Wes and Stu had pulled him into their circle. Why he wanted so badly to move up. To meet Paul.

Paul was someone he could really admire. He and his Dark Warriors had a purpose. They had focus. They were doing something that Kevin could get behind. That he could be proud of.

And if he could prove that to Andy, he would. For once he'd be the one doing the explaining, and not the other way around.

Except he hadn't been bullshitting when he'd told her

he didn't have a way in. He'd thought that Wes or Stu would come by today, that they'd ask him to hang with them. At the very least they'd be able to talk about last night. Better yet, they could go to Paul and tell him all about it. Wes knew Paul, he'd told Kevin so himself.

But there had been no call. Nobody had dropped by. Just Kevin, the television, and a bunch of bullshit shows. He picked up the remote, intending to find something with some action, then dropped it when the shrill ring of his phone startled him. For a second he didn't look at the screen, afraid it would be a bill collector or his mother or a wrong number. But he couldn't stand it, and he finally snatched it up on the third ring. *Please be Wes. Please be Wes.*

It wasn't. It wasn't Stu, either.

It was better.

TEN

Paul Vassalo knew about evil. As a child, he'd looked it in the face. He'd gagged from the stench of it. He'd watched as the people he loved best had died, ripped apart at the hands of monsters. The kinds of monsters who shouldn't exist. Shouldn't, but did.

At the time, he'd been too young to do anything about it. But he'd waited and watched and learned.

Now, he was the one the monsters needed to watch out for. And not just him—one man couldn't expect to stand against the monsters. But a team? An army?

That was the way to fight the devil. And that was what he was fighting, after all. Evil incarnate. The physical manifestation of dark spirits upon the earth. Demons, monsters, whatever you wanted to call them. The creatures weren't human, and they were poisoning the world.

Paul stood now at the north end of an underground bunker hidden deep within the Mojave Desert. In front of him, a dozen men stood at attention, his most promising soldiers. Each of them would recruit four more to their cause within the month, and those four would do the same in turn. With that type of exponential increase, his army would be massive within a year.

But it wasn't the future he was concerned with now. His father had always said that a man should look toward the future only if his feet were firmly planted on today.

Today.

He smiled, because today he'd set the wheels soundly in motion. Soon, every other cell leader would know that Paul was the man to watch. That he was the one who would lead the charge for the ultimate eradication of the dark creatures.

"Gentlemen, your stakes."

The men raised the plastic stakes that they'd been supplied with for training purposes.

"Bryce? If you'd do the honors."

To his left, Bryce Lowell stepped forward, his face wind worn and craggy. Bryce had served his country for twenty-five years, and even though he was officially retired, he was serving it still by training Paul's Dark Warriors.

"If you men will step off the mat," Bryce said. The men complied, each stepping backward until they were no longer on the oval-shaped mat that had been constructed out of hematite. An interesting metal, it affected vampires quite dramatically, sapping their strength and eradicating their ability to change into mist.

At the same time, Bryce spoke into a walkie-talkie. Moments later, two uniformed men led a pale woman into the room. She wore a metal collar and had long dark hair, and her sharp eyes cut straight into Paul, promising retribution. She wouldn't have the chance to follow through, of course. Paul would use her for training purposes until she was too weak to provide a good workout for his team. Then he'd move on to one of the other two vampires he had trapped in the cells below the bunker.

He used the females for battle training; he had to ensure that his men wouldn't go easy in combat simply because they were fighting a woman. The male vampire that was currently imprisoned in the bunker served another purpose. Paul used it for training the men to withstand a vampire's ability to control a human's mind. At first, the vampire had refused to assist Paul in that very necessary operation, but once Paul had explained— through the use of a syringe filled with liquid hematite and acid—how painful noncompliance could be, the vampire had become much more amenable. And the men now had a 98 percent success rate in withstanding a vampire's compulsion.

"Private," Bryce said, pointing to one of the men. "You're up."

The blond-haired private stepped onto the mat just as the handler shoved the vamp toward him. She snarled. She didn't, however, attack. Just stood there, staring at the private.

"This is a training exercise, female," Bryce said. "Attack."

"Fuck. You." Her voice, raw and hoarse, grated on Paul like sandpaper.

He reached for the small control box in his pocket and pushed the button. Immediately, she was on her knees, her hands clawing at her throat, as if she was trying to rip off her own head.

"Attack," Bryce said again, but once again the female only looked up at him, her face now curled into a pain-filled sneer.

"Go," Bryce said, this time to the private. "She'll defend herself."

The blond man shot a quick glance at the other men,

then moved forward. He was experienced in hand-to-hand, but it was obvious that he wasn't used to attacking a downed opponent. Finally, he kicked her in the ribs. She grabbed his foot, and was on top of him with incredible speed, fangs bared, head bending toward his neck.

Paul crossed his arms and watched. He didn't want her to win, obviously, but he had no use for soldiers who couldn't prevail. They all understood the risks. Training was training—but it was also for keeps.

The private got his hands under her and shoved, pushing her off of him. He was on his feet in seconds, using the momentum of his rise to propel himself forward and into her. They went tumbling, him on top of her. In the next instant, his stake came down, the hard plastic slamming straight into her heart.

She went limp, blood spilling onto the mat. She'd be given blood to revive her, and then the next soldier would have a go.

The private backed away, breathing hard, as the other men applauded.

"Excellent," Paul said. He turned his attention to the other men. "Tonight, you train. But tomorrow ... tomorrow I'm sending six of you on a mission. Tomorrow night, you take the first step toward our prime objective."

"Name?" The tuxedoed doorman held a clipboard, his finger poised to scroll down a list of names.

"K-Kevin. K-Kevin Whalton."

He sounded so nervous that Andy took his hand and squeezed. "We're invited," she told the doorman. "For the cocktail party."

"Of course. Here you are." The doorman made a quick check mark, then stepped aside to call the elevator down from the penthouse. A moment later, the Warford Hotel's ornate elevator doors slid open, and Kevin and Andy stepped inside. The doors closed, and Kevin turned to her, grinning like a fiend.

"Holy shit, is this cool or what?"

"It's pretty snazzy," Andy had to agree.

"Can you believe it? I mean, he's throwing this party for me. For us. Wes and Stu, I mean. Not you and me."

She laughed, amused by how nervous he was, and at the same time worried that his nerves would give her away and he'd do something foolish like mention that she was a reporter.

He'd stumbled into her apartment last night and told her that Paul Vassalo himself had called to say that he was holding a special cocktail party to congratulate Kevin and his friends on their defeat of the werewolf. She'd held her breath and she hadn't pushed, but she'd been desperate to go with him.

And then, miracle of miracles, he'd invited her. Granted, the reason he'd done so was that he wanted to prove to her that werewolves really did exist and that the Dark Warriors were doing God's work, so he hadn't just extended the invitation out of the goodness of his heart.

Didn't matter.

The point was that Andy was riding with him in the elevator of one of the West Coast's most prestigious hotels. They were heading to the penthouse—which dozens of movie stars and heads of state had stayed in over the years. Heady stuff, but even better was the fact that she'd be mingling with the infamous Paul—a man who just might be the key to another career-making story. She'd be charming and flirtatious and interesting and whatever else was required to get in Paul's good graces and stay there. Because at the end of the day, she was getting this story. Whatever it took, she was getting it.

"So, uh, do I look okay?"

His red hair stood up in spikes, and he was so pale from nerves that his freckles seemed to float off his skin. But his suit was snazzy and his smile was bright and she couldn't help reaching over and squeezing his hand. "You look awesome."

The elevator's walls were mirrored, and she took the opportunity to check out her own appearance. She'd learned long ago to play up her pale eyes with dramatic liner and tonight she'd paired it with a shimmering silver eyeshadow that matched the metallic sheen of her simple, shift-like cocktail dress. Other than that, she wore little makeup. Just some powder and pale lip gloss. Her dark hair was piled on top of her head and held in place by an ornate clip that used to be her mother's. A few tendrils fell loose to frame her face. On the whole, she thought she looked party-ready. Hopefully she also looked like a girl to whom Paul would wish to divulge all his deepest secrets.

Beside her, Kevin was shifting his weight from foot to foot as he reached up to loosen his tie, the expression on his face suggesting that the thing was about to choke him. She smiled fondly at him. He hadn't dated much since high school, and sometimes she wondered if he'd ever find the balls to ask a woman out. Maybe a new reputation as a macho werewolf hunter would do the trick. So long as the women didn't think he was insane, it probably couldn't hurt.

The doors opened to reveal the stunning suite. Candles covered every surface, lending the room a fairy-tale glow. It looked like it was lit by fireflies. Despite her nerves about the party and her impression that Paul was either running a scam or was some sort of nutcase, she had to admit she was charmed.

"Kevin!" A gangly man with bushy blond hair and a frat boy grin hurried up, hand outstretched. He started pumping Kevin's arm, and immediately began talking. "Stu's not here yet—the idiot isn't answering his phone—but isn't this amazing? And all for us. What did I tell you, buddy? What did I tell you? I'm Wes, by the way, and who are you?" He focused on her, his smile going wider and his voice turning oilier.

"Andy," she said, taking the hand that had dropped Kevin's and reached for hers.

"The hell it is. You're too beautiful to have a man's name."

"It's Andrea," Kevin put in.

"It's Andy," she said firmly, tugging her hand free.

"She's a looker, Kev, and a spitfire, too."

"She's my cousin," Kevin said.

"And that makes her even prettier," Wes said, sidling closer.

Andy fought back the urge to show him another meaning of spitfire. Instead, she smiled thinly and reminded herself that this was one of the boys that had seen the werewolf. He was a source. An asshole, but a source. "Can you tell me about it? The werewolf, I mean."

"Oh, man, it was fucking ferocious. I mean, he started out looking like anybody, you know? And then—whammo—he turned into a monster. Right in front of us. I tell you, if we hadn't moved fast, we'd be dead."

"Don't exaggerate, Wesley." The voice was honey smooth and it came from behind Andy. She turned, and found herself staring into the rugged face of a man who seemed to command the entire room with nothing more than a glance. "I think our young Wesley is trying to impress you," he said to Andy, his mouth curving into a smile. "And who can blame him."

"You're very kind," she said.

"Paul Vassalo. And you're Andrea Tarrant. I've heard a lot about you."

"You have?" She looked sideways at Kevin, who seemed bewildered.

"I told him I was bringing you as a date, but—"

Paul laughed. "Don't worry. I didn't run a background check. It's just that your name comes up often."

"My name?" This was making no sense whatsoever.

Paul spread his hands expansively. "What else do family men talk about but their family?" He turned slightly, and Andy shifted in the same direction, then gasped.

She glanced sideways at Kevin, but he looked as bewildered as she did. "Daddy?" she whispered as the floor shifted beneath her feet.

Her father crossed the few yards that separated them, then hooked an arm around her and pulled her to him in that familiar way he had. "Hello, sweetheart," he said, then kissed the top of her head. "And you look spiffy, Kevin."

"Thanks," Kevin said, but there was a vertical crease of confusion between his eyes.

Andy looked up at her father, who was smiling at her and the cluster of people who stood around them as if he didn't have a care in the world. She knew better, though. This was the man she knew best in all the world, and she could see the strain on his face and feel the tension in his arms.

"What a surprise—I didn't expect to see you here," she said brightly, because she couldn't think of a single thing else to say.

"I could say the same thing," Andrew Tarrant said. "Imagine my shock when I arrive early to share a drink with Paul and he tells me that not only is one of the guests of honor my nephew—" He cut off for long enough to raise his glass in a silent toast to Kevin. "—but that the same young man is bringing my daughter as a date."

"He wasn't happy at first," Paul said to Andy. "He's been struggling for months with whether or not he should tell you about what we do here."

"You mean fighting the monsters?"

"Exactly." He aimed a smile at her father. "You see, Andrew? I told you she'd take it in stride. After all, considering what killed her mother, she has a vested interest, too."

CHAPTER

ELEVEN

er mother?

Her mother had been mugged. What the hell was Paul talking about?

Her father's arm tightened against her. "It's not something she likes to talk about."

"No," she said, shaking her head and not even trying to hide the tears that began to well in her eyes. "No, it's really not."

Paul's brow furrowed, and he looked genuinely distraught. "I'm so sorry. Of all people, I should know better than to bring up such a painful memory." He pressed a hand to her arm in a gesture of genuine sympathy. "The pain of losing a mother never goes away; it only sinks beneath the surface. I'm sorry to have dredged it up again."

"It's okay. Really."

"I think I'll take my daughter to get a drink."

"Of course," Paul said, turning to Wes and Kevin. "And I'll take these young men around the room and introduce them to their admirers."

Kevin shot her a glance that she interpreted as a ques-

131

tion: Was she okay? Could he leave? She nodded and managed a small smile, then watched as Paul led the two college boys away.

"Daddy," Andy said as soon as Paul was gone. "I don't —why are you here?" She could tell the question surprised him—why wasn't she asking about her mom? But she couldn't tackle that question straight on. If she came at it sideways, maybe it would hurt a little less.

There were only a dozen or so people in the room, so it was easy for them to find a seat in a quiet corner. "I've told you, sweetheart. My ministry is about fighting evil. And evil walks the earth."

"I thought you meant by, you know, prayer. And bake sales. And evangelical preaching. Not—oh, jeez, Daddy, I don't even know what this is."

"This is war," her father said, with an intensity she'd rarely seen in his eyes. "This is the war that rages in heaven."

"Does that make us the angels or the demons?"

"Don't be flippant, Andrea." He drew in a long, noisy breath. "I never wanted you on the front lines like this. Not you, and not Kevin. I only learned today what Kevin's been up to—and what happened to him the other night." He closed his eyes and pressed his fingers to his temples. "He told you what he saw?"

"He told me a story about a werewolf. Daddy, I came tonight because Kevin needed a friend—he was so nervous." She deliberately didn't mention the story that she'd been hoping to walk away with. "But I don't believe in this stuff."

"Whether you believe or not, it's true. I've seen one myself. I saw the one that killed your mother."

"One what?" she asked slowly.

"Andy." Her father's tone was gentle. "A werewolf killed your mother."

She hugged herself against a sudden wash of cold. "I don't want to hear that."

"I didn't want you to hear it, either. I wanted to keep you safe, away from this world. I wanted you to walk far away from evil and stay only in the light. You deserve that, Andrea, and it's what I want for you." He sighed. "But the truth is, I should have told you long ago." He brushed her cheek. "You deserve to know what happened to your mother."

"So tell me now." She wasn't sure she really wanted to know—not yet. But once the words were out, she couldn't call them back.

"Your mother was an exceptional woman," he began. "I think you already know how we met. I was traveling, preaching in small communities across the South. She lived in New Orleans and she came to one of my iced tea socials."

Andrea smiled, imagining her mother in a crisp cotton dress and her father in his suit, probably melting in the Louisiana heat, but unwilling to take off his jacket, because it would have been bad manners.

"We knew right away—sometimes it's like that. You see someone, and suddenly there's a warm knot in your heart, as if God is telling you that he's made it easy and put the other half of your soul right there in front of you."

Inexplicably, she thought of Agent Doyle. Of the way she'd gotten all twisted up looking at him. But that wasn't the same—she'd been pissed off, and that was a different kind of knot than the one her father was talking about.

"She was a true New Orleans girl. Magic and voodoo and portents. Now you know I don't cotton to that kind of thing, but I loved your mother, and she loved me, and when I moved on she came with me. We were married six months to the day that we met, and to her credit she never talked about zombies or vampires or the living dead. Not at first, anyway."

"She used to tell me about fairies," Andy said wistfully.

"I remember. I asked her to stop. She believed they were real, and I was afraid she'd make you believe, too." He frowned. "She told you about other things, too. Dark things. I had to beg her to stop telling you stories. You had nightmares—she stopped when she realized she was scaring you. You really don't remember?"

"No."

"She stopped talking, but it didn't stop her from thinking about it. She became obsessed."

"Why?"

"I don't know. She started arguing with me. Telling me that my thinking was one-sided. That being human didn't make someone good."

"It doesn't."

"No, of course not. But she also said that being a vampire or a werewolf or a demon didn't make you bad."

Andy licked her lips. "She went looking for them?"

Her father nodded. "She went looking, and what she found killed her."

The words seemed to hang flat between them. She felt cold again, and wished she'd brought a shawl. "That's— that can't be true."

"Why are you here if you don't believe?"

"I told you," she said. "Kevin asked me to come."

But he didn't seem to hear her. Instead, he sat back with wide, disappointed eyes. "Oh, no, Andrea. Please, no."

A tight fist seemed to squeeze around her heart. "No, what?"

"Are you writing an article?" His voice was low, barely audible even though she was sitting just inches away from him. "Andrea, what Paul is doing—what I'm doing—it's important work. But stealth is a requirement. You write an article and his entire operation is at risk. People aren't ready to—"

"Daddy." She clutched his hand. "I'm not chasing a story," she lied. Except was it a lie? True, that's why she'd come. But that was before she knew her father was involved. Anything she wrote now would expose her dad as a nutcase, too. Even if all this stuff about vampires and werewolves was true—dear God, could it be?—no reader would believe it. The world at large would still label them all crazy.

And yet at the same time, how could she walk away? Could she find a new angle? A way to write about this without getting her father involved? Somehow this strange subculture had killed her mother, and didn't that deserve some attention?

She pushed the questions away, her mind spinning too much to think. She didn't have to decide right now, all she had to do was protect her access.

Her father looked at her for a long time, then finally nodded. "Paul can't know."

"Know what?"

"That you're a reporter. I trust your word," he added, and she felt guilt rise hot in her throat. "But Paul doesn't know you. If he finds out about your pen name—"

"What? What would he do?"

It seemed to take a moment for her father to answer. "He's a friend and he trusts me. I don't want to violate that trust."

"Of course. I can keep a secret."

"And Kevin?"

"He can, too. I promise."

Her father didn't look convinced, but he nodded. "So this is a one-time thing? You came tonight simply to support your cousin? And after this you're walking away from Paul and all the rest of it?"

The question caught her off guard. She couldn't walk away—but she couldn't explain why without admitting that she'd lied about wanting to find a way into a story.

But there was more to it than that. Whether he was right or not, her father really seemed to believe that a werewolf had killed her mother. She couldn't quite wrap her head around that possibility, but she also trusted her dad. How could she trust him about everything else and think he was a mental case as far as Gretchen's death was concerned?

Suppose—just suppose—that all of this freakishness really was true. Suppose that werewolves and vampires did exist.

And suppose that one of them had really killed her mom.

She drew in a breath and faced her dad. "I can't do that, Daddy. I don't know what I believe yet, not really. But if werewolves really do exist, then I'm not walking away." Because then it wouldn't be about the article anymore.

Then it would be about revenge.

TWELVE

Kyle Creevey was a list maker. Before he'd been imprisoned, he'd made lists of every girl he'd ever fucked. Of every girl he'd ever killed. And of every asshole who'd looked at him the wrong way. During the trial he'd made lists of all the lies the witnesses spread about him. Of all the pompous lawyers who had it in for him. And most especially of all the reporters who wrote about him in their articles as if he was some sort of goddamned freak of nature.

Top of that list was Andrea Tarrant. Or, as she liked to be called, Allison Stahl.

He grinned. Little bitch thought she could keep her identity a secret? It had been so easy to find out the truth. A chat with his defense attorney. A conjugal visit with one of the bitches he kept on the side. A clever little girl who earned her living picking pockets, and who'd been more than happy to slide in next to Andrea during the trial and sneak a peek at her driver's license. And the bitch reporter had been none the wiser.

What fucking bullshit. Little bitch thought she was so

smart. But he had his eye on her. Oh, yes. He had his eye on all of them.

The whole death row thing was a problem, no doubt about that. But there were ways.

Oh, yes … there were ways.

It was good to have friends in high places, and Kyle had made friends with some of the best. He'd heard through the grapevine that Rhys had been captured—and that was some fucked-up shit—but Rhys had introduced him to some pretty fine folks. Folks who'd made Kyle's blood stronger. Who would make him stronger yet. Oh, yeah, they would.

No, Kyle didn't fear death row. All he regretted was the mind-numbing boredom. But that was going to change. Yeah, that was going to change real soon.

At the moment, he was wearing an orange jumpsuit and his wrists and legs were shackled to the rail on the third seat from the back on the prison bus. And the bus was on a lonely section of highway heading toward San Quentin. The sun had set hours ago, and they were so far from the city, that the only lights on the horizon came from the occasional far-off house.

He was the only prisoner, and he bounced in the empty shell of a bus, his bony ass, too thin from prison food, coming down hard on the worn-out springs.

They were transferring him. Prison crowding, they said. Whatever. He didn't care why; he only cared about the opportunity. Because they were watching, weren't they? They had to be. They'd promised him freedom. They'd promised him life.

They'd come for him, Kyle was sure of that. They'd come, and he'd become magnificent.

He sucked in some air and started to whistle.

"Shut the fuck up, Creevey," the driver shouted back to him. The guard, sitting in the first seat right behind the driver, just shook his head, a smug little smile on his mouth. Another asshole. Not that Kyle was in a position to do anything about it. Sometimes you just had to accept the fact that you were up to your asshole in assholes. Better than alligators, he supposed.

Suddenly, the bus stopped, and Kyle was thrown forward, his chest slamming into the back of the seat in front of him. "What the fuck?" he yelled.

"Car stopped short in front of us," the driver called back. "We'll be moving in a minute. What the he—"

He didn't finish his sentence. The bullet that blasted through the front windshield tore off the bottom of his jaw. The second one went through his brain.

"Holy fuck!" The guard was on his feet in a second, but it was a second too late. A shotgun blast, then the door burst open. Three men in bulletproof vests leaped on, guns aimed. Two shots, and the guard went down. The three ran forward as two more entered, guarding their backs. Kyle yanked at his arms, but the chains that bound him held tight.

"Kyle Creevey?" the third one asked.

"You fucking know it."

"You're coming with us."

"You're vampires?"

The men looked at each other and laughed. Then one of them plucked a syringe from a sleeve pocket. "Not exactly," the man said, then jammed the needle into Kyle's neck.

"Cut the restraints," the man said, and as another one hurried to comply, the world started to spin around Kyle.

He wasn't dying—he couldn't be dying.

But then the world went black.

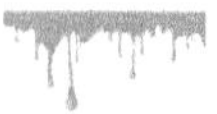

Doyle leaned against the bar, a drink in his hand and his eyes on the crowd. Travis was on the balcony with Paul, and the crowd was mingling. So far, everything was going to plan, but he hadn't yet spoken with Paul himself. Just in case the big man decided to kick him to the curb, Doyle was making a point of familiarizing himself with the faces in the crowd; he wanted to be able to recognize Paul's inner circle by sight.

The trouble was, his attention kept pulling back to one face. An elegant face, with a strong jaw and prominent cheekbones and dark hair that seemed to both absorb and reflect the candlelight like angel fire. *The reporter.* She was sitting with an older man on a silk sofa. He couldn't hear their conversation, but he could see the look on her face, which was filled with both pain and incredulity. Whatever the subject of conversation, it was a good bet it wasn't Disney's latest movie.

He started to shift his attention, but for just an instant, her gaze swept the room. *Those eyes.* He slammed back the rest of his drink. Those damned eyes that kept pulling his focus, not to mention his memories.

The first time he'd seen her—ages ago when she'd been in the crowd that had gathered around a body—he'd thought they were Kathryn's eyes. And he'd thought the same when they'd crossed paths at the prison.

But they weren't Kathryn's eyes. Not when you looked closer, and damned if he didn't want to look. The color and shape were the same, but this woman's eyes were sharper and set more widely on her face than Kathryn's had been. Her eyes were soft, even slightly vulnerable, but there was strength there, too.

Without thinking, he took a step toward her, then stopped cold. What the hell was he doing?

He lifted his glass to toss back some more Scotch, then remembered that he'd already polished it off. Shit.

The woman was messing with his equilibrium, and that pissed him off. He told himself that any spark he felt was simply because she reminded him of Kathryn, but he didn't really believe it. Better to just walk away. He wasn't here about the woman. Hell, he had no reason to even be thinking about her.

Except he did.

For one thing, she knew what he was—an agent, if not a para-demon. Of course, since he was using his job as his cover that hardly counted as a reason for him to go talk to her. Simple logic, but it left him disappointed.

But then there was the reality of what she was—a reporter. He had to assume that she was here writing a story, some huge investigative piece on Paul and his operation. And while Doyle couldn't give a shit if she blew the lid on their group, he did care if she exposed them before he was ready.

She was still talking with the older man on the sofa, but after a moment, he squeezed her shoulder, then stood up and stepped out onto the patio. This was an interesting development, since it suggested that the man ranked highly in the group's pecking order. Paul, Travis, and this anonymous man. Were they the holy trinity, or did others also hold powerful positions in Paul's Dark Warriors?

He was mulling the question over so deeply that he didn't notice her gaze shift to him. But when he looked up, those pale eyes were looking right at him, luminescent in the flickering light. He considered looking away, but he didn't want to. He didn't know if the compulsion was good, bad, or indifferent, but he did know that he wanted to do nothing but get lost in her eyes.

In the end, she was the one who looked away, her gaze darting downward. He felt a tight sense of satisfaction, though he wasn't entirely sure why. Winning a staring contest was hardly the most impressive feat of his career.

She stood, and he felt his pulse quicken in anticipation. This time, he did turn away. If she was coming toward him, he damn well needed another drink.

He turned and poured himself another Scotch. When he looked back, she wasn't even close to him. She was standing with the two young men whom Paul had been parading around when Doyle arrived. Wes and Kevin, Travis had told him. Two of the three who'd killed Jordan. He needed to talk to them—but before he did, he needed to make sure he could keep his temper under control. Revealing the demon here would not only be counterproductive to his overall mission, it would most likely be suicidal.

After a moment, she squeezed the hand of the redheaded kid, then stepped away. She turned, paused, and looked straight at Doyle. She had a trim figure that she held with grace, shoulders back and her chin up. She walked toward him slowly, but with undeniable purpose, and as she did, one eyebrow arched up, as if in question. Doyle didn't know what the answer was.

"You've been watching me."

"You look familiar."

"That's because we've met. At the prison. Or don't you remember, Agent Doyle?"

"I remember," he said. "And I've seen you in the crowd around some crime scenes. Ms...?"

She hesitated for just a moment, then said, "Tarrant. My name is Andrea Tarrant. Andy."

"You're a reporter?"

She stepped closer to him, her expression tight. "I'm not here as a reporter."

He looked at her, trying to judge whether she was telling the truth. "No? Then why are you here?"

She stood even straighter. "I'd appreciate it if you'd keep the reporter thing between us. I write under a pen name, and my job isn't something I advertise."

"I won't blow your cover."

"I'm not undercover." She drew in a breath. "Look, are you going to be a jerk or aren't you?"

He couldn't help his laugh. "Chances are I'll be a jerk several times over. But I will keep your secret."

"Oh." Her expression had been shifting into something argumentative. Now her face relaxed. It was, he thought, a stunningly beautiful face. "Thank you."

"My pleasure."

"Right. So." She reached up, her fingers touching the cross that hung around her neck. He didn't think she was aware of the movement. "If you'll excuse me, I think I'll get a glass of wine."

"I'll join you."

She glanced down at his drink.

He took a sip, then smiled. "For the company, not the Cabernet."

Her brow furrowed, but she nodded, then shrugged. "Suit yourself." She turned and moved toward the side of the room, then took a glass of wine from the serving table. He followed, telling himself that he needed to find out more about the man she'd been talking with, but knowing damn well that he really just wanted to be near her.

She took a sip. "So is Paul Vassalo a national security risk? Is the hotel being invaded by terrorists?"

"Excuse me?"

"I'm just wondering why Homeland Security is interested in a cocktail party."

"I get the feeling you don't want me here."

Her expression softened. "I'm sorry. I just—I've

worked very hard to keep the fact that I'm a reporter a secret, and here you are. I feel a little edgy."

"I said I'd keep your secret."

"So you did." She shrugged. "But it's not like I know you. And in my experience, people lie."

"Yeah? That's been my experience, too."

She laughed. "You're not exactly helping your own case."

"So wait and get to know me. In the end you'll figure things out."

"How long is this party going to go on for?"

"Are you suggesting we won't see each other again after this party?"

She swallowed, and her hand fluttered up to her necklace again. "Are you suggesting we will?" He heard the softly flirtatious tone of her voice and felt a stab of purely male victory in his gut.

"Maybe I am," he said.

"Oh. Well." Even in the dim light, he could see a hint of pink stain her cheeks. She cleared her throat, then took a sip of her wine. "So, how'd you end up here?" Her voice had a forced casualness, and he felt a kick of disappointment. "Did you come with someone?"

"Travis Sullivan."

"Really? The attorney who prosecuted Creevey?" Her neck craned as she searched the room, clearly intrigued by that bit of info. "I don't see him."

"He's on the balcony. Talking with Paul and the man you were with. Who was he?"

"Not that it's any of your business, but he's my father."

That little piece of information sliced through him like a knife. If her father was here, then it was possible she was a part of all this, not just an observer on the sidelines like he was.

And what do you care, Doyle? Why should you care what she thinks about the Shadowers? About you?

Because for whatever reason, this woman got under his skin. But he couldn't blow this mission simply because a beautiful woman messed with his head.

She was looking intently at him. "You never answered my question—are you here on official business?"

"Official business?"

"You know what I mean. You're a cop," she added, her voice so low it was barely audible. "Is this a sting? Are you undercover? Are you about to pull out handcuffs and make an arrest?"

He laughed her off. "I know Travis from work. He knows perfectly well that I'm with Homeland."

"Really?"

"You sound surprised."

"I just—nothing."

"What?"

"I guess I assumed that agents were more ... skulky about things."

He could tell that it wasn't what she'd intended to say —and her coyness made him wonder how much she knew about the Dark Warriors' activities. At the very least, she apparently knew enough to think that they might have caught Homeland's eye.

He didn't call her on it, though. Considering who her father was, Andrea Tarrant could turn into a solid asset. "Did you really just suggest that the federal government is skulky?"

Her lips twitched. "I guess I did. So, if you're not here for work, why did you come? Just to keep Travis company?"

"I'm interested in what Paul's doing."

"Oh."

He knew he hadn't given her a straight answer—and

he knew she knew, too—so he was grateful when he saw Kevin peering at them from across the room. It gave him a chance to shift the conversation. "We're being watched."

She turned to glance over her shoulder. "That's Kevin."

"I know. The man of the hour." Doyle worked hard to keep the contempt from his voice. "You know him?"

"My cousin."

Doyle couldn't ignore the sense of relief that flooded him. From the familiar way he'd seen her touch the guy earlier, he'd thought—

Not that it mattered. But, yeah. He was relieved.

"Man of the hour?" she repeated. "So you know what happened?" There was a touch of ambiguity in her voice, and he realized this was a test. Her way of finding out if he was in with the rest of them. If he was safe to talk to.

Hell yes, he was.

He met her eyes straight on. "You mean about the werewolf?" His words came out casual, but he felt anything but. His head was filled with Jordan, and he had to force himself not to look at Kevin, for fear his contempt would show on his face.

"That's exactly what I mean," she said, almost too brightly. It made him wonder if she really believed the story. "The whole thing's pretty amazing."

"It's difficult when your entire view of the world shifts."

"Yes. It is." She took a sip of her wine and looked over at the balcony. "But that wasn't really what I meant. It's just that Kevin's not the fighting kind. I don't think he's had a fight since kindergarten. Joanie Myerson stole his Cheerios. It was ugly."

"Those things usually are."

"So an alley fight—when I heard, I was thinking there was no way. But it just got weirder." She leaned against the wall and took a sip of her drink. "I don't know about you, Agent Doyle—"

"It's Ryan. But you can call me Doyle. Everyone does."

"Well, I don't know about you, but when he told me that his fight was with a werewolf..." She trailed off with a shake of her head. "Honestly, I thought he was a loon. And now—" Her brow furrowed, and she blinked, as if fighting back tears. "Sorry. I'm feeling a little bit overwhelmed tonight."

"Are you saying you just learned? That werewolves exist, I mean?" He hoped the answer was yes. Because that would mean that she was new to the Dark Warriors, and any culpability for what the group had done so far wouldn't fall on her shoulders.

"I'm still not sure that they do," she said. She shifted her weight against the wall. "No, I learned something else that was disturbing tonight. Actually, the whole evening has me on edge. I'm sorry—I usually make better small talk."

He moved to share the wall with her and took a sip of his own drink. The Scotch was smooth and it slid down easily. "Do you want to talk about it?"

"No," she said. "I really don't."

There was a familiar kind of pain in her voice. The kind that cut through a person when their world was shattered. He barely knew her, but despite all reason, he wanted to reach out and hold her and protect her. From what, he didn't know.

But he swore to himself that somehow, someway, he was going to find out. And if it was within his power, he would find a way to ease her pain.

THIRTEEN

Andy tried to shake off the memories of her mom, not to mention the dark fear that everything her father had just told her was absolutely true. She wanted to go home and curl up in bed, but she couldn't. Maybe later she'd have time to process everything she'd learned today, but right now she didn't. Right now she was here, she was with Doyle, and she needed to keep her head.

Doyle.

She shifted her position against the wall to look more directly at him. He'd come here with Travis Sullivan, an assistant district attorney with an eye on a senate seat. Exactly the kind of hook she'd been looking for when she asked Kevin to tell her which meet-up groups to join. Exactly who she'd wanted to meet when she begged him to get her in even deeper.

She watched as he stepped in through the balcony door, then poured himself a drink. She could walk over right now and introduce herself.

Except that now, with the news about her mother's death and the revelation that her father was in deep with the Dark Warriors, ferreting out information about Travis was the last thing on her mind. The article that had seemed so important only an hour ago now seemed far-off, like something she'd once dreamed. Maybe the dream would solidify again, but for the moment, her priority list had changed.

"Deep thoughts?" Doyle said from beside her. He was watching her intently, and his gaze felt like fingers softly stroking her. There was an uncomfortable pleasure in the thought of that imaginary touch.

"Only as deep as this glass," she lied, lifting her wine. From across the room, Kevin waved, and she thought about the expression she'd seen on Doyle's face earlier, after she'd told him that Kevin was her cousin. He'd seemed pleased. Almost relieved. And she couldn't help but wonder about it. Was he attracted to her?

The possibility swirled pleasantly inside her. She was probably reading too much into things, but she'd be lying to herself if she didn't at least admit that she felt a little buzz when she was close to him. And that she'd felt it from the first moment she saw him at the prison. Hell, even a little at crime scenes. That instant zing of attraction that made her want to smooth her hair and check her makeup. Stupid, she knew, but she couldn't help but think of what her father had said about the instantaneous connection between him and her mother.

Come on, Andy, get a grip.

Her emotions were all over the place. She knew why, of course—it had been a crazy day. But she needed to rein it in.

"Andy—" Doyle began. Her name hung between them, full of promise. But she didn't get the chance to find out what he was going to say, because Kevin came bounding up, breaking the spell.

"Some party, huh? Everyone wants to talk to me and

Wes. I wish Stu was here. I can't figure out why he'd blow us off." He turned to Doyle and stuck out his hand. "I'm Kevin Whalton. I'm one of the guys that took down the werewolf."

Something harsh crossed Doyle's face, and for a moment she had the impression that he was going to refuse to shake Kevin's hand. Then the moment faded and he clasped her cousin's hand in his own. "You must be very proud," he said blandly.

"Are you one of Paul's friends?" Kevin asked.

"I came with Travis," Doyle said. "But I'm hoping to meet Mr. Vassalo. He's got something very unique going on here."

"So, how much of this stuff do you know already? I mean, for me, the other night was my first time. Have you ever fought a werewolf? A real one, I mean? Or a vampire?"

"As a matter of fact, I have. Both."

Andy looked at him in surprise.

"Then you know what I'm talking about," Kevin continued. "They're evil, pure and simple. And there's nothing to be done about evil except to destroy it." He cocked his head toward Andy. "She's still a skeptic."

Doyle glanced sideways at her. "Is she?"

"You've piqued my curiosity," Andy said, sidestepping the question. "How exactly does one recognize a were-wolf? I mean, if I were to meet one in a dark forest? Or a vampire, for that matter, traipsing through a cemetery?"

"It isn't easy," Doyle said seriously. "Most vampires and werewolves look just like you and me. They have their day-to-day lives. They blend in."

He was looking at her, only her, and the rest of the world seemed to fade away.

"That's what makes them so hard to fight," Kevin said, his voice breaking the spell. "Evil walks among us. Just like your dad always says. You have to be on guard all the time."

"Is that right, Mr. Doyle?" She wanted him to look at her that way again, but he'd shifted his attention to Kevin, and she felt a sinking disappointment.

Paul stepped up to join the group. "Is what right?" he asked.

Kevin lit up like a shiny penny, all youth and eagerness. "Andy was just asking Mr. Doyle about how vamps and werewolves hide in plain sight."

"Ryan Doyle," Paul said, extending his hand. "I'm Paul Vassalo. Travis speaks highly of you. Tells me you'll be an exceptional asset."

"Doyle's fought vampires," Kevin said, his voice overflowing with awe. "Werewolves, too."

"Is that a fact? How did you get sucked into our elite club? Most people are blissfully unaware of the danger that surrounds us."

"My mother," Doyle said flatly. "She's the one who got me interested in fighting demons."

"Demons?" Kevin asked.

"Aren't they the common denominator?" Doyle asked. "All of the creatures you're fighting—we're fighting—are creatures of the night. The kinds of demons that live in hell. That animate the monsters that prey on the innocent."

"And you've actually fought these creatures?" Paul asked.

Andy stared at Doyle, as interested in the answer as Paul was.

"I have. You could say it's been something of a mission with me. I get pissed off when someone steps in and hurts the innocent."

"I know how you feel. So tell me what you've done. What kind of monsters have you taken down?"

For a moment, Andy thought that Doyle wasn't going to answer, and she fought the urge to intervene. This was a test, obviously, even if he didn't realize it. And if he didn't impress Paul, then he wasn't going to be in the group. And for good or for bad, she wanted him in the group.

"Vampires," Doyle finally said. "They're the worst. The most vile. They were human once, but they let the darkness inside take over." He shifted his attention from Paul to Andy. "They destroy lives, and leave the survivors with hearts like charred ash."

"Poetic," Paul said. "And I must say I agree. You've actually taken one out? How?"

"More than one," Doyle said. "And there are only two ways to kill a vampire. A stake through the heart works best. Nice and clean since it leaves no trace."

"What do you mean?" Andy asked.

"Ashes. Just like in the movies."

"And the other way?" Paul prompted.

"Well, that would be beheading. That does leave a body. A much messier business. I used a chain saw once. It wasn't pretty."

Andy was certain she'd gone as pale as Kevin, but neither Doyle nor Paul seemed to notice.

"I had a similar experience once," Paul said. "I was in Argentina and trapped without a weapon in a closed hotel. I ended up stabbing the werewolf that attacked me, getting him through the heart with a steak knife. Imagine my surprise when I discovered that the utensils weren't silver."

"What did you do?" Doyle asked.

"Fortunately, the salt shaker was sterling. I snatched it up and thrust it and my fist into the hole left by my knife. The werewolf died with my hand in his heart."

"Well," Andy said. "This has certainly been educational." She felt like she needed to put a stop to it before they tugged down their flies and did some serious measuring. "I'm going to go freshen my drink." She looked at Doyle. "Need a refill?"

For a moment, she thought he was going to accept, but in the end he shook his head. "I'm fine. I should probably go find Travis. He was kind enough to bring me here, and I've all but abandoned him."

She hoped her disappointment didn't show as he moved across the room away from her. She stayed with Kevin, and they spent the next hour sipping drinks— Kevin sipping a few too many—and mingling. The spotlight shone brightly on her cousin, and despite the bizarre circumstances, she couldn't help but be delighted for him. He wasn't used to being the center of attention, and tonight he was eating it up.

As the crowd started to thin, her father appeared by her side. "Have I done good?"

She looked up at him, confused. "What?"

"I've been giving you space. It's what all the parenting books say you should do for children."

"I'm pretty sure those books are referring to toddlers. But, yes, you've done good. And I did need space."

"Did?"

"Do," she admitted. She rose up on her toes and kissed his cheek. "I'm not shell-shocked anymore, but I'm still trying to wrap my head around all of this. It would be easier if the basic premise wasn't so insane." She gave her dad a hug. "I'll come over tomorrow. Daylight and coffee will help. We can talk more then."

"Good. I'm going to give Kevin a ride home. You came in his car?"

She nodded.

"It'll be fine with the valet. He can get it tomorrow."

He pulled out his wallet and handed her a fifty. "Cab fare. Unless you'd like me to drive you home, too?"

Doyle drifted into view across the room, and she shook her head without thinking. "No thanks. I'm going to stay a little longer."

She watched as her father left, his arm supporting Kevin. Wes, she realized, was already gone, as were most of the other guests. The ones who remained were gathering their things and saying their goodbyes. Paul was in a corner, his phone pressed to his ear.

She fingered the fifty-dollar bill in her pocket and took a step toward him, ready to say her own goodbyes. He hung up as she approached, looking stricken.

"What is it?" she asked, as Doyle and Travis joined her.

"That was Stu's girlfriend," Paul said. "He's dead."

The body sprawled on the back patio of the tiny Northridge apartment was so mangled that Doyle thought it could easily have been mistaken for raw meat. They were standing a few feet from the body, held back by the LAPD officers who'd responded to Stu's girlfriend's frantic call. Andy was standing next to Doyle. Her eyes were bloodshot, and her hands were pressed to her mouth. She was shivering.

He took off his jacket and pulled it over her shoulders. She looked up with stormy eyes, then slid her arms into the sleeves before reaching out and clutching his hand. She squeezed tight, and he squeezed back, using her as an anchor to calm himself, knowing that she was using him as an anchor against her fear.

It was a werewolf attack—and a particularly brutal one. Despite the fact that this was one of the three kids who had killed Jordan, Doyle felt a cold surge of fury. There were laws, goddammit. There were rules. And this vigilante crap was nothing more than rage-filled bullshit.

He wanted to know who had done this, and it frustrated him almost more than he could stand that he couldn't bend down, press his hand to that bloodied forehead, and try to get a look at the face of the weren or werens who'd so boldly crossed the line.

And Tucker. Dammit, he wanted his partner to be here with him. Wanted him working the damn case. Stu was a shit, but he didn't deserve this. Nobody did. But that wasn't part of the plan. Tucker was out on the street, waiting nearby in a black, unmarked van so that he and Doyle could pull off an elaborate sting—a sting designed to absolutely convince Paul of Doyle's value to the Dark Warriors. They'd intended for it all to go down in the suite after Paul's guests had departed, but that sure as shit wasn't happening now.

Well, just add it to the list of things the werens had screwed up.

He thought of Luke's remarks about a war that was brewing, and his gaze drifted toward Andy. He met her eyes and for a moment he felt comforted. Then he remembered where he was and what he was doing, and he knew there really wasn't any comfort to be had.

"There's nothing more we can do here," Paul said, his voice heavy with grief. He looked between Andy and Doyle. "Come on. I'll give you both a ride home."

Travis stayed behind as a representative of the district attorney's office. Doyle and Andy followed Paul, the silence unbroken until they were seated inside his Mercedes.

"It's so unreal," Andy said. "So brutal."

"I'm going to pull in somewhere. An all-night diner. I think we could all use a cup of coffee. Maybe some eggs." He met Doyle's eyes in the rearview mirror. "Any problem with that?"

Doyle shook his head, then shifted in the seat and casually glanced out the back window. In the distance, he could see the van's headlights as Tucker slid into traffic and followed them.

The night's business wasn't over yet.

He only wished that Andy wasn't right in the thick of it with him.

FOURTEEN

Tucker parked the van at the far side of the mostly deserted parking lot. Doyle had already gone inside with Paul and that reporter from the prison—Tucker couldn't wait to hear Doyle tell him about that—and now it was time to get busy.

He'd rather this went down without the girl, but there wasn't any time to be picky. They might not have another opportunity as perfect as this one. Near-empty coffee shop. Deserted parking lot. Late at night. And there were other reasons why it needed to happen now.

With a frown, he glanced toward the back of the van where Rhys was bound in hematite. He had gotten into the vamp's head, and deep. But Rhys was strong. If the compulsion faded, Tucker wasn't sure he'd be able to go as deep a second time.

"Fucked up," he said to himself. "This whole thing is completely fucked up."

It wasn't—not really. Hell, it was a brilliant plan, and he had to give Doyle kudos for coming up with it. The whole operation hinged on his partner earning Paul's trust, and fast. And what better way to earn the trust of a self-professed monster hunter than by rescuing him from a monster that was trying to kill him?

When Doyle had suggested the plan back at Division, Leviathan had initially been skeptical. But the need had outweighed his hesitations, including Sara's protestations that Rhys hadn't yet been convicted. That little fact hadn't bothered anyone else, though, and even Sara had come around when Luke reminded her that the Shadower world operated differently than the human world. Under the Covenant, the Alliance Chairman had the authority to render judgment on suspected criminals. Usually, that power was delegated to the PEC, but it didn't have to be.

That meant that Luke—Tiberius's proxy—could be Rhys's judge, jury, and executioner—and he'd swung the proverbial ax with gusto.

Now it was up to Doyle to put the plan into action. If he failed—if Rhys somehow managed to get away—they'd all be up shit creek.

Tucker got out of the van and pulled the panel door open. Time to set the scene.

Fucked up, he thought again as he aimed his dart gun at the street lamps, preparing to shoot out the bulbs. Yeah, this was definitely some fucked-up shit.

Andy's coffee had gone cold, but she didn't care. Especially since despite the fact that she was a card-carrying coffee addict, she kept forgetting to drink it.

Her mind was too full of the bloodied mess that had once been a boy.

Doyle and Paul sat across the table from her. Doyle hadn't touched his coffee either, and hadn't had a bite to eat. Paul was the only one who'd managed that task—polishing off most of his scrambled eggs.

He took another bite, then looked up, his mouth curving into a frown. He reached out and laid his hand over Andy's. "It's not easy."

"It's really not." She felt Doyle's eyes on her and she tugged her hand away, using it to lift the coffee to her lips. The liquid was cold and unappealing, but she took a long sip anyway, then looked at Paul. "My dad didn't tell me about any of this, you know."

"I gathered as much."

"It all started because of Kevin. He told me about the werewolf. And I didn't believe him. I thought he and the other guys were being mean. By attacking Jordan, I mean. That was his name, right? Jordan?"

Paul nodded.

"I thought it was just a case of guys with too much testosterone playing at being monster hunters. It seemed unfair and barbaric. Three against one. Knives against nothing."

"Your reaction's not atypical," Paul said. He looked at Doyle. "Don't you agree?"

Doyle nodded, his expression tight. "The monsters look human. It's natural to think of them that way. They're not."

"But that's exactly my point," Andy said. "I didn't think the monster looked human. I thought he was human. This whole thing—I couldn't wrap my head around it."

"It's a difficult thing to grasp," Paul said. "Some people never do."

"I believe that," she said. "Even at the party—even after Daddy told me about my mother—I still wasn't sure what I believed."

Doyle, she noticed, looked at her curiously when she mentioned her mom.

"And now?" Paul asked.

"Now I want to know what you're doing about them. How you're fighting them. These—these things that killed Stu."

Doyle's face was hard, but Paul chuckled. "That's a big question you're asking."

"The whole thing's pretty big," she said. "Kevin said you're well organized."

"We are."

She signaled for the waitress to top off their coffee. "No offense, but I didn't exactly get a monster-hunter vibe at the hotel."

"No. That was what we call a party."

"Sorry. I don't mean to sound critical. And I know I could just wait and ask my dad about all of this, but we're here and what we saw..." She shivered.

"Are you okay?" Doyle asked.

She nodded, willing it to be true. "Yeah. I am. Or I will be." She gave him a wavering smile, then shifted her gaze to Paul. "I'm genuinely curious, and I want to know what's going on. What you're doing." She looked back at Doyle, hoping she was right in assuming that he was an ally. "Don't you?"

"Hell, yes. Anything you're doing to bring these monsters down, I'd like to hear about it. For that matter, I'd like to help."

"Are you set up like an army?" Andy asked. "Do you recruit people into basic training?"

She leaned back against the booth and took a deep breath, realizing as she did that she really did believe these creatures existed. And she really did want to help fight them. A werewolf had killed her mother—so help her, she believed it. Seeing Stu's ripped-up body had twisted something deep inside of her, like tumblers falling in place in a lock. The rose-colored glasses she had worn her entire life had been soundly smashed under the heel of reality.

She shook her head as if to settle her thoughts. "I'm sorry. I'm hammering you with questions, but I—"

"You're eager," Paul said. "That's good. And I promise, you'll learn. But slowly. To answer your questions, yes, we train. And yes, we do have ranks like the army does."

"How do you find recruits? It's not like you can just put out an advertisement."

"No. We recruit from among those who already know the truth. Who've seen it with their own eyes. There's more of us than you might think."

"But how do you find them? Kevin went to a meet-up, but that can't be the only way."

"It's not. Which makes recruiting a slow process. Ultimately, it comes down to word of mouth. Making connections. Learning people's secrets."

She caught Doyle's eye across the table. "That's not always easy."

"It's not," Paul said. "Which is why our group grows slowly and carefully."

"So what happens after someone joins the team? Then you train them to do what? Handle a stake? Fire silver bullets?"

Paul laughed. "Something like that. It's a shame Bryce wasn't at the party. I think you would have enjoyed talking to him."

"Bryce?" Doyle asked.

"I consider him my right arm."

"Why wasn't he there?" Andy asked

The corners of Paul's mouth tightened. "He had something to attend to."

Doyle, she noticed, was eyeing him curiously. But if Paul was aware of the scrutiny, he didn't show it.

"So, how big is all of this? I mean, what's your goal? To eradicate all of the monsters?"

Paul appeared to genuinely consider the question. "No, that's more what I would call a corollary. Our mission is to protect. Sadly, we failed Stu."

"We need to find the werewolves who did that," Doyle said, his voice tight. "And we need to make them pay."

Andy looked at him, moved by the passion in his voice. He spoke with such vibrant intensity that it seemed like he had actually known the boy. She knew he hadn't, though. What he wanted was justice. Or revenge.

She thought of her mother and knew that, yes, she wanted those werewolves to pay, too.

"How did they find him?"

"My guess is that he bragged to the wrong people," Paul said.

She shuddered, thinking that it could easily have been Kevin.

"And I think that's enough talk. I can see from the look on your face that I've said too much."

"No—really," she protested. "I was just remembering Stu. The way he looked..."

"Exactly my point." Paul's voice was soft, fatherly. "Let me take you home. Get a good night's sleep. You'll have more questions, and I'm happy to answer whatever your father can't." He glanced at the bill and left some cash. "Breakfast is on me," he said, as he slid out of the booth.

She followed him out, and Doyle was close behind her. She didn't pay much attention as they walked, and she only half-noticed that the parking lot was pitch black; the streetlights had all been snuffed out.

She heard the beep when Paul pressed the unlock button

on his key-chain fob, then she hurried to keep up as he moved across the lot. Suddenly, a dark shadow leaped into her field of vision, and she felt Doyle's hand on her arm, yanking her backward even as Paul's surprised cry filled the air.

"Stay down," Doyle urged, and then he was gone, and she was left behind, terrified by the knowledge that something horrible lurked ahead in the dark, and Doyle was rushing right into the arms of the monster.

Doyle had no trouble seeing in the dark, and he watched as Paul thrust a stake toward Rhys. Just like a good little vampire hunter, he had come prepared.

But Paul had never been up against a vamp like Rhys, and with one brutal blow the vampire not only knocked the stake out of his hand, but shattered his arm as well. Doyle knew; he heard the bones cracking.

As much as Doyle wanted to stand back and watch Rhys destroy the human, it wasn't part of the plan. Paul's death would only make him a martyr, and Doyle was certain that Bryce or Travis or Andy's father would step in to fill the gap.

A bag of trash was gaping open just a few yards from Paul's car, a broken chair leg protruding from it. It would have been a nice coincidence, except it wasn't a coincidence at all. Tucker had put it there, ensuring that Doyle would have the tools he needed to fight the vampire, keeping in mind that he would need to come across as human if this bluff was going to work.

Now the pseudo-human Doyle lunged forward, stooping only long enough to grab the stake, then leading with it as he broadsided Rhys, who was leaning in for a second attack on Paul.

"Doyle!" Paul cried out as Doyle and Rhys crashed to the ground. The vampire rolled them over, his massive strength reduced by both the hematite injection and the influence that Tucker had planted in his mind. The bastard was still strong, however, and Doyle found himself cheating a bit and calling upon his own preternatural strength to fight back. One good thrust and—yes—he had Rhys flipped over. The stake was in hand, and he thrust downward. Nice and clean and fast.

The kind of quick in-and-out that was sure to impress Paul.

Unfortunately, Rhys had other plans. They'd landed on a piece of cardboard, and as Doyle drove the stake down, Rhys pressed his palms to the asphalt on either side of their corrugated pad. A quick push and he slid down, knocking Doyle's aim off and forcing the stake to embed a solid three inches above his heart.

Well, shit.

He still had a grip on the thing, and he tightened his fist to pull it out. As he did, Rhys's brow crinkled. "You," he said, and Doyle had to lift his other hand and send his knuckles crashing down into Rhys's mouth, breaking his jaw.

It wouldn't do for Paul to know that Rhys and Doyle had history.

His maneuver shut the vampire up, but it also made him lose the pressure he'd been keeping on Rhys's chest. Without that steady pressure, the vampire burst up, driving his forehead into Doyle, the whole thing happening so fast that Doyle could only react, not think.

At the same time, Rhys rolled sideways and yanked the stake out of his body, sending it flying off into the parking lot. Doyle scrambled off the vampire and was about to sprint for the stake when Rhys grabbed him by the back of the neck and jerked him back.

A manageable situation for the para-demon Doyle. For the fake-human Doyle, it was more dangerous, especially since Rhys was digging his fingers into the side of Doyle's neck. One quick twist, and he'd snap the bone, and that was definitely something Doyle wouldn't be able to explain away.

The stake. He could summon the wind. Blow it toward him. Maybe Paul wouldn't notice.

Except Paul was watching. Though his face was twisted with pain, he was still conscious. That was good—Doyle needed him to see this. Bad, though, because he needed the damn stake.

The vampire's fingers tightened, and Doyle cried out with genuine pain.

He tried to spin around, but Rhys's grip was too strong, and Doyle had to wonder if they'd injected enough hematite. If Tucker's compulsion was holding.

He struggled, trying to jerk free, but his attacker's grip held fast.

He had to risk going for the stake. With luck, maybe Paul wouldn't—

"Stop it!"

Andy's voice rang out, and Rhys tossed his head back in pain, before whipping around and smashing her hard across the cheek.

Her anguished cry rallied Doyle like a battle hymn. She went down, and Rhys pounced immediately, the broken chair leg she'd tried to embed in his back still protruding from it.

Doyle didn't waste any time. He leaped onto the vampire and ripped out the stake. Then—using all of his demonic strength—he thrust it through Rhys's back and straight into his heart. More force than a mortal could have conjured, but Doyle was over this bastard.

With any luck Paul wouldn't question him. Even if it compromised the mission, though, Doyle knew he wouldn't have done it any other way. A second's hesitation, and Rhys might have killed Andy, and Doyle couldn't let that happen. He didn't know why—and he sure as hell wasn't going to analyze it now—but she'd gotten under his skin, and he couldn't bear the thought of losing her.

Slowly, he bent down and extended his hand. "Are you okay?"

Her eyes were wide, her expression panicked. But she took a breath and calmed herself, and after a moment, she nodded slowly, brushing at the Rhys-dust that now covered her. He had to admire her strength. "I'm going to have one hell of a bruise, but I'll survive. One thing's for certain—if I had any doubts left, they're gone now."

"Seeing is believing?"

"Almost getting killed works well, too." She took his hand and he pulled her up, stopping short of pulling her into his arms. Instead, he forced himself to release her and hurried to Paul's side.

"Bone snapped," Paul said through gritted teeth.

"Shattered is more like it. Come on. I'll get you to a hospital." He hooked an arm around the injured man and helped him to his feet.

"Pretty damn impressive," Paul said.

"I'm an impressive guy."

Paul looked at him seriously for a moment through eyes hooded with pain, then he nodded. "That you are. We should talk."

"Right now, we don't need to do anything except get you fixed up." His tone was restrained, but inside he was cheering. Their plan had worked.

Hopefully saving the world would go just as smoothly.

FIFTEEN

Kyle Creevey knew he wasn't dead, because his head hurt too damn much.

He peeled open his eyes, squinting against the light that shot into his head like knife points. That was pretty much all he could see. Just burning white light. And shadows. Tall, moving shadows.

Fuck. They were men. And now he could see their uniforms. Military. Just like the guys who'd pulled him off the bus.

"Who the fuck are you?" His voice sounded far away, like it was coming from someone else.

"Guess you could say we're your guardian angels," a voice replied from just as far away.

"You pulled me out?"

"We did."

"Think I'm going to thank you?" He tried to sneer, but his voice still wasn't working right.

"I don't give a fuck what you do." The shadow that was talking shifted closer, and as he did, he came into better focus. "At least not as long as you do what you're told."

"That right? And what are you telling me to do?" The man in front of him was short and dark.

"My employer needs some information."

Creevey barked out a laugh. "And why would I help you?"

"Tit for tat, I'd think. We gave you your life, after all. I'd think a rescue from death row is worth a bit of tangible gratitude."

"That was always in the bag," Creevey said. "You people just got to me first."

The man glanced back at the soldiers who were lined up behind him, then returned his attention to Creevey. "Be that as it may."

Creevey sat back. The world around him was becoming crisper. He was in a room with metal walls and, as far as he could tell, only one door. And he was strapped to a chair, with electrodes attached to his temples. The wires led to a machine, and a man sat at the machine, his eyes trained on the guy who was speaking.

Not a lot of options.

"So tell me," he said. "What is it you want to know?"

"The vampires you admire so much—they're centralized. We believe they have some sort of local base of operations. We think you know where."

Creevey barked out a laugh. "You think I know that?" He knew they were right—Rhys had told him about something called Division 6 and the PEC. Apparently it was all over the globe, but there was an office in Los Angeles. An actual fucking office where the vamps and shit showed up each day in suits to play cops and robbers with the Shadowers gone bad. Some fucked-up shit, that's what it was. But Creevey didn't have a clue where it was. "I don't know shit, asshole."

The man doing the talking turned to look at the man sitting behind the machine. "He's telling the truth."

"That's a start, Creevey. Stick with the truth and we'll get along okay."

"What the fuck?"

"You don't know the location. Fine. But I think you can find out."

"Even if I could, why would I help you?"

"How are you feeling, Mr. Creevey?"

Kyle frowned, confused by the shift in the conversation. "Better. Whatever shit you people injected in me is wearing off."

"It's not. I assure you."

Kyle cocked his head, not liking the tone of the man's voice. "What are you talking about?"

"We injected you with poison in addition to the sleep agent. You do this one little favor for us, and we'll do a favor for you. The antidote."

Creevey nodded. He needed to look cooperative even though he was anything but. Idiots. As if poison would have any effect on him. Not when certain promises had been made. When his friends changed him, they'd push him beyond death.

Poison—such a ridiculous notion.

But playing along would mean freedom. And for that he was willing to play their games.

He lifted his head and met his captors' eyes. "You want me to get the location? Fine, I'll get the location." It was the god's honest truth.

What he didn't say was that he wasn't about to share it with them. He didn't say it, because that would be a lie.

Since Paul had received a nasty bump on the head along with his broken arm, the hospital admitted him overnight for observation. Andy stood next to the beeping equipment by his bed and smiled down at him. "I haven't been to a party that turned out this wild since college."

"Neither have I," Paul said.

She hooked her thumb toward the hallway where Doyle was waiting. "Looks like you have quite an asset on your team." She'd been astounded by how skillfully Doyle fought. And she'd been almost paralyzed with fear when the vampire had cornered and disarmed him.

"Two assets," he said, looking at her.

"I don't know about that." She gently touched her swollen cheek. "I was terrified."

"And yet you acted."

She nodded but kept silent. The truth was that the only thing that had given her the strength to move was the undeniable certainty that watching Doyle die would be like having a stake driven through her own heart.

"I should let you rest." She squeezed his uninjured hand and then hurried out the door to meet Doyle.

"So," he said. "Alone at last."

She was mortified to realize that she was blushing. "Not that alone. There's a hospital full of people around us."

She fingered the fifty-dollar bill that was still in her pocket. Doyle had driven them to the hospital in Paul's Mercedes, but they'd have to leave it in the garage so that Paul could use it in the morning. "I've got cab fare. Want me to have the driver drop you at the hotel? You left your car there, right?"

"Why don't we both go?" he asked. "I can give you a ride home."

"Oh, I don't want to be any trouble." What she wanted was to spend time with him, and she kicked herself for being coy. What if he agreed and told her he'd pay for his own cab back to the hotel? "Actually, yes. That would be great."

At such a late hour, the traffic was sparse, and they were back at the Warford in no time. The lobby was abandoned—at 3 A.M., it wasn't that surprising, and they walked in silence toward the parking garage elevator.

"That's it," Doyle said, as they emerged on the first parking level. He was pointing across the lot, and she saw a candy-apple-red Porsche parked next to an ancient Pontiac Catalina, a mustard-yellow boat of a car.

"The Pontiac?"

He looked at her with a smile. "What? You don't think I drive a Porsche?"

"No," she said, amused.

"Smart girl."

She laughed, then followed him, pleased that she'd so accurately pegged his car. "I'm in Burbank," she said. "That's probably out of your way."

"Not in the slightest."

He pulled out, then maneuvered the downtown streets before sliding easily onto the highway. The Catalina was a 1963 model, so it was older than she was. It had bench seats and no shoulder seat belts and the kind of radio where you had to punch the buttons. She loved it and told him so.

"It's usually much spiffier."

She surveyed the immaculate interior. "Looks pretty spiffy to me."

"She needs a bath. My workload's been crazy. I've neglected her."

"There's a gas station near my house with one of those drive-through washes. You could pull in?"

"It's awfully late."

"I think it's open twenty-four hours," she said, then yawned because she just couldn't help it.

"I should get you home."

"No, really." The words were out before she'd thought them through, but she didn't regret them. She wanted to spend time with him. She wanted normal. She wanted conversation. She wanted to forget about what she'd seen tonight and just be with this guy that, dammit, she was attracted to.

She wanted her mind to be less of a muddled mess, but that was hoping for the impossible.

"The car needs a bath, Doyle. I don't want to stand in the way of a man and his clean car."

She almost sighed in relief when he grinned at her. "Fair enough."

"There," she said, pointing toward the gas station.

He plugged in the money, slowly drove into the car cave, and set the brake. A moment later, the water began to shoot out at them and the huge brush descended. A loud, rhythmic roaring filled the car, and she could see far off streetlights reflected in the drops of water.

"If this were a date, it would be romantic," Doyle said, eyeing her sideways.

"It would," she agreed. Her stomach was fluttery, and not from hunger or from the strangeness of the day.

He looked at her, just looked, and she found that she couldn't look away. All she could think about was what it would feel like to kiss him. To have him hold her in his arms—arms strong enough to protect her from all the nightmares out in the world.

Almost—almost—she got up the courage to shift toward him on the bench. But then the brushes stopped moving and the green light blinked on, and the moment seemed to dissolve around them like mist.

"Time to go," he said, easing the car out of the cave.

"I'm just over there," she said. "The next left, and then all the way down. Second house from the end."

"Cute," he said, as he pulled into her driveway.

"That's another word for small. But I love it. And you're right. It is cute." The house was a pale pink stucco bungalow that she'd bought when she turned twenty-one with the money that had been put in trust for her after her mother's death. It had cost a small fortune because in California even tiny homes were pricey, even when they were in crappy condition.

But that was the benefit of working freelance. She'd had a lot of time to fix the place up herself and she even got paid to write articles about the rehab. During that same period, the market went crazy. And when it was all over, her property had ballooned in value, and she was sitting pretty.

It wasn't a house in Malibu, but it was hers and she loved it. She even had an avocado tree in her backyard, and that was nothing to sneeze at.

She pushed open the heavy Catalina door. "So, this is me. Thanks for driving me home."

"Any time."

She stepped out, and was about to shut the car door, but somehow she couldn't manage it.

"Andy?"

She drew in a breath for courage. "Listen, I know it's late. And you probably want to get home. But, oh hell. The truth is I don't want to be alone." That wasn't exactly the truth. If it was anyone other than him, she'd be fine with being alone. When the option was Doyle, though ... well, she wanted him with her. "Would you—would you like to come in for a drink or something?"

For a second, he just looked at her, and she started thinking of ways to backpedal. "It's okay if you don't. It's just that—well, tonight was a little crazy, and—"

"You're scared?"

"Yes. No." She drew in a breath. "I'm a little freaked out, but I'm not scared. I guess I'd just like the company."

"I'd love to come in." And her relief—and delight—were palpable.

"There's not much sense giving you the grand tour," she said after pushing open the door. "This is pretty much it."

"I like it."

She looked around, trying to see it from his eyes. The walls were each a different color, and she had flowers everywhere. Books covered pretty much every surface, and a package of Chips Ahoy sat open on the table, left over from her last snack attack. "It's kind of a mess."

"I like it," he repeated firmly.

"Coffee?"

"It's almost four. If we're not going to bed, I think coffee's a necessity."

"Oh. Right." She could feel her cheeks heat up, and she wished she wasn't so tired. If she hadn't been exhausted, she would have had a better comeback. As it was, she could only stand there and absorb his words, getting lost in what must have been an unintentional double entendre. Because surely it had been unintentional. "I have stale cookies to go with it. Or, let's see, I think there's a coffee cake in the freezer."

"Are you hungry?"

"I'm antsy."

"That's understandable."

"It is?"

"After the night we had?"

"Right. Fighting vampires." At least he wasn't commenting on the real source of her antsyness. Himself.

She ended up heating up the coffee cake and making a

full pot of coffee. Half-caff in honor of the late—or early —hour.

"It's good," he said, taking a bite from the plate she'd set on the coffee table in front of him.

"Thank Sara Lee. I had nothing to do with it."

"Well, then, I applaud your shopping skills."

She grinned, then settled back against the couch cushions. "I should probably apologize. I don't usually need a babysitter."

"No," he said firmly. "I want to be here. Do you want to talk about it?"

"It? There are too many its to choose from. And the truth is—" Was she really going to admit this? "The truth is that I mostly wanted to spend more time with you."

"Really?"

She watched as he seemed to absorb her words. He had dark brown eyes with golden flecks that seemed to catch the light as she shifted on the couch to face her more directly.

"And why is that?" he asked. She barely heard his words. She was too busy looking at his mouth. He wasn't a classically attractive man, but she thought his mouth was perfect. Wide and firm, but quick to smile. She wondered what his lips would feel like under hers. And she wondered if she was losing it from a lack of sleep.

"Andy?"

She jumped. "What?"

That mouth curled into an enticing smile. Yeah, definitely kissable.

"I asked why you wanted to spend time with me."

"Oh." She licked her lips and felt a tug at her neck. She realized she was clutching her necklace and she forced her hand back down into her lap. He sat up, leaning a bit toward her as if encouraging her to answer. He reached out, his fingertips resting gently on her bare knee. She was suddenly aware that her cocktail dress ended midthigh. And that she wasn't wearing a bra under the thin, shimmery material.

"Andy? Did you want to spend time with me because you're nervous?"

"I'm nervous," she admitted. "But not about the monsters."

"Then what?"

"I—" She bit back nervous laughter. "I don't know."

He slid closer to her on the couch. The movement pushed his hand higher on her thigh, and her entire body stiffened, her pulse increasing, her skin burning.

"You don't know?" he repeated. "I have an idea. Do you want me to tell you?"

"I'd love to be enlightened," she said—or she started to say. Before she could get the last word out, his mouth closed over hers, and she went from being grounded on the couch to floating out there with the stars. His lips were soft but firm, and he pulled her close as his lips parted and his tongue sought hers. He was tasting her, teasing her, and she was soaking it in, her mind spinning, her whole body more awake than she could ever remember it being, and all because of a kiss.

It seemed to last forever, and when he gently pulled away, she had to remind herself to breathe.

"I like the way you kiss," he murmured.

"I'm glad. Considering that my dad's a preacher, I didn't get much practice growing up. Except on pillows. Mannequin heads. That kind of thing."

"How do I compare?"

"Remarkably well," she teased. "And unlike pillows, you taste good. Minty. Not sure if it's peppermint or spearmint. I should take another taste test," she said, then pressed her mouth against his, her tongue seeking entrance as the rest of her body began to burn with need.

One hand cupped her head, and he unclipped her hair, letting it fall in loose curls around his fingers. His other hand stroked her bare thigh, and she felt hyperaware—his finger, his lips, the sweetness of his breath. Slowly, his hand inched up. She was wet—she knew it. Her body was swollen, craving his touch.

She wanted him, but couldn't have him. Not yet.

Regretfully, she pressed her hand over his, stilling his progress up her leg. "Not that fast," she whispered, her voice breathless with longing.

He pressed his forehead to hers, and she felt the rise and fall of his body, the steadiness of his breathing as he gathered himself. Then he slipped an arm around her shoulder and settled a soft kiss on her hair.

"I'm sorry," she said as he pulled her close against him.

"No," he said fiercely. "Don't be sorry." He held her, his fingers stroking her arm. "I just want to hold you."

She tilted her head up to look at him. "Really?"

He matched her incredulous tone with a sly grin. "For now," he amended. "For now, I just want to hold you."

She snuggled closer, pulling an afghan from the foot of the sofa over her legs and enjoying the warmth that seemed to emanate from him.

"Tell me about the first vampire you killed," she said.

He stiffened, and she shifted around so that she was facing him. "I'm sorry. It's probably none of my business." And it also threw a big bucket of ice water on the mood—although she supposed that was a good thing. She was far too eager for his touch ... and Andy wasn't a girl who usually let things move as quickly as she wanted them to move with Doyle.

"No," he said. "No, it's all right. It's just ... well, it's not a pleasant story."

"You don't have to tell me."

For a minute, she thought that he wouldn't, because he didn't move. He just kept his arms around her and stayed silent, letting her soak up his warmth and strength. She closed her eyes, content to drift off like that, then she was pulled back to consciousness by the low, steady tones of his voice.

"I was only ten," he said. "But I'd already been going on expeditions with vampire hunters for years."

"Oh my God—why?"

"My mother," he said. "She was raped by—by one of them. One of the dark creatures that Paul's fighting. It made her hard. She became obsessed with hunting down and destroying anything she considered evil. Anything nonhuman. It became her driving force, and she made it mine, too. She'd recruit men—hunters—to teach me what to do. To take me out with them, so that I could not only see how vile the dark ones were, but could kill them myself. When I was ten, she had the man who was training me lock me in a vampire's crypt right before sunset. It was a test. I survived. Barely."

Her hand was a fist around her mother's necklace, and she felt the hot sting of tears in her eyes. "I'm so, so sorry. I'm sitting here all eager to get started, and you were forced into it in the most horrible way."

"I've made peace with it. More than that, actually. Hunting the evil creatures that live among us—bringing them to justice—it's what gets me up in the morning."

"Bringing them to justice." She smiled. "Is that why you joined Homeland? Why aren't you, I don't know, a professional vampire hunter?"

"There's all kinds of evil in the world. Believe me, I've dealt with my share."

"Right. I'm sorry. I didn't mean to suggest that your job was less important. It's just that if hunting these dark things takes up so much of your time anyway—"

"Yeah, but the health insurance sucks."

She grinned. "Right. Dropping the subject. What happened to your mother?"

His expression darkened so quickly that she instantly regretted asking the question.

"There came a point when she realized that she'd never win. She'd never completely eradicate the darkness. I was twelve when she jumped from a very high rooftop, and ended her fight that way."

"Doyle." She took his hand. "Oh, Doyle, I'm so sorry."

"It was a long time ago."

He was so stoic, but she was certain that underneath he had to be hurting.

"I volunteer at a center for teens," she said. "A lot of them have gone through some horrific things. It always amazes me how strong the human spirit is." She squeezed his hand. "You're incredibly strong."

"That sounds like a good cause," he said, clearly trying to latch on to a new subject. "How did you get involved with that?"

"My dad's ministry. I was never very active in his church growing up. I mean, I did what I had to do, but none of the extracurriculars, if you know what I mean. But when the ministry set up the Pacific Teen Center, I knew I wanted to be a part of it. I lost my mom when I was eleven, and so I felt a bond with those kids, you know? Even if they have both parents, a lot of them are at risk." She shrugged. "Anyway, I like doing it."

He reached out and brushed his fingers over her necklace. "Did your mother give you this?"

She nodded. "She was dying. And she told me that it would protect me." She managed a thin smile. "I guess I need it now. If there's ever a time you need God on your side, it's when you're up to your elbows in demons."

"Is that what you think we're fighting?"

"Well, yeah. Unnatural creatures. Isn't that what you said was at the core of all of them? Demons? Mom gave me this to protect me from them. And I know it doesn't really have magical power, but it makes me feel safe. Like she's looking out for me."

"You said at the coffee shop that your dad had told you something about her. The way your face looked then—I could tell it was painful. Do you want to talk about it?"

"It's Daddy I should be talking to, but I'm not sure I really know how. It's got to be as painful for him as it is for me."

"You can tell me, if it helps."

"A werewolf killed her." The words still sounded strange. "I just found out tonight." She smoothed the blanket in her lap as if the motion could smooth out her jumbled thoughts, too. "I found out a lot of things tonight. I went from thinking evil is something inside of us that we need to control if we want to get into heaven to learning that real evil—demons, vampires—is out there walking around."

She waited for him to say something, but he was just watching her. "I've always believed that demons and angels are real—maybe that comes from growing up with a preacher for a father—but I never thought of them walking among us. I just thought of demons as the opposite of guardian angels. The antithesis of spiritual guides, you know?"

"The angel and the demon on your shoulders, whispering into alternate ears," he said.

"Exactly. When I interviewed Creevey, I saw evil, but he's human. And that's the only type of evil I believed in before tonight."

"Of course. You said you used a pen name. You're Allison Stahl? The one who wrote those articles about Creevey?"

"That's me, at your service."

"Creevey's a scary son-of-a-bitch. And you're right. He's as evil as they come."

"I don't dispute it," she said. "But it turns out there's more. It has a face. It's out there and real. I learned the truth today, and I already feel like I'm a different person. It's a big job, getting rid of these creatures, but by God, after what happened to Stu, I know it's necessary."

He stood up and walked over to her sliding glass door. She couldn't see his reflection, but his back seemed rigid.

"Doyle?"

"I'm sorry you've had to see all of this darkness in the world."

"I'm not," she said. "I feel like I've been walking around with my eyes closed, and now they're finally open."

"Maybe so," he said. "But you're wrong about being a different person. Seeing evil—getting close to it—doesn't change you. It just underscores who you already are."

She pulled her knees up and hugged them to her chest. "Maybe I've never really known who I am. But I do know that I've always wanted to understand it. And fight it." She moved to stand behind him. "Lately, I've felt like the articles I write are my way of fighting evil. The same way my dad does from the pulpit. But now that I know about all this, I want to do more. Do you feel like that? Like you just want to step in and do more because you're one of the few people who know the truth, and it's your obligation?"

He turned to her, and his eyes were sad. "Every day," he said. "I feel like that every day."

"I lied, you know."

His eyes narrowed. "When?"

"I told you I wasn't writing an article about the Dark Warriors. But I was. That was the plan, anyway. To get in deep and shine a light on this freakish group that thinks vampires and werewolves are real. Only now…" She trailed off with a shrug. "Well, suffice it to say I won't be writing the article anymore. And I meant it when I told Paul that I wanted to help him."

She saw the way his face tightened and the pained expression in his eyes. She moved to stand beside him at the door, then pressed a hand to his cheek and felt the prickle of his stubble against her palm. "Doyle? What is it?"

He closed his eyes, and for a moment the connection lingered, a soft sizzle that arced between them. "You have a good heart, Andy. Promise me you'll keep your eyes open. That you'll really pay attention and learn about what it is you're fighting."

"Of course I will."

"I just mean that when you first see this world, it's so bright it can be blinding. Don't think you see something just because you expect it to be there."

"I don't understand what you're talking about."

He stepped back with a shrug, breaking the contact between them. Slowly, he turned back to the door and pressed his palm against the glass. "I'm tired," he said. "And I'm talking nonsense."

"Do you want to go home?" She hoped he didn't.

"Do you want me to?"

"No." The word came out so fast she had to cover it with a laugh. "Sorry. I didn't mean to sound so eager."

"I like that you're eager. I like being here."

"Oh." A flush of pleasure shot through her. "Me too."

He took a step toward her, and she was suddenly totally aware of her body. Of every breath, every tingle, every hair standing up on end, anticipating his touch. His touch, his touch, yes, how she wanted his touch again.

Finally, he slipped his arm around her, and with a sigh of absolute contentment, she leaned against him.

"So you have a choice," he said, his normally gruff voice taking on a soft tone.

"I like choices."

"We can keep talking, or I can kiss you again."

"Let's go with option two," she said. And then his mouth was on hers, and she was losing herself, sliding into the wonder that he desired her as much as she desired him. That she could touch him, that she could kiss him, that she could—

Oh, yes, she wanted it all.

"Doyle," she murmured, breaking the kiss just for long enough to say his name. He clutched her tight, pulling her close, his kisses filled with an almost desperate need, like he had to drink her deep before she disappeared, and she wanted to pull back and tell him to slow down, but dear God, she didn't want to let go for even a second.

But then they were apart, and she looked at him with bafflement. "What—"

"I'm sorry," he said, his eyes not meeting hers.

"About what?" She was breathing hard, feeling desperate.

"This," he said softly, his words cutting into her heart. "We can't do this."

SIXTEEN

The Club Rouge was a shithole of a place—at least if you stayed in the main part of the club. Kyle had no intention of staying there, though. The main part was nothing more than a hunting ground, and he saw at least three sweet young things upon whom he'd be more than happy to lavish his affections. But that could come later...

Right now, he had someone to meet and a life to end. His own.

He whistled as he headed toward the back of the club, then down the hallway leading to the restrooms. He turned into one of the perpendicular hallways, then slowed his pace, letting his fingertips trail over the wall as he searched for the mark that Rhys had once pointed out to him. It was somewhere right around—

There.

The gilt S on the wall signaled that a much more interesting club lay hidden within. Carefully, he searched the wall for a hidden latch. It took him a few minutes, but he finally found it. He looked up and down the hall, confirmed that no one was watching, and slipped inside.

"Well, well," a feminine voice said. "Look what the cat dragged in."

Another woman eased up behind the first, then leaned forward and sniffed. "Human." She grinned. "Guess it must be snack time."

"I'm here to see Voight," Kyle said. "He'll be pissed if you don't take me to him."

"Did you hear that, Millicent? Voight's going to be pissed."

"Guess we better take him," Millicent said. She reached out and grabbed Kyle's collar. "Come on, human."

He didn't shake her hand off, but only because he knew they'd soon be equals. He'd have her then. Have her kneel in front of him. He'd show her how powerful he was, and she'd apologize for thinking that he was ever less than her, even when he'd been human.

"Well, well." Voight was sitting at a table sipping blood from a wineglass. "My good friend Rhys's little, lost puppy dog. I thought you were in the kennel, little puppy dog."

"I thought you were going to get me out."

Voight shrugged. "That was Rhys's grand plan. And it doesn't look like you needed help anyway. You're out, aren't you?"

"I want the change," he said.

Voight lifted his brows. "Do you? Did you hear that, friends? He wants the change." He looked at Millicent. "Would you like to do the honors, my dear?"

She lifted her middle finger in a fuck-you gesture. "Screw you, Voight. I'm only here to detox. Those PEC assholes dragged me downtown and kept me in an inter-view room for five hours asking me questions about that fucking werewolf. I've already got a bad taste in my mouth. I don't want to add to it with the taste of him."

She sneered at Kyle, and he lunged for her, ready to rip her throat out.

"And now you want to hurt poor Millicent," Voight said. "So many wants. So many desires. I understand completely," he added. "I want a lot of things, too. Things I haven't gotten even in all my long centuries on this earth." He shrugged. "These things happen, pup."

A low rage bubbled up in Kyle, and he looked around at the pale, harsh faces of the vampires. The same vamps who'd given him blood. Who'd made him stronger so that he could do his work. So that he could take his pleasure with all those girls, and be stronger and faster than the cops.

They'd fucking helped him. And now they were going to ignore him? They were going to just toss him back into the cesspool that was humanity? They were going to force him to continue to be mortal after Rhys had promised— promised—that he would walk the earth until the end of time.

"I deserve the change." He took a step toward Voight, refusing to show his fear. Refusing to think about the poison running through his veins. "I was promised the change."

"The vampire who promised you is dead. And to be honest, puppy dog, I've never much liked you."

Andy pushed away from Doyle, her hands smoothing her clothes, and Doyle wanted to kick himself for being a complete asshole.

"Andy." He reached for her hand to stop her from

walking away. "Please, I'm sorry. That was harsh. I didn't mean it to be harsh."

Goddamn the hunger. It was growing in him. Not demanding yet—not enough to put her in danger—but enough to remind him of what he was.

And why he took human women to bed.

He didn't want to use Andy that way. Didn't want to use her to prove to himself that he could keep up the façade of his humanity. Especially when he knew she not only despised what he was inside, but was terrified of it.

And that really was the crux, wasn't it? Even as pure and perfect as the past few hours with Andy had been, the ending was the same as always—Doyle had to feed the demon. He was one of the monsters she was so eager to fight. And no matter what else happened between them, that fundamental truth could never be changed. He'd learned that the hard way from his mother, who'd never managed to beat the evil out of him despite her best efforts.

He clenched his fists at his sides, wanting to lash out. Wanting to rage against the unfairness of it all. But most of all, wanting to pull Andy back into his arms.

Goddamn him for wanting it so bad. Goddamn him for letting her get under his skin.

"I should go," he said.

"Yes, you probably should." She was facing away from him, and her words, so flat and lost, cut into him, stealing his reason.

He should walk out the door. He should walk right through it and get into his car.

Instead, he moved in front of her. He hooked his finger under her chin and lifted it until she had no choice but to either look at him or close her eyes.

She looked, and he saw strength behind her embarrassment. "I don't understand," she said. "I thought—"

"I want you," he said firmly, though he knew that he shouldn't speak. "I want to rip every stitch of your clothes off and lose myself inside of you. I want to kiss you until your mouth's raw. I want to forget everything except you, Andy." And dammit, even that didn't quite cover it. He didn't fully understand what it was about her, but there was no denying that she'd snapped something inside of him. Maybe it was her eyes that had first caught his attention, but now it was so much more.

"Then why?"

Because he couldn't hide what he was forever. Because he didn't want her to be one in a long line of women whom he'd left in the morning.

Her embarrassment had been replaced by concern. "I don't understand," she said.

He took her hand and led her back to the couch. "I want you," he repeated, "but not like this. You stopped me earlier. I don't want to cross a line that you've drawn." It was a bald-faced lie—he didn't give a damn about crossing her line—but there was no other explanation he could give.

She looked at him as if he were the only true gentleman in the world, and he felt like the lowest of heels.

"What would you say if I told you that I'd like to move that line?"

He closed his eyes and swallowed. He needed to go. Needed to push this thing between them away, because it couldn't go anywhere and he couldn't risk her finding out the truth about what he was.

But at the same time, she didn't know Doyle the PEC agent, the one who had something to prove every time he slept with a human woman.

No, she only knew Doyle the Homeland Security agent. Doyle the Dark Warrior.

But you won't be undercover forever.

He wouldn't. But right now he wanted her too badly to think about the future. How could he, when Andy blocked everything else from his sight?

"Doyle? What would you say?"

He was surprised to find his voice still worked, so thick was his need. "I'd have to say that I'm a uniquely lucky man."

"Don't pull away again," she said, hooking her arms around his neck.

"No," he promised. He hoped it was a promise he could keep.

"Doyle?"

"Yes?"

"Make love to me."

Her words—their boldness—shot through him, making him hard and needy. With a low groan, he reached down and scooped her up, curling her slender body against him. The barely there cocktail dress rode up, and he felt the soft skin of her hip against his palm as he carried her into the bedroom.

It was small—the house had been designed so that the living and dining areas were as large as possible—but she'd made it cozy. The bed filled the room, and every surface was covered with either a green potted plant or a vase with cut flowers. A fish tank with a small light provided the only illumination, and the bubbling lull of the filter added a sensual soundtrack.

He set her down on the bedspread, and he toppled onto her when she tugged at his collar. "I'm not risking you getting away," she said. She took his hand and pressed it against her thigh. "I stopped you once tonight. I won't do it again."

He trailed his fingers up, stroking her soft skin, and he was lost, absolutely lost. He shifted his position, leaving one hand resting softly on her thigh, while he slid his other up her belly until his thumb brushed the swell of her breast.

She moaned, arching up as if in silent demand. "Don't stop," she whispered, and he almost laughed—he had no intention of stopping.

Slowly, he let his fingers stroke higher between her legs until the pad of his thumb met the soft material of her panties.

She moaned softly, her hands ripping at his shirt, as if she was desperate to feel his skin against hers.

He knew exactly how she felt.

Gently, he slid his finger under her panties, feeling her damp curls brush his skin. "Spread your legs," he said, and when she complied, he slipped his fingers inside of her, using the pad of his thumb to stroke and tease her until she cried out with a desperate passion, trembling against his hand.

"Doyle—oh, God, Doyle."

He bent over her, his hand cupping her sex, and pressed his lips to her mouth, then leaned down to cup her breast through the thin material of her dress. Then lower still until his lips were tracing patterns on her soft belly, exposed now because of the sheath dress bunched up around her waist.

He wanted to taste her, wanted her nails digging into him as she came.

Mostly, he wanted to be inside of her.

"I can't wait," he said.

"Then don't."

He yanked her panties down, somehow managing to get his own clothes off. He stroked his hands up the inside of her thighs, and she spread her legs as if inviting him home. She was slick and wet, and he thrust inside, almost losing himself in the pleasure of filling her.

He stayed still, afraid that if he moved he'd come right then. But she wasn't having any of that. Her hips rose, and she pistoned against him, forcing him into a corresponding motion. "Please," she whispered. "Oh, yes, please."

They moved together, finding a natural rhythm, hard and fast, as her body closed around him, drawing him in, claiming him.

And then she shattered, tightening around him and sending him over the edge with her. He lost himself to pleasure, swallowed up in the stars and in the sweet, soft sounds of the woman in his arms.

"Wow," she said, when they'd both stopped shaking. He wrapped his arms around her and held her close. "Wow," she repeated, her voice soft and dreamy.

She rolled over, shifting her position to get even closer, and he pressed his lips to her brow. "Doyle," she murmured, her voice little more than a breath as she curled herself next to him and drifted off toward sleep. "I'm so very glad you stayed."

He lay still, relishing the rise and fall of her body. This was not something in his repertoire. Usually he'd be sitting up, pulling on his slacks, and heading out the door right about now.

It felt good to stay. Gently, he pressed a kiss to her hair. "So am I," he whispered. And for the first time in more than two centuries, he closed his eyes with a human woman next to him, and settled in for the night.

It was, Paul thought, good to be home.

He'd been discharged from the hospital after morning

rounds, and he'd rolled through the gate of his Beverly Hills compound only minutes after eight in the morning.

Now he was in his study, and Bryce was sitting across the desk from him. Bryce's second in command, a young soldier named Aaron, stood behind him at attention.

"Our asset?"

"It wasn't a problem," Bryce said. "We intercepted the prison bus, and the extraction went off without a hitch."

"Good. They've been training hard, working as a unit. They'll need that discipline when we make our move against the enemy." He looked at Bryce. "Do we have the location?"

"Not yet."

Paul reached for a paperweight on his desk and curled his fingers around it, squeezing hard to quell the flare of irritation. "Did I not make myself clear that time is of the essence? They know that we exist and that we're planning something. If we don't move fast, we'll be defending rather than attacking, and that is an unacceptable turn of events."

"I know that," Bryce said. "Creevey didn't have the location. But I explained to him that it would be in his best interest to find it out and give it to us."

"How much time?"

"The poison will stop his heart in forty-eight hours. Of course, we told him thirty-six. I expect we'll see him soon. And once we have the location, we're ready to move immediately. The men are fast and sharp and tight. Isn't that right, Aaron?"

"Yes, sir. And if I may say so, sir, we're looking forward to kicking some vampire and werewolf butt."

"I don't blame you," Paul said, laughing. "I'd like to be in the thick of it with you."

"You're much too valuable to be in active combat," Bryce said. "And you damn well know it."

Paul grinned. Bryce was right, of course. "I want you to add Doyle to the team."

Bryce did not look pleased. "We've trained down to the wire, Paul. Adding another player at this stage would be foolhardy."

"He's exceptionally talented. And unlike most of your team, he's got field experience killing these creatures. Not just controlled training."

"If everything goes well, we won't be engaging in hand-to-hand."

"And if it doesn't go well?"

Bryce frowned. "It means that much to you?"

"You should have seen him in action. Bryce, he saved my life."

"You're the boss," Bryce said. "But I don't like it."

"The more experience we have on this, the better. Especially since we're going to be moving in hard and fast."

"Of course." Bryce nodded, though he clearly wasn't thrilled. "We'll bring him in immediately."

"Good. And Wes and Kevin?" Paul added. "You sent someone to guard them?"

Bryce swallowed and drew himself up straighter. "No, sir. I didn't think—"

"Dammit, man, no, you didn't think. Those boys are assets. They're poster boys. Walking fund-raisers. And if the werewolves took revenge against Stu, don't you think it's likely that they'll also seek out the other two?"

He pulled his phone toward him and dialed Kevin's number, followed by Wes's. Neither boy answered, and a rope of fear knotted through his gut.

He pushed himself out of his chair. "Come on," he said to Bryce. "And hurry."

SEVENTEEN

The buzz of Doyle's phone woke him, and he reached slowly for it, careful not to wake Andy. The display showed that the call was from Rand.

"What have you got for me?"

"You're going to want to kiss me, Doyle. But I'm not going to let you."

"Considering I can't imagine ever wanting that, I'm going to go out on a limb and guess that you ID'd the werens who took out Stu."

"That's affirmative," Rand said. "The kid went out drinking. Bragged in a few bars he had no business bragging in, and a couple of werens who have a rep for acting first and thinking later heard about it and decided to show Stu just how little they thought of him."

"Two perps? We sure we got them all?"

"We'll know once we get them into custody and question them," Rand said, "but they weren't careful at all. They told pretty much the entire weren community what they had planned. And I've got a traffic cam placing them one block from Stu's apartment. I'm confident they're our guys, and that they worked alone."

"*When* we get them into custody? You're telling me they're still at large?"

"That's what I'm saying. We've issued an all-points. I'll call as soon as we locate them."

"Damn straight," Doyle said. "Stu may have been a little prick, but he was a human. There are rules, goddammit, and those fuckers broke them."

He ended the call and put the phone down quietly. Then he gently wrapped his arm around Andy's shoulders, wondering if she was ready to withstand the depths of the world into which she was diving.

Andy woke in Doyle's arms, more at peace than she could remember feeling in a very long time. She kept her eyes closed, enjoying the rise and fall of his chest against her cheek. Breathing in the scent of him, soapy with an undertone of cinnamon. She smiled to herself. That was probably from the coffee cake.

"Are you awake?" he whispered.

"If I say yes, does that mean I have to move?"

"We could stay here forever," he said. "But our food options would be rather limited."

"You'd be amazed by how many places deliver in my neighborhood." She rolled over in his arms and grinned up at him. "I enjoyed last night."

He stroked her cheek, and she felt a shiver travel all the way down to her toes. "It was my pleasure."

She forced herself to sit up, then glanced at her watch, shocked to discover that it was almost noon. "I should go talk with my dad. And I'm betting you have a job to go to. Or do they just let you run free at Homeland Security?"

"They tend to keep us on a short leash."

"That's the beauty of freelancing," she said. "My time is my own." She made a face. "Or not. I need to see Daddy, hit the grocery store. I should check on Paul, too. Thank him for the party and make sure his arm is okay. And Kevin. At the very least I need to give him a ride back to the Warford, because you have never met anyone who is more lost without a car."

She ran her fingers through her hair, hoping she didn't have a serious case of the morning frizzies. She turned to him as a new thought hit her. "The cops aren't going to find anything, are they? About Stu's murder?"

Doyle shook his head. "What could they find? They're looking for humans. The attackers were werewolves."

"I still can't believe it. I think I would have had nightmares about it if you hadn't been here. I'm so glad Kevin wasn't with us to see what they did to—" She clapped her hand over her mouth as a new thought struck her. "Paul said that he thought they went after Stu because he bragged to the wrong people. But what if that wasn't it? Or what if he included Kevin and Wes in his bragging?"

Doyle didn't waste any time. "Get dressed," he said, and within minutes they were in his car.

"His apartment's in North Hollywood," she said, her foot pressed to the floor of the Pontiac, as if that could make it go faster.

Doyle reached over and took her hand. "We'll find him. He'll be okay."

"You don't know that," she said, hating that he didn't rush to contradict her.

"Here," she said, when he hooked a right onto Whitsett Drive. "That one. There, there! Pull in there."

Doyle slammed on the brakes, pulling the Pontiac into a fire zone. They both leaped from the car, and she raced toward Kevin's apartment, upstairs and in the back. Doyle was right beside her, and he rested his hand on her shoulder for support as she pounded on the door.

Nothing.

"It's locked. Could they have gotten in through the back? He's on the second floor and there isn't a balcony." She turned to Doyle, desperately wanting him to say that of course Kevin was locked up safe and sound.

"If they wanted in badly enough, the second floor wouldn't stop them."

"Shit." She pounded more.

"Back," Doyle said.

"What?"

"I said get back," and even as she was scrambling out of the way, Doyle kicked up and out, his foot intersecting the lock. The doorjamb splintered, the door sprang open, and inside the room, Kevin screamed.

"What the fuck! Jesus, Andy, what the fuck?"

A towel was wrapped around her cousin's waist and his hair was sopping wet. She didn't care. She raced toward him and threw her arms around him.

"We were a little worried about you," Doyle said.

Kevin patted her back. "Okay. So, you wanna tell me why? And you wanna do something about my door?"

To Kevin's credit, he didn't go too pale when Andy told him about Stu's brutal murder, though he did have to sit down.

"But I'm okay, right? I mean, I didn't brag to anybody." He looked between Doyle and Andy.

"I don't want you to stay here alone," she said.

Doyle pulled out his phone. "I'll have someone take you into protective custody."

She turned to gape at Doyle. "You'd do that?"

"Of course," he said. "Under the circumstances I don't see another option."

"But are you allowed to? I mean—you know what? Never mind. If it'll keep him safe I'm not going to argue."

He didn't bother answering because he was already talking. She tuned out his conversation and took a seat next to Kevin.

"Ripped up?" Kevin said. "Like—"

"Like you really don't want to hear the details." She took his hand. "Do what Doyle says, okay? I want you safe."

"Yeah," he said, looking a little shell-shocked. "I can get clothes, right?" He gestured at his towel. Doyle snapped his phone shut and nodded, and Kevin went into his bedroom to pull on some jeans.

"He'll be safe?"

"I promise," Doyle said.

A few minutes later, Agent Tucker appeared in the doorway. He looked at the splintered wood and lifted a brow. "Forget your key?"

"This is my partner, Severin Tucker."

"I remember him from Lompoc. Thanks for doing this."

"His wish is my command," Tucker said, nodding at Doyle. "And where is our happy houseguest?"

Kevin reappeared a second later with a duffel slung over his shoulder. "I didn't know how much to pack."

"Andy can get anything you forgot," Doyle said. "Hopefully, you won't need to be under for long."

"Where's he going?" Andy asked.

"All you need to know right now is that he's going to be somewhere safe. Fair enough?"

She hesitated, uncomfortable with the secrecy. She wanted to know where Kevin would be. But this was Doyle, and she trusted him. She nodded.

"Kevin?" Doyle looked at him.

"Safe works for me." He followed Tucker to the door,

then paused. "But what about Wes? You're checking on him, right?"

Doyle caught Andy's eye. "He's our next stop."

It didn't take them long to get across the valley to the small house that Wes rented in Van Nuys.

"Wow," Wes said as he opened the door for them. "If I'd known I was going to be throwing a party, I woulda bought more beer." He stepped aside, and Doyle saw that Paul was sitting inside the small living room. "Come on in."

"Doyle," Paul called as he crossed over to them, then shook Doyle's hand and kissed Andy's cheek. "I see that you had the same worry that I did. Kevin?"

"We went there first," Doyle said. "He's fine."

"I'm relieved," Paul said. Doyle waited for him to ask where Kevin was now, but he didn't. Instead, he turned and gestured to the two men who were sharing the room with him. "I believe I told you about Bryce? And this is Aaron, who's fast following in his footsteps."

Both men nodded in greeting.

"And Wes?" Doyle said. "What are we going to do about him?"

"We were just discussing that," Paul said. "I've got plenty of room. He can stay with me for a few days."

"And after that?" Doyle asked.

"A few days should be plenty," Paul said, in a voice that left Doyle with no doubt that things were heating up. But what was being planned, dammit? And when?

"There's room for Kevin, too, of course," Paul added.

"I've already sent him to a safe house," Doyle said.

"Did you? Where?"

"If I tell you that, Homeland might find out I'm playing in a different sandbox. Trust me, though. He's fine."

"Good," Paul said, seeming satisfied. Bryce, however, peered at Doyle.

"Why are you playing in our sandbox?"

"Bryce." Paul's voice was sharp.

"No, it's okay," Doyle said. "I'm new and he doesn't know me. It's a fair question. Why am I with Homeland? To protect this country. Why am I aligning myself with Paul? For the very same reason. There are things out there that the government is blind to. And it's not in my nature to leave it to others to fight something evil when I know it exists. I need to be in the fight, too."

Right now, actually, he was itching for a fight—for the release that came with the violence of a kill. It was the hunger, of course. He could feel it growing stronger inside of him—he should have gone to Orlando's last night after he felt the first hint of it, but he wouldn't trade the time he'd spent with Andy for anything. And this morning had been out of the question, too. He'd needed to protect Kevin and come here.

But Doyle wouldn't have to wait for too much longer. Paul would take care of Wes, then Doyle would take Andy home, and he could go to Orlando's and do what needed to be done.

In the meantime, he tamped down the hunger. Or at least tried to. There was still an edge in his voice as he took a step toward Bryce. "I think you understand that. The need to fight. Don't you?"

For a moment, Bryce only stared at him, the silence stretching out for so long that Doyle almost feared that the demon half he kept so well hidden was starting to rise to the surface. But then Bryce nodded.

"Yes, I do." He studied Doyle for another long moment. "You've got quite the reputation. Paul says you saved his life."

It was a peace offering, and Doyle accepted it. "I'm just glad I was there to help."

Bryce looked at both Doyle and Andy in turn. "It's my belief that the attack wasn't random. That vampire sought Paul out. He's making an impact, as all powerful leaders do. He's a threat."

"Clearly," Andy said. "But this is where it starts to fall apart for me. A threat to what?"

"Their organization, of course," Paul said.

"Their what?"

"They're everywhere, you see. In our lives. In our government. They're a solid network. A tangible entity."

Andy was staring at him, and Doyle could see the horror that was written all over her face. "You're serious?"

"He is so totally serious," Wes said.

Paul nodded. "I even have proof. Just the other month I managed to acquire a tape from a reporter who'd been present at the scene of a crime. On it, you can hear someone telling the crowd to forget. To destroy all of their pictures and their tapes."

"I don't understand," Andy said, but Doyle did. Somehow Paul had managed to get his hands on a tape that had captured Tucker or some vamp telling the lookey-loos at a PEC crime scene to forget what they'd seen. *Shit.* That shouldn't have happened.

"They were covering up the crime," Paul said. "A vampire or a werewolf killed someone and left the body, and the press showed up at the crime scene, and these creatures swooped in and used their mind tricks to make them forget."

"Sounds like something from Star Wars," Andy said.

"Besides, it obviously didn't work. You have the tape, so it wasn't destroyed."

"Because the reporter got into a car accident leaving the scene. Purely coincidental, but it meant that the tape wasn't destroyed. And it found its way to me."

Andy shivered visibly. "This is all overwhelming."

"It is. But it's real, too," Paul said.

Out of the corner of his eye, Doyle could see that Bryce was looking at him, and Aaron was looking at Bryce. He took a step forward, presenting a façade of determined solidarity. "Then we need to take decisive action. Do something to bring these monsters down once and for all."

"Exactly," Paul said. "And I'm glad that's your attitude. I'm hoping we can get you more involved in the organization."

"Do you have anything particular in mind?"

"We have something big in the works. I expect to have more details soon, but let's just say that within the next few days, things are going to change dramatically for our dark friends. Trust me when I say it's an operation that's going to make history."

"That may be too soon," Bryce said.

"I agree," Aaron added. "Doyle needs time to train with the other men."

Doyle hid his excitement under a calm façade. This was the prize in the cereal box. "Of course I'd like to participate," he said. "But I don't want to risk the operation." He looked at Bryce and Aaron, but the person he was really speaking to was Paul. "If you feel like your team is a well-oiled machine and that I'd mess things up, just say the word. I can sit out one operation—so long as I know I'll be in the thick of it eventually."

Paul laughed. "Didn't I tell you? A true team player. No, Doyle. You're in this with us. You'll meet the men. And they know damn well they can use a fighter like you. Isn't that right, Bryce?"

Bryce nodded, the gesture deferential. "Of course."

Doyle took care not to smile. His little bit of reverse psychology had done the trick perfectly.

The doorbell rang again, and Wes laughed. "Shit, I'm popular today."

He started in that direction, but Doyle called him back sharply.

"What?"

"There's something—" But what could he say? That his preternaturally keen sense of smell had told him the Big Bad Wolf was at the door?

He grabbed Andy's arm and gave Wes a shove toward the back door of the house. "I just have a bad feeling about this," he said as the sound of the front door crashing in echoed throughout the house.

EIGHTEEN

"Run!" Doyle yelled, his hand clutching Andy's wrist so tight she was certain he was going to bruise it. In front of them, Aaron, Bryce, and Paul veered to the left, crashing down a small hallway into what she presumed was Wes's bedroom.

Doyle was leading her and Wes in the opposite direction, through the kitchen. A door at the back stood half-open, and Doyle urged them both through it, then slammed it behind them. A garage.

Wes's car took up most of the space, and they had to scramble over the hood to get to the other side and the door that stood closed. To their left, at the rear of the car, was the huge overhead door, but Andy assumed Doyle didn't want to go out that way. She'd seen those doors as they'd driven up to the house, and like in most structures, the garage was only a few feet from the front door.

"Alley?" Doyle asked, pointing to a small door at the other end of the garage. "Can we get out that way?" His question was quickly answered when the door burst open and two men in leather pants and biker jackets rushed in from the alley—but they weren't typical gangbangers.

They were werewolves. Andy could tell because they seemed to be in the midst of some horrible change, their bones elongating as she watched, and their faces sprouting hair like demonically possessed Chia pets.

"Go," Doyle said. He smashed a fist through Wesley's car window, then punched the button on the dashboard control box to open the garage door.

Nothing happened.

"It's broken!" Wes shouted.

"Get back," Doyle said, gesturing behind him.

Andy complied, scooting down the narrow path between car and clutter toward the big folding door.

Wes didn't. Instead, he rushed past Doyle, leading with a knife—and tossed himself at the two werewolves.

"Fuckers!" he cried. "Are you the ones who did it? Are you the ones who killed Stu?"

"Dammit, Wes, no!" As Andy watched, Doyle lunged forward to grab the kid and pull him back, but one of the werewolves got to Wes first. He clutched Wes's shirt in his hand and tugged him up so that he was right in his face.

"His eyes!" Doyle yelled, lunging forward. "Wes, go for his eyes! You need to—"

But he didn't get to finish the sentence, because the second werewolf launched himself at him, and over and over they went, a flurry of hands and hard bodies and fists.

"Eyes, Wes!" Andy screamed, but the kid's bravado had evaporated in the face of reality. He was freaked, and he stabbed his hand out blindly, missed the werewolf's eyes, and opened himself up for a brutal attack. The werewolf's hand had warped even more—it was all razor-sharp claws and long bones—and as Andy watched, it slashed out, slicing Wes from his neck down through his chest. The kid's mouth hung open, but no cry of pain came out. Instead, he just looked shocked as he stumbled backward. He dropped his knife, then fell, his blood spilling out onto the concrete floor.

Andy screamed.

In front of her, Doyle and the second werewolf were a messy tumble of arms and legs and fists.

Beyond them, the first werewolf turned his attention from Wes to her. She saw his eyes glint with dark glee, and then he sprang forward, launching himself over Doyle and the second werewolf like he was playing some freakish game of leapfrog. He landed on the hood of the car, and then made one more leap directly at her.

She stumbled backward. The garage was tight, and she didn't have room to maneuver. The car was on her right and a series of shelving lined the space to her left. Stacks of newspapers took up most of the shelf space, but interspersed with the papers were gallon jugs of paint. Andy grabbed one and flung it, tossing it hard at the attacking werewolf and catching him in the face.

He howled, and she felt a sense of deep satisfaction, but she didn't have time to enjoy it. She needed to find another weapon—and fast.

Behind them, she saw Doyle slam the werewolf he was fighting against the side of the car, before jabbing it in the eye with his thumb. "You—" The werewolf's words came out in a pain-filled gasp. "You're a—"

But Doyle didn't let him finish. He silenced the werewolf with a knee to the crotch, and when the creature sank to the ground, Doyle dropped down on top of him.

That was when a solid wall of werewolf blocked her view.

"Bitch." He grabbed her by the neck and yanked her close, and she found herself staring, terrified, into a face that was half-human and half-wolf, with terrifying gold eyes. His mouth hung open, all sharp teeth and menace. She struggled, kicking and scratching, but she might as well have been doing nothing for all the good it did. Then she felt a tug from behind, and she was tossed aside into the shelving like a bag of groceries.

She realized Doyle had leaped over the car and shoved her aside so that he could move in for the attack.

She sat up, gasping and sore, and though half of her field of vision was filled with the fighting men, beyond them she could see the body of the werewolf that Doyle had kneed in the crotch. He was dead—of that she was certain. His chest was sagging open and his heart had been ripped out. She rolled to her side and vomited, then realized she couldn't stop shaking. She fought through it, and crawled the long way around the car, circling back to the hood where Wes had fallen, hoping that he'd somehow survived.

He hadn't, and a cry of anguish and fear slipped from her lips as she tried to force her mind to order her thoughts. The silver knife Wes had wielded was on the ground next to her, and she clutched it tightly. A small part of her told her she had to help Doyle—that she couldn't bear it if he ended up like this—but another part told her there was nothing she could do. That he had it under control. She believed that last part—she didn't know why or how, but he really did seem to be holding his own.

Through the fog of her horror, she watched him battle it out with the werewolf that had attacked her. Fists and teeth and fury and—most strange—she saw that Doyle's skin had taken on an orangish glow. Exhaustion, she assumed. The blood that was rushing to her head must have altered her perception.

A wild wind whipped around them, kicking up the newspapers, and even though she knew she was in shock, she still couldn't understand how there could be wind in a garage.

And then, when the werewolf got in a solid blow and sank his teeth deep into Doyle's shoulder, she saw his eyes turn red with fury. Red.

She cried out, and he turned to her, his face still Doyle's, but at the same time not. *Oh, dear God, he was one of them. Not a werewolf, but something.*

"Knife," he groaned, and it took a second for her to realize that he wanted the silver blade she'd snatched from Wes.

For a split second she hesitated—he'd lied to her in the most fundamental way. He'd taken advantage of her belief that he was human, and he'd slid so self-righteously into her bed. But that didn't mean she could let him die. Dammit all, he might be a prick, but she was better than that. After all, he'd saved her life.

She tossed the knife.

Fortunately, she hadn't moved too slowly, but her aim had been crap. The knife got caught in the wind, though, and it seemed to fly straight into his hand. She had the oddest feeling that he'd made it do that. And then he had it in his fist and was thrusting it down, straight into the werewolf's heart.

The wolf's scream echoed in the enclosed space, and Doyle backed away, stumbling, his shoulder bleeding, his face returning to a more human color, only even paler than usual.

As the werewolf fell—hopefully dead—to the pavement, Andy crawled to Doyle's side. His breathing was ragged, and his face splotchy. His skin looked, well, off, and she realized now what was going on. He was like Jordan. Doyle was a spy—he was getting inside Paul's organization so that he could scope it out.

She stumbled to her feet and forced herself to move toward the door. She had to get out of here. Had to get clear so that she could think, dammit, think.

Her hand closed around the doorknob. She was ready to push through into the alley, but she hesitated. She squeezed her eyes shut, not sure if she was being stupid or kind, then turned back around to face him.

"What are you?" she whispered. The voice of reason told her to stay back, that he was dangerous, but her heart fought back, twisting in grief at the sheen of blood that covered him.

"Go," he said. "Trust your instincts, and get the hell out of here."

She almost did. Probably would have, too. Except that she saw the way he was shivering. His body was trembling as if he were covered in ice. Only moments earlier, he'd been her savior, strong enough to fight the creatures that were attacking them. Not anymore. Now he was weak, and she couldn't help the gnawing fear that if she left him, he'd fade away into nothingness.

She moved closer.

"I told you to get out of here," he said. "I want you gone."

"You told me to trust my instincts. I'm staying." She shifted to get a better look at his shoulder, and he winced. "This doesn't look too bad."

"Deadly to my kind," he said. "Werewolf bite. Curable if I get what I need, but otherwise..." His voice trailed off.

"Otherwise? Otherwise, what?" She bit her lower lip. "What is it you are? No, never mind. What is it you need?"

Again, he only looked away.

"Dammit, Doyle, I am seriously pissed off at you right now. But at the same time, I'm the only help you have."

A muffled ring surprised both of them, and she realized it was coming from the phone in the back pocket of Doyle's jeans. She pulled it out and saw that it was Paul. She answered. "Are you okay?" she asked. "Where are you?"

"A few blocks away. Bryce and I are fine. Aaron's dead, but so are two werewolves. Where are you? How are you?"

"I'm not sure where we are," she lied, not wanting him to know they were still in Wes's garage. Not when Doyle was ... well, the way he was. "Wes is dead. It was horrible. The werewolf, he—"

"I know. I know what they can do. How are you? How's Doyle?"

"I'm fine," she assured him. "Doyle is—" She looked at Doyle, who tensed, undoubtedly certain that she was about to tell Paul everything that had happened. "Doyle is hurt. He says it's not bad, but I'm going to get him to a clinic or a hospital or something."

"Was he bit?" Paul's voice took on a harsh, demanding tone. "Did the werewolf bite him?"

She wasn't sure what compelled her to, but she knew she had to lie. "No. It was a knife. Slashed him in the shoulder."

"Can you handle it?" She heard the relief in his voice. "Do you need us to find you?"

"No. I can handle it. I'll—I'll call you later."

He hung up, and she quickly did the same.

Doyle looked at her, his expression bleak.

"You slept with me," she said, her voice low and dangerous. "You knew what I believed about you, and you slept with me."

"I did," he said, and she couldn't tell if the regret in his voice was for the act or for the lie. "What are you going to do now?"

She punched out a loud breath. "Dammit all, I'm going to do exactly what I said. I'm going to get you help." She rocked back on her heels. "So what exactly do you need?"

What did he need? He needed souls. He needed strength.

The battle had drained him, but the wound had destroyed him.

So what he needed was souls ... but he could hardly tell her that. As it was, he was astounded that she hadn't run. That she hadn't told Paul what he was, then stood back as the human and his team rushed in with their knives and their stakes and their wretched fury.

"Why are you doing this?" It took a huge chunk of his energy to force the words past his lips. But he had to know. Because she was right—he'd lied by omission. And if she wanted to turn her back on him, he damn sure couldn't blame her.

Her forehead creased in what appeared to be confusion. "You need help. God, Doyle, you're a mess." She knelt down next to him, and he could smell the urgency and fear she was feeling along with her anger and disappointment. "Tell me. Tell me what it is you need."

"Need ... to feed." He hadn't wanted to speak the truth, but he was fading. He wanted Tucker to help him, not her, but that would take too long. If he'd fed more recently—if he hadn't already been fading before the werens' attack—but none of that mattered now. He was here, and what he needed was souls.

Crouching beside him, she licked her lips and nodded, all practical, though the smell of fear still clung to her. "Right. Okay. Blood? Is that what you need?"

He managed a shake of his head. "Car. There's a place…"

"A place? What place?"

"Pico … on Pico."

"It'll take forever. Dammit, Doyle, just take my blood. Take a little, please, and then we'll get you there. You don't look good, you really don't." She was tripping over her words and tears glistened in her eyes.

He drew in a shaky breath. "Just go. Leave me."

"Screw that." She got in his face. "I'm not leaving. Do you hear me?" Wildly, she looked around, then pulled the knife from the chest of the werewolf. "You're feeding, damn you, whether you like it or not." She lifted the knife over the pad of her thumb, then bit her lower lip in concentration.

"Don't," he said.

"Shut up."

"Not blood." He blurted it out, the thought that she would bleed for him both unacceptable and absolutely amazing.

"What?" The knife was still poised to cut.

"Not blood. Essence. Energy."

"Oh." She stared at him for a moment, then dropped the knife. She rocked back on her heels and her mouth moved as if she were forming words, but no sound came out. "Oh."

"Orlando's. Take me there."

Through his darkening vision she looked hazy, like a

ghost. But he could see her swallow. "Is there time? Tell me honestly—is there time?" Her voice sounded as if she were talking underwater.

He didn't answer. He didn't know.

"Do—do I have to die?"

"Not feeding off you."

"Do I have to die?"

"No."

"Then do it."

"No."

"Why the hell not?" She straddled him, a blurry, dark vision with beautiful pale eyes. "Do it. Whatever it is you do, do it."

She was right in his face, and he turned away. He couldn't bear to tell her what he truly fed upon. He could remember too clearly the horror in his mother's eyes when she'd learned the truth of it. The way she'd dropped to the ground, praying for God to take him away.

"Doyle. Now, dammit, now." He could smell it—hell, he could practically taste it. Her soul. Rich and deep and as sweet as honey. He couldn't, though. God, how could he do that?

She slapped him hard. "Doyle! Do it! Whatever it is, just do it."

He opened his mouth to argue, to tell her to go, that he couldn't bear for her to know what it was he needed, but she was too close. Too there, and he was so damn hungry.

Half-mad from need, he gripped her shoulders and pulled her close, then closed his lips over hers.

She tensed, then relaxed, her mouth opening and a soft moan escaped into him, along with the sweet, deli-cious threads of her soul.

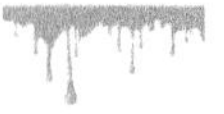

She was floating.

She twined with him, not her body, but her essence.

Her eyes were closed tight, but it didn't matter. Andy could see the two of them and they were bathed in a glow of light.

No, it was her light, and it was spilling out over him. Vibrant, shining colors twisting around him like silken threads.

She could feel it, like the brush of satin against bare skin and it was the most erotic sensation she could ever remember feeling. Magical and pure and—

He broke away. "Enough."

The spell shattered, and she scooted backward, unsettled. This wasn't right. He'd done something to her. Put some kind of spell on her. He'd taken her energy, her essence. Pulled out the essential strands of her.

And dear God, she'd enjoyed it.

She scrambled to her feet, confused and scared. And not just of Doyle—whatever the hell he was—but of her own roiling emotions. Of this desire to pull him close and hold him instead of running as far and as fast as she could.

That's what she was running from. From herself as much as from him.

An old flannel shirt hung from a nail, and she grabbed it and pulled it on, covering her blood-spattered shirt. Then she hurried back to the alley door and pushed it open. A stream of light burst in, illuminating Doyle's battered, bruised face.

She hesitated.

"Go," he said. "Just go."

"What about you?"

"I'll be okay."

She pushed on the door, undecided. Then she let it swing shut. "Did you get enough?"

"I'm not taking any more from you. I got enough to survive. I'll be fine."

"Orlando's? That's where you need to go? Where is it?"

He was silent.

"Dammit, Doyle, how are you going to get there? Drive? You going to call Tucker? In case you hadn't noticed, this place looks like a war zone. What happens if someone else gets here first? Tell me where Orlando's is. I'll take you there. I'll take you," she added, "and that's the end of it."

His eyes met hers. "Head north. I'll tell you where to turn."

"Keys in your pocket?"

He nodded, and she leaned close, trying to ignore the intimacy of her hand in his jeans. She found the Pontiac's key, then slipped out the alley door and ran around the house. It was bigger than any car she'd ever driven, and she moved slowly, afraid she was going to scrape the sides on the narrow bricks of the alleyway. Finally, she brought it to a halt by the door leading from Wes's garage.

She opened the car's back door, entered the garage, and helped Doyle to his feet. He was weak, damn him. No way could he have managed on his own. Together they stumbled to the Pontiac, and she helped him crawl inside and stretch out on the backseat.

"Phone," he said. She still had his in her pocket and she passed it to him. As she pulled out of the alley and onto the street, she heard him telling someone named Lissa that he was on his way and that she should have a room ready for him. "And call Tucker for me," he asked, before ending the call.

"Where now?" she asked, then followed his directions. She could have looked it up on her phone, but she wanted to keep him talking. Maybe it wasn't the same, but she felt a bit like he was a concussion victim, and she needed to keep him awake.

"Use the parking garage," he said when she told him they were close. "It's off the side street. You'll see the sign."

"Right. Okay."

She maneuvered the boat of a car down the twisting drive, then pulled into a nearby space.

"This is where I get out," she said. He had his phone. If he needed to call for someone to come help him inside, he could. But Andy had reached her limit on all things strange and disturbing, and she didn't want to meet anybody who ran a business designed to sell Doyle the kind of sustenance he needed.

"Andy," he said, and she stopped before slamming the driver's door shut. She forced herself not to turn around. Not to look at him. And she forced herself not to cry. "Thank you."

"Goodbye, Doyle," she said, then she let the heavy door swing shut and she jogged across the parking lot.

She knew she should walk away, but despite all her talk about getting the hell away from Doyle, she couldn't quite bring herself to abandon him. She found a dark alcove, and she slid into the shadows. She'd wait there to make sure someone came out and took care of him.

Two minutes passed, and she thought that she was going to have to go back or call Orlando's herself and tell someone to get their ass to the parking garage.

Then she saw headlights. A moment later, a sleek black car with tinted windows pulled up next to the Pontiac. The doors opened, and Tucker stepped out, followed by another man. Without thinking, Andy took a step forward, trying to get a clearer view. She knew that man. The massive build. The dark hair. The scar that slashed across his right cheek.

She even remembered his name, because it was so damn unique. Luke Dragos.

What the hell was CeeCee's guardian doing with Doyle?

Just go. Not your problem anymore. Go.

Good advice, and she decided to take it. She cast one more look back toward the Pontiac, where Luke and Tucker were helping Doyle out. Then she headed up the exit driveway, being careful to stay in the shadows.

There was a convenience store at the end of the block, and she bought a T-shirt with the logo for some band she didn't recognize. She changed in the bathroom and left her soiled shirt in the trash. Then she called a cab.

She sat on the curb drinking a Slurpee as she waited the full twenty minutes for it to show up. She'd intended to have it take her home, but once she slipped into the backseat, she found herself giving the driver her father's address, and then she leaned back against the sticky upholstery and tried to figure out what the hell had happened. How she could have misjudged a man so dramatically. Because on the surface, Doyle was everything she'd ever hoped to find in a man—attractive, strong, funny, and a damn good kisser. He'd even stepped into the knight in shining armor role, rescuing her from an evil beast that was out to kill her. And that wasn't just metaphorical, either.

Everything she could want—except he wasn't what he seemed.

Instead, he was—what?

She didn't know. Or maybe she did, but she just didn't want to think about it. It was too sad, too scary, and as the cab bounced along the surface streets she hugged herself and thought of her dad and hoped that he'd have some wisdom to offer her, because right then, she was fresh out.

"Sweetheart." Her dad's wide smile greeted her at the door. She gave him a tight hug, closing her eyes and relishing the feel of his arms around her. "What's wrong?"

She pushed back and looked up at him. "That obvious, huh?"

"You never could cry without your eyes swelling."

She managed a sniffly laugh; it sucked to be so transparent. "There's no keeping anything from you."

"And you shouldn't even try. Besides, you didn't come here so that you could not talk to me. Are you okay?" He pulled her inside and they sat down next to each other on the couch. "Is this about your mother?"

She made a noise that was a cross between a laugh and a snort. "That and a million other things." She licked her lips, realizing that he didn't know half of what had happened. "Did you hear about Stu?"

His brow furrowed, and she told him the story, watching as his face shifted through a variety of emotions. "Kevin?" he finally asked.

"Safe."

He nodded. "Thank God."

"I'm surprised Paul didn't tell you."

Her father shook his head dismissively. "I was at the church all morning. He left a message, but I haven't called him back yet."

She almost told him about the attack at Wes's house, but decided against it. He'd just worry, and it was too late to do anything about it. Besides, that wasn't why she was here.

The truth was, she wasn't entirely sure why she was here.

"I met this guy..." She trailed off with a shrug and she realized she'd been touching her mother's cross, silently pleading for it to give her strength. To protect her against everything—and everyone—that was swirling around her. "Considering everything that's going on, I guess a guy sounds pretty trivial."

"Relationships are never trivial. Can you tell me what's wrong?"

"I'm just—" Her voice broke. "I'm just really frustrated. I thought there was something there, you know? He's strong and funny and capable and we can sit and talk for hours. But we're different." Her smile was beyond ironic. "Really, really different."

"Sometimes a couple's differences strengthen their relationship. Your mother and I seemed very different on the surface, but it was what was in our souls that really mattered."

She shivered. "I don't think this—" She cut herself off and leaned against him.

"All right, tell me. What's this big chasm between the two of you?"

But she couldn't tell him. Not this. "It's—it's a lifestyle thing. He's a cop. It's—well, he looks at life differently. And it's dangerous. And, I don't know. It's just difficult. And all this stuff with Mom and Paul and everything, it's just making the differences seem that much bigger. Does that make sense?"

"Anything that distances you from someone can be a challenge. Give him space. Maybe the two of you can find a way to work past it."

She nodded, wanting to take that next step and tell

him exactly what the trouble was. But she couldn't. He was in tight with Paul, and that meant Doyle was the enemy. Oh, God. The enemy. She knew what her father would say. That he was evil. That he was the devil incarnate. That Andy needed to run far and fast before Doyle got his claws into her soul.

She pressed her hand to her mouth, afraid she was going to be sick.

"Sweetheart?"

"I—I saw what happened to Stu." She took three huge, gulping breaths. "I think I understand what happened to Mom." *Doyle's kind did that. He's like them. He's one of them.*

Her father's arms tightened around her, but he didn't say anything.

"Do you think they're all like that?"

"What do you mean?"

"Werewolves. Do you think they're all vicious? All the werewolves? All the vampires? All of these creatures that the Dark Warriors are fighting? Or are there some that are, I don't know, just better, I guess, you know, like what Mom thought."

He didn't let go, but she felt the tension in his body, and she knew that her question had made him uncomfortable. "Why would you ask that?"

"I don't know," she lied, her mind focused on Doyle. "I was thinking about Creevey."

"Creevey?"

"He's a monster, right?" She pulled out of his arms and shifted on the couch, because this was important and she wanted to see his face.

"Of course he is."

"But we don't judge all people by him. We don't look at a man and think that since Creevey's evil, that man must be, too."

Her father shook his head, his expression infinitely sad.

"Daddy?"

He reached out and cupped her cheek. "You're always looking for the good in people."

"Is that bad?"

"Not when it's actually people you're looking at. But these creatures—sweetheart, they're not human. They're demons. I realize it's difficult to wrap your head around it, but you have to."

"But—"

"No," he said, and this time his voice took on the tenor of the pulpit. "Think, Andrea. Think about who was the most beautiful of all. The most tempting of all. Lucifer may shine like a light, but that doesn't change his nature, what's at his core. Evil is evil, Andrea. And that basic nature cannot be changed."

TWENTY

Andy borrowed her dad's second car to go home, but as soon as she pulled out of the driveway, she knew that she wasn't ready to go. She'd heard what her dad had to say. But although she loved and respected him, his words had rung false in her ears.

His answers weren't her answers, and it was time for her to put her reporter hat back on and figure out exactly what was going on—what Doyle was, and what that meant.

The trouble was, a reporter needed sources, and Andy wasn't exactly well stocked in that department. She didn't know anybody outside of Paul's crew who even knew that this other world existed. And Paul was definitely not the man she wanted to talk to right now.

So where did that leave her? Libraries? The Internet? No.

The realization hit her with such force that she slammed on the brakes, almost causing the car behind her to careen into her. The driver shot his middle finger into the air and burned rubber getting around her, something that would normally piss her off.

Today, she ignored it. She eased back into traffic, her mind going a million miles a minute. *Luke Dragos.* He'd been right there at Orlando's. She'd seen him.

And he was CeeCee's guardian.

She could be wrong—maybe CeeCee really was just your average kid—but Andy would have bet a full year's supply of Chips Ahoy that CeeCee was as different from teenage heartthrob Kurt Wiley as Andy was from Ryan Doyle.

It was already early evening, and she knew that it was a long shot that she'd find CeeCee at the Pacific Teen Center, but she had to try, and she broke about a dozen traffic laws getting there. She slammed the car into park, then raced inside, standing in the doorway as she scoped out the room.

All of the kids looked up at her, a few with concerned expressions. A few more waved.

CeeCee just frowned.

"Can we talk?" Andy asked, approaching her.

"Am I in trouble?"

"No, but I need your help." She cocked her head toward the door and led the girl outside. This wasn't official, and she didn't want to have the conversation in a building owned by her father's ministry.

"So what's going on?" CeeCee asked, when they were both settled on a low stone wall, their feet dangling as they looked out at the ocean.

Wasn't that the question of the hour? Now that she was here, Andy really wasn't sure how to broach the subject. She drew in a deep breath and decided to dive right in. "I was thinking about you and Kurt," she said. "What's so different about you two?"

"Huh?"

"You told me you were too different—that was why you could never date. But you look the same. You're both teens. You both live in California. So what's different?"

CeeCee's nostrils flared a bit, and then she frowned. "It's complicated," she said.

"Would it uncomplicate things if I told you that I think I understand."

"Oh, please. I promise you, you don't."

"Do you know a guy named Ryan Doyle?"

That got CeeCee's attention. She turned sharply and looked at Andy. "What makes you think I know him?"

"He's a friend of your guardian's, isn't he? Of Luke's?"

CeeCee laughed. "Hardly. Those two haven't been friends for a really long time." She shrugged. "But they work together, so I guess they have to tolerate each other. How do you know him?"

Andy ignored the question and dove straight into the deep end while her courage held out. "What is Doyle? He's not a vampire or a werewolf, so what is he?" She squeezed her hands into fists, hoping against hope that she hadn't just scared off a perfectly human teen.

CeeCee jumped down off of the wall and started walking away. "Oh, whoa. I don't do this crazy talk stuff—"

"Bullshit."

The girl stopped in her tracks, but she didn't turn around.

"Please. I need to understand. I—I like him. But I don't understand what he is. I don't understand any of it at all. And you're the only one I could think of to ask."

Slowly, the girl turned back around. "Why do you think he's anything?"

It was Andy's turn to hesitate. "I saw him do things. His skin changed. His eyes, too. And he was able to control the wind."

"Yeah, well, I think that goes with the package."

"What package?"

"Doyle's a para-demon."

"A demon?" Oh, dear God, her father was right. Doyle might seem human, but he came straight up from the bowels of hell.

"What? You mean like all fire and brimstone? It can get pretty gritty in here," the girl said, thumping her chest, "but none of us are cousins of Beelzebub."

Despite the flippancy of the girl's words, Andy felt a million times better. Except at the same time, Paul's voice was in her head, telling her about the darkness inside vampires and werewolves. Telling her they needed to be eradicated.

"Oh, please," CeeCee said, after Andy had said as much. "Did you know I ran away from home? My stepfather beat me. That was evil. Not what I am now or what the family I have now is like. They're good folks, you know? I mean, yeah, there's bad shit out there, but I don't think Doyle's bad shit. I think maybe he did some bad things—I think Luke did, too, a long time ago. But they both fought to be good, you know? And I think that if you fight, then you can't be evil. Because evil would just give in."

"You're sixteen, right?"

The girl sighed. "This year, yeah. And next year, too. Apparently I'm going to be sixteen forever."

Andy laughed. "The age suits you." She paused. "My mother knew about your world. And she knew that it was like mine. Some folks are good, some aren't. Some are bad, some aren't. She tried to prove it, and it ended up getting her killed."

"I'm sorry," CeeCee said. "That must've been hard."

"I didn't realize it at the time. But it's colored my dad's whole world."

"He's seeing what he wants to see," CeeCee said. "It's

not like it's hard to see how things really are if you just open your eyes."

Andy considered that, and had to admit that she agreed. And if Doyle wasn't pure, walking evil...

She cleared her throat. "So, um, does it ever happen? One of your kind dating a human?"

"Oh, sure," CeeCee said easily. "Sara was human when she and Luke got all hot and heavy."

"Really? What happened?"

"She was a prosecutor and I guess there was a case that involved Luke. And they fell for each other, but she almost died, so Luke turned her into a vampire." CeeCee shrugged. "I guess that worked out pretty well, huh?"

"Yeah," Andy said, though the solution wasn't really one that appealed to her. "So you're saying—wait. Sara? Sara Constantine?"

CeeCee cocked her head. "Yeah. You know her?"

Andy nodded. "Casual friends. I covered a lot of press conferences for the DA's office."

"Oh. Well, you should go say hi or something."

Or something, Andy thought. Sara would definitely have a unique perspective on all of this.

"And Serge is like me," CeeCee said, clearly warming to the topic. "And he's with Alexis now and she's totally human."

"What about later?"

CeeCee shrugged. "Dunno. Guess they'll figure it out." She looked sideways at Andy. "So what are you going to do?"

"I don't know," Andy admitted. "But this has helped. Thank you."

"Sure. I guess it's pretty cool you came to me. You're the first person I've ever really given advice to."

"Then it's an honor. How about you? What are you going to do?"

"You mean with Kurt?" Her voice rose to a squeak, the former confidence disappearing.

"That's what I mean."

"Duh. Nothing."

"So you're trying to get me and Doyle together, but you're not even going to see what happens with Kurt?"

"You know about Doyle. Kurt doesn't have a clue about me."

"So?"

She frowned, then shrugged. "Maybe tomorrow I'll buy two hot dogs and see if he wants to share."

"Can't hurt, right?"

"I hope not," the girl said. She made a face, then blew out a noisy breath. "So, what started all of this, anyway? The way he kicked up the wind? Seriously?"

Andy hesitated, but CeeCee had helped her too much. She couldn't play coy now. "He was hungry," she said, wanting to spare the girl the part about the fight. "And he ended up feeding off of my essence." She told her the rest of the story, ending up with dropping him at Orlando's.

"Your essence? Oh, you mean your soul?"

Something cold and terrifying uncurled in Andy's gut. "What?"

"Doyle feeds on souls. Even I know that."

"Souls. As in—souls?"

"Yeah. You should know that—why else would you take him to Orlando's?" She must have noticed Andy's clueless expression, because she continued. "Duh. It's a soul-trading bar."

Andy swallowed, her father's sermons running through her head, sermons about the sanctity of the soul and the devil's ploy to steal it. "Did—did he hurt me by taking it?"

CeeCee shrugged. "Well, I wouldn't think so. I mean, that wouldn't make much sense, would it?"

"Are you sure?"

CeeCee just stared. Apparently, she wasn't sure.

And that meant that Andy wasn't finished yet.

And she knew of only one place she could go to get the answers that she still needed.

Doyle kept his eyes closed, breathing deeply of the soul that was being pumped through the feeding machine. Usually, it was the machine he wanted.

Today, it wasn't enough for him—he wanted living soul.

He wanted Andy.

He squeezed his eyes closed, hating the direction of his thoughts.

He'd taken just a little from her—only enough to give him the strength to survive the trip to Orlando's. But it had been momentous. The sweet sensation, the glorious taste. The heady knowledge that her very essence was twining with his—that they were sharing something even more intimate than sex...

He shuddered, longing now for something he couldn't have. Because while the moment itself had been amazing, he'd seen her face in the aftermath. The horror reflected there when she'd realized the full extent of what he was— a dark creature. A monster.

Fuck.

Slowly, he pushed the machine away, then sat up, rubbing his temples. He was full now, but he still felt ripped. Not physically, but emotionally. Andy had come into his life and she'd knocked him sideways. He'd had her for just the briefest of moments, and he'd lost her as quickly as he'd lost Kathryn when she'd tumbled from that window.

But Andy's not dead.

Maybe not, but she might as well be. To her, he was the enemy. Her enemy, the world's enemy, Paul's enemy.

Paul's enemy. The thought jolted through his head again, and he cursed as he jumped off the table. Shit, how could he have been so stupid?

He pulled open the door and stepped out of the private room and into the posh hallway that led to the main part of the club. It looked like any number of night-clubs, with multiple dance floors, beautiful waitresses, and tables scattered about for the guests.

He found Tucker sitting around a table upon which a scantily clad succubus was dancing. "I'm in love," Tucker said.

"I thought you were immune to a succubus's charms," Doyle said.

Tucker looked the girl up and down. "A succubus, sure. But I'd have to be dead to be immune to that." He shifted his attention to Doyle. "You got your tank all topped off?"

"We need to go see Andy."

Tucker's eyes widened, and Doyle saw his partner come to the same conclusion. "Oh, fuck me," Tucker said, then slammed back the last of his drink before standing. "You think she's talked to him yet?"

"I hope not." He was betting she hadn't. He'd come to know her pretty well in the short time they'd known each other, and he didn't think she'd run to Paul right away. She'd want to get it straight in her own head first. Hopefully that would buy him some time.

"You'll need to ask her," he said, catching Tucker's eye. "And you'll need to make sure she tells us the truth."

"I can do that. And afterwards?"

The question hung in the air between them. Doyle hesitated at the club entrance, wishing there was another way, but knowing there wasn't. "Afterwards, you wipe her memory," he said, and then he pushed out into the night.

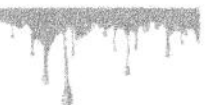

Orlando's was bustling, and Andy stood in the thick of it, her back ramrod straight, hoping that she didn't look so out of place that someone would come over and decide to unceremoniously suck out part of her soul.

A beautiful woman with long blond curls glided toward her and stretched out her hand, the gesture punctuated by a welcoming smile. "My doorman says you'd like to speak with me?"

"You're Lissa?" Doyle had mentioned the woman's name in his call to Orlando's, and she'd asked for her specifically when she walked in the door.

"I am. I'm the owner."

"I'm Andy. Thanks for seeing me. I should say right off that I'm not—well, I'm human."

Lissa's laugh rang out. "Yes. I can tell. Come with me."

She led Andy to an office that overlooked the main floor of the club. She sat behind a desk and gestured for Andy to take the chair opposite her. "Are you here about Doyle?"

"How did you know that?"

"Doyle was parched when he came in, but he'd fed enough to allow him to keep his hunger under control. I asked him how. He told me about you."

"Oh. What did he say?"

"That he was afraid he'd terrified you, but that you

were exceptionally brave to help him. He thinks you're quite remarkable."

"Oh." She felt her cheeks warm and realized she was blushing. "The thing is, I don't think he told me the exact truth about what he took from me."

One eyebrow arched up. "No? What did he say?"

"That he needed some of my essence."

"That's a fair statement."

"Really?" Andy asked, afraid to get her hopes up. "I thought maybe what he really took was some of my soul."

Lissa folded her hands on her desk. "That's a fair statement, too."

"Oh." Her mind filled with the images she'd grown up with—vibrantly colored paintings by Renaissance masters depicting souls writhing in hell. "But—"

"You're limited by what you think you know," Lissa said gently. "Your soul isn't like a gold ingot that you have to protect. It's like a fruit tree that blossoms and grows. Sharing a part of your soul willingly won't hurt you. It happens all the time. You share your soul with the people you love every day. It grows, it changes. And if it's not tattered or broken, then losing part of it won't harm you. If anything, it will grow back even more robustly. Like pruning a tree."

"Do you mean that?" It went against everything she'd ever believed, and yet she couldn't escape the memory of what it had felt like. Wonderful. Like starlight on a summer night.

"Of course I do. A soul given willingly can be an amazing shared experience. Sensual. Even erotic."

"And if the person's unwilling?"

Lissa's face darkened. "That can damage both the giver and the taker. Is that what happened between the two of you?"

"No," Andy said immediately.

"Of course not. Doyle wouldn't do that to you." Lissa smiled. "Have I calmed some of your fears?"

"You have. Thank you."

"Most humans wouldn't have the courage to walk in here and demand to see me, much less start questioning me."

Andy resisted the urge to lick her lips. "I hope I didn't offend you. But—well, it's important that I understand this. Because..." She trailed off, frowning.

"Because you don't want to run away from a man you care about for the wrong reasons? I understand. And I won't tell Doyle you came to me."

"Thank you."

"You're a lucky woman to have your eyes opened to a whole new world. Who knows what amazing things you'll see?" Lissa stood. "Come on. I'll give you a tour. I think you'll find it fascinating."

TWENTY-ONE

Andy lay in bed, her body burning with need, her back arching up, her lips parting. *Please. Please, now.*

His hands were on her, his brown eyes on her face, so intent on seeing her. Rough hands slid beneath her nightgown and stroked her, brushing hard nipples, sliding over soft skin.

Doyle, Doyle, oh yes, please, Doyle.

She knew somehow that this was a dream. That she'd wake up and be alone. That when the morning dawned he'd be gone and her courage to confront him would be gone, too. Because despite everything she and CeeCee had talked about, despite the calming words from Lissa, things between her and Doyle were complicated. And scary. And truly messed up.

But in dreams? She could lose herself to him in dreams, and that's what she was doing right now, giving herself over to pleasure, to him, to the sweet sensation of his touch. To the simplicity of being with him.

In her dream, his hand stroked her belly, fingers dancing over soft skin. She moaned, feeling half-awake, like this was really happening, but keeping her eyes tightly shut because she knew that was impossible.

But oh, dear Lord, that touch.

That touch was real.

Doyle?

Her eyes flew open with joy—and a hard hand stifled the scream that rose from her mouth only an instant later.

"Hello, beautiful," Kyle Creevey said. "Told ya I'd make you come for me. I think now's a damn good time, don't you?"

The fingers on his free hand stroked her stomach some more, then inched down to snap the elastic of her panties.

She tried to speak, to scream, but he tightened his grip over her mouth. "No, no, no. Now don't struggle." His mouth quirked up. "Actually, what the hell, struggle if you want. That only makes it more fun."

She swallowed, trying to think. Trying to remember everything she knew about him. He took his time, she knew that. But in the end, he always killed his victims.

She squeezed her eyes shut, and realized her mind was still focused on Doyle. On the desperate fantasy that he'd rescue her. On the wish that he was here to hold her and make her fear go away.

She didn't know what he was—all she knew was that she wanted the chance to know him. To see if what she'd felt for him was real—and if he'd truly felt it, too. And now, dear God, she'd lost it.

"You want me," Creevey whispered. "Oh, yeah. You know you do. Now come on, baby. Open up for daddy." His knee was between her legs and he was trying to pry them wider apart. She tensed, fighting him. She knew it would ultimately be futile, but she had to try. Had to fight. Had to pray that somehow, someone would—

"Andy!" Doyle's voice, along with a sharp pounding at the front door of her house.

"Doy—" She cried out, but Creevey clapped his hand over her mouth before she could fully get the word out. He wouldn't know. He'd knock and she wouldn't answer, and he'd leave, and even if he thought to come back later, she'd be dead, and—

Crash!

The echo of splintering wood filled the tiny house.

Creevey was off her in a second, and she watched as he slipped through the open window that had been his entryway. An instant later, Doyle was at her side, and she was clinging to him, tears flowing freely.

Someone else rushed past, and she realized that it was Tucker, and he was climbing through the window in pursuit. But she couldn't think about that now, didn't even care. All that mattered was that Doyle was there and that he was real and that he was holding her.

"I heard your cry. Dear God, I could smell your fear."

"You came. I wanted you, and you came." She clung to him, holding him tight, finding it impossible to believe that he was real.

Gently, he pushed her away, then pulled up the sheet so that she could clutch it tight over her nightgown. "Did he hurt you? Did he—"

"He didn't get that far." She shuddered. "But he touched me." She felt the hot tears stream down her face. "He—"

"Shhh. It's okay. You don't have to tell me."

"I'm so sorry," she said.

"You don't have anything to be sorry about."

"Not about him. About you. I was scared. I shouldn't have been scared of you." She drew in a breath, thinking about everything her father believed, everything she'd seen. She loved her dad, but he was wrong. Doyle wasn't evil. He fought evil. And so help her, she wanted to be right by his side.

"I don't know what you are," she said. "Not really. But I'm not scared anymore." She brushed her lips over his. "I'm not scared at all."

Paul watched as Bryce paced the length of the training floor in the Mojave bunker. Behind them, a half-dozen men were working out on the mat. In an hour, formal training would begin. They'd captured a new female, and they were planning to let her loose on the soldiers.

The men, Paul was certain, would show the little bitch just how powerful a human could be.

In front of him, Bryce stopped. "I'm short a man now," he snapped. "Was it really necessary to take Aaron out?"

"He was bitten," Paul said. "He would have changed."

"Not until the next full moon," Bryce countered. "We could have used him until then."

"We couldn't guarantee his continued loyalty," Paul said. "Once someone's crossed that line, eradication is essential."

Bryce nodded. "Yes, yes. I know. But dammit, Aaron was a good soldier."

"We have Doyle to take up the slack."

"We could postpone the mission," Bryce said.

"Not an option, and you damn well know why. Besides, we're almost ready. We have the ordnance, we have a plan, we have an exceptional team—which will be even better with Doyle on it. Soon we'll have the location. A day of reconnaissance and we'll be ready to go."

Bryce didn't look happy.

"Am I to understand you need more time?"

"My team is set. I don't need Doyle."

"You're wrong to distrust him," Paul said.

"Perhaps you're wrong to trust him so easily."

Paul tamped down the irritation that flared within him. Certain things were nonnegotiable with him, and saving somebody's life was cause for undeniable loyalty. He had no intention of breaking that code. Nor did he have any intention of explaining himself yet again to his subordinate. "This discussion is over. I'm going to look in on Travis's progress."

He crossed the room, stopping outside a hematite door with a small porthole-style window. He peered in the window. Travis was sitting in a chair across from the male vampire, who had a collar around his neck. One of the soldiers stood near, holding the collar's control.

"Again," the soldier said. "Compel him to dance."

"This little prick doesn't have the brains to withstand what I can do," the vamp said. "You're wasting my time. And you're pissing me off."

"Strong words from a neutered vamp," the soldier said, and he pressed a button on the control box. Immediately, the vampire's body went into convulsions. Paul smiled. Electricity was his strongest weapon against the vampires. It didn't kill them, but it definitely slowed them down. Even better, it had proven to be useful against all manner of creatures. Paul patted the Taser in his pocket; he'd learned to always be prepared.

He closed the porthole, confident that the soldier would convince the vampire to continue with Travis's training. At this point, though, Paul was beginning to think the vamp was right. Perhaps Travis's politician's mind simply wasn't designed to withstand compulsion.

One of the soldiers from the training floor jogged over to him. "Sir, I've been asked to inform you that a visitor is being escorted to your office."

"Creevey," Paul said, glancing at his watch. "And he's here with time to spare."

Kyle Creevey followed the uniformed pretty boy into the bunker. At first, he hadn't believed the bullshit story about the poison. He'd brushed it off, not much caring if it was true or not, because he was going to get turned, and poison couldn't do shit to you if you were already dead.

Then the fucking fangers had gone and flat-out denied him, which had really got him riled. Got him needing a release. Got him needing a kill.

He'd wanted to kill one of the vamps, but it would have been too dangerous to try. He wanted to live long enough to find a vamp willing to change him.

So he did the next best thing and started working his way down his list, starting with the very top name.

Woulda worked, too. Woulda taken the edge off if his little party with Andrea-Fucking-Tarrant hadn't been interrupted.

He'd barely gotten out of there without being caught. Then he'd raced down the road on the Harley those fuck-ass soldiers had given him so he could get to the club and back to their safe house. As the wind whipped around him, he'd felt the familiar rage stirring inside him. The kind that made him stronger. Only this time, he felt sick, even a little dizzy.

And that's when he remembered the poison. When he got to the safe house, they'd tossed him in a car and drove him here, to the fucking desert. So now here he was, staring at the guy who'd fucked him up in the first place, along with some other asshole he'd never seen before. "Who the fuck are you?"

"You can call me Paul," the man said. "I believe you have some information for us?"

"You got an antidote for me?"

Paul looked over at the other guy—Kyle never had learned his name. "How much time left?"

"Twelve hours."

"We have plenty of time to bargain," Paul said. "Give us the information, and we'll give you the antidote."

"I don't have it," Kyle admitted.

"That's a pity. Bryce, would you escort Mr. Creevey out?"

"But I can get it," Kyle said. "Or rather, I know how you can get it."

"I'm listening."

"The vamps," he said. "Capture one. Torture one. I'll happily help you do it." Oh, yeah, he would. "You jack them up full of this shit called hematite, and they'll start rattling off whatever they know."

"We've tried that," Paul said. "We routinely capture vampires. We use them to train our men," he added, and Kyle had to admit he was impressed. "It's our policy to interrogate every captive. So far, none have given us the location for the creatures' center of operations. They were either extremely well conditioned, or they knew nothing."

"That a fact?" Kyle shifted his weight, mulling over his options. He wanted the damn antidote. He also wanted the vamps who'd shot him down to suffer. If he could manage to do both, that would be sweet.

"It is a fact. One that's been particularly troublesome. If you can help us out here, it would be worth the anti-dote. If you can't ... well, I can't say it was nice knowing you."

"I think maybe we can work something out," Kyle said.

"Is that so? And what do you suggest?"

"There's a particular vampire I know of," he said. "She's been inside their headquarters. You want a location? Capture her."

TWENTY-TWO

Her lips were soft beneath his, and Doyle held her tight, tasting her, holding her, the horrible fear fading now that she was safe in his arms.

He heard a throat clearing and he reluctantly broke their kiss, turning his head to look at his partner. "Creevey?"

"Bastard got away," Tucker said. "Had a motorcycle." He lashed out, smashing his fist down on the windowsill. "Shit."

It was the kind of reaction Doyle himself would have had except that right now nothing mattered to him except for the woman in his arms. The world would start up again soon enough. For now, he needed these few minutes.

"Head on over to the office," Doyle said. "Have tech fire up the traffic cams. See if they can chart a path. Pull his file and see if we can figure out where he'd hole up."

"Creevey's not technically our case."

"I'm making it our case," he snapped.

"I'll take care of the paperwork." Tucker looked at Andy, his eyes soft. "Do you still want me to...?"

"No," Doyle said, hoping he was making the right decision. "Not now."

Tucker nodded. "I'll be in touch."

As soon as Tucker was gone, Doyle stood. "You should get dressed. I'll make you some hot tea. And then we'll talk."

She nodded, the sheet clutched around her. He paused in the doorway to look at her, so small and vulnerable on the king-sized bed, and he felt rage build up inside of him. A killing rage—and there was only one man he wanted to take it out on.

The PEC had to find the bastard, because Doyle wanted blood.

A few moments later she padded into the kitchen. She was wearing threadbare jeans, a T-shirt, and no shoes. She sat down at the breakfast table, one foot tucked under her, and curled her hands around the tea he'd fixed for her.

"What was Tucker asking you about? He asked if you still wanted him to do something."

Doyle considered not telling her, but he changed his mind. This was the time for brutal honesty. "I came over here so that Tucker could wipe your memory."

She sat back, her eyes going wider. "Really. Wow. Why?"

"You know what I am. I couldn't risk you telling Paul." He sat down opposite her. "Have you told Paul?"

"No. Honestly, it didn't even occur to me. He's not ... he doesn't really understand what he thinks he's fighting, does he?"

"No."

"So I get to keep my memory?" The words were serious, but her expression was playful.

He stayed serious. "Are you sure you want it? I won't lie, Andy. What you said—about not being scared, about wanting me with you—it was everything I wanted to hear. But you were terrified. Creevey was—"

"No," she said firmly. "This has nothing to do with Creevey. It's just you and me." She drew in a long breath. "I did a lot of thinking. I did more than thinking, actually."

He shifted, suddenly on alert. "What do you mean?"

"I'm a reporter, remember? I poked around."

He looked at her, still not understanding. "Poked around? Where? And why?"

"I know someone. Someone from your world, I mean. I didn't realize it until last night after I dropped you off at Orlando's. He stepped out of a car, and I recognized his face. He has a scar, and he's an imposing guy. Hard to miss. I've seen him before at the Teen Center."

For a moment, he had no idea what she was talking about. Then he thought of Luke and the girl who'd recently become his ward. "CeeCee? You know CeeCee from the Teen Center?"

"Until I saw Luke, I just assumed CeeCee was your typical teen trying to fit in."

"And now?"

"Now I think exactly the same thing." She met his eyes and he saw nothing but honesty there.

His heart twisted, and he reached for her hand. "Andy."

"I did more, too. I went back to Orlando's." She told him all that she'd learned about soul lore. How she knew her soul would recover after letting him feed—and how it might even blossom if there was a connection between them.

"Is there a connection?" she asked him. "Is there, or did I destroy anything we might have started by being so damn scared and running away?"

"Scared?" The word hung false on his lips. "Is that how you see yourself? Andy, scared is the last thing you are. Look at you. Right here. Right now. You could have chosen to believe every horrible story you've ever been told. You could have turned your back and told your grandchildren stories about the time you brushed up against evil."

"No, I—"

"But you didn't," he said firmly. "You were scared—of course you were. Who wouldn't be? But you asked questions. Hell, you walked straight into the abyss. A human just walking into Orlando's and demanding to see Lissa? Andy, my God, you're the bravest person I know."

He meant every word he said, and he could tell she knew it from the small smile that touched her lips.

"She was very nice, actually."

"Lissa? She's awesome. But all you knew was that you were going deep into a place where your soul just might be ripped from you. Tell me you weren't afraid."

She shook her head. "I can't tell you that. I was terrified."

"And yet you went anyway." The words hung in the air, their full import finally hitting him. She'd gone in because of him. Partly because she was a reporter, sure, but at the end of the day, this was about him. "No one's ever done that before," he said. He was speaking more to himself than to her, but she answered anyway.

"Done what?"

"Believed in me. No," he corrected. "That's not what I mean. No one's ever cared enough to try to figure me out."

The tiny smile bloomed. "I haven't got you completely figured out," she said. "Not you or the world you live in. But I know you're not evil. And neither is Lissa or CeeCee or Tucker." She sat up a little straighter. "There's a whole other world out there that I know hardly anything about."

"There is."

"It's not evil," she said. "It's not vile or wretched or a slice of hell the way that Paul wants to make it out to be."

"No, it's not."

"But there's evil in it," she said. "Those werewolves who killed Stu, for example. But there's evil in my world, too."

"Kyle Creevey," he said.

"And a whole lot more like him."

"You've been thinking a lot," he said.

"I have. And I want to know more. Will you tell me?"

"Of course. Whatever you want to know."

"Let's start with you. CeeCee said you're a para-demon, but I don't really know what that means."

He hesitated, not quite able to believe that they were having this conversation. That she'd seen the demon inside of him. And yet she wasn't afraid of him. It was a miracle, and it humbled him, filling him with an emotion he hadn't felt in a very long time—hope.

"Go on," she urged.

"I should probably tell you that I'm a lot older than you," he began.

"You look like you're in your late thirties."

"Close," he said. "I'm three hundred and eighty-two."

"Of course you are." She frowned at her tea. "I have bourbon. Maybe we should have bourbon."

He couldn't help but laugh. "Maybe we should."

"Keep going," she said as she got up and headed to the cabinet beside the refrigerator. "You told me about your mom. Was that true?"

He frowned. "You're starting with the hard questions," he said. "The truth is I exaggerated a bit. But, yes, what I told you was true. I just left some things out."

"I'm listening."

"I told you she was raped—she was. By a horrible creature. A demon."

"And that's like what my dad preaches about?" She brought the bourbon and two glasses back to the table. "Evil spirits?"

"Evil, yes. But flesh and blood, although essentially immortal. And while we believe that demons come from another dimension, I don't think it's the same as what you'd think of as hell. And the truth is it doesn't matter. They've walked this earth for a very long time. It's fair to say they're natives now."

She nodded, but he wasn't sure she completely understood. "But the bottom line is that he raped your mom, and that got your mom started on her quest. She wanted to eradicate him and the others like him, right?"

"Not exactly. The part I left out of the story was that she got pregnant." He focused his attention on her face. "She got pregnant with me."

TWENTY-THREE

Andy didn't like what he was saying, but she realized that she should have expected it. CeeCee had told her what he was after all—a para-demon. And that meant part demon.

"But you're not—I mean, you're nothing like your father."

"My mother thought I would be. She used to try to beat the evil out of me."

"The bitch."

"Mmm," he said. "I happen to agree with you, but she wasn't entirely wrong. Except that you can't beat it out. Not really."

Andy swallowed. "What do you mean?"

"It is there. Inside me. Something dark. It lives inside. It writhes and fights and tries so hard to come out to play." His smile was thin. "You've never seen my temper. Not really."

"A temper isn't evil."

"No, it's not. You've never seen the demon, either."

"I saw something. It was scary, I'll grant you that, but —" She cut herself off.

"But what?"

She thought of what she'd learned from both CeeCee and Lissa. And she thought of what she knew in her heart. "But it's not fire and brimstones. It didn't come from hell."

"Do you think that matters?" he asked softly. "Evil is evil. There's darkness in Creevey, but he didn't sprout from Lucifer's head, either. So you tell me. How are we different?"

For a moment she couldn't speak—the idea that he would compare himself with that human filth was appalling. He had to be exaggerating to make a point, but when she looked at his face, she saw that he wasn't.

"You fight it," she said. "Creevey embraces it."

He nodded, but the gesture seemed tired. "I fight it because I have to. But believe me when I say that it would be easy to give in. As easy as going home."

She stared at his face, at the haunted look in his eyes, and for a moment she didn't see the man but the little boy. An innocent child who didn't understand what he was and had no one around to help him. "Your mother was the evil one." She spoke softly, more to herself than to him. But it was true, and the words gave her strength. "She was a first-class bitch," she said, more strongly. "I don't know what she did to you, but I'm certain she wasn't a real mother to you."

"No," he said. "You're probably right. But that doesn't mean I didn't learn from her. I kept the demon down, all right, if only to save my own skin."

She heard it then, an unmistakable tinge of fear. No, not fear—self-loathing. "You think that without her, you would have just let go. You think you owe your humanity to that horrible woman."

It was a statement, and he didn't bother answering. It didn't matter. She was certain she was right.

"After you learned to keep the demon down, did she leave you alone?"

"She did. For a while."

"But something happened?"

"I turned twelve."

She waited for him to speak—the pain on his face was palpable, and she desperately wished there was something she could do to soothe him.

"I turned twelve," he repeated, "and the hunger hit me."

"For souls," she said. And even though she understood more now, she couldn't help but shiver.

Doyle noticed, and he looked away.

"I'm sorry," she said. "I didn't mean—"

"Of course you did. By its very nature it sounds vile. That's why I don't feed on humans. Not if I can help it."

"Orlando's," she said. "Lissa told me about the machines. And about the girls." During the tour, Lissa had explained how most of the Shadowers who lived off of souls chose to take them directly from one of the succubi on Lissa's staff. It had been a strange conversation, but what had been stranger was the way it had made Andy feel. "Doyle?"

He looked at her, and she couldn't believe what she was about to say, but he needed to know. "When Lissa explained to me how it worked—about the girls, I mean —I wasn't scared. Well," she corrected, "maybe a little. Mostly, I was jealous."

His brow furrowed with an unspoken question.

"What I felt—what we shared—it was amazing. Sensual and sweet, and the thought of you sharing that with another woman..." She trailed off with a shrug. "I didn't like it. I was glad when Lissa told me you prefer to use the machines."

He reached across the table and took her hand. "Andy." That simple word held a wealth of emotion.

She wanted to move into his arms. Wanted him to hold her and comfort her—and she wanted to do the same for him.

But she also wanted to know the rest. No, she needed to know. Needed to understand. And so she stayed at the table, her fingers held tight in his. "What happened when your mother learned about the hunger?"

"She lost it," he said. "The Church was our life, and she was as devout as any woman alive. More, probably, since she'd been schooled in a convent and would have taken vows had she not been raped by my father."

Andy realized that she'd released his hand and that her fingers were now clutching her cross. Doyle's voice was level, matter-of-fact, and she got the impression that he had to tell the story that way. That to let himself really feel it would be too painful—or too dangerous.

"It's still not an excuse," she said. "You were her child."

"The world was different then," he said. "I'm not excusing her, but everything she knew came from the Church. And do you really think it would be so different today? Would a woman raped by such a vicious creature keep her child? Or would she think it was vile and either end the pregnancy or abandon her baby?"

"You would have been better off if she had abandoned you."

"Maybe. But she didn't. And when the hunger first hit me—you have to understand that I didn't know what was going on. I was weak. Lost. Literally dying. And a school-girl came upon me. A little girl I knew from the village. She bent over to help me and I—" He cut himself off, then waved the words away.

"She survived. And I know now that her soul did grow

back, but because she hadn't consented, she always bore a mark. But at the time I believed I'd utterly destroyed that little girl. My mother came upon us at the end, and she screamed that I was the devil. That I'd brought desolation upon the earth. She hit me over and over and over again." Andy cringed, watching the way Doyle's expression tightened as he pantomimed his mother's lashes.

"And that's when I lost it."

She was certain she didn't want to know, and yet she asked anyway. "What happened?"

"I fought back. With my mind." He drew in a noisy breath. "I didn't know until that moment that I had the power, but with a single, brutal thought I set fire to our barn."

"You can control fire?"

"Wind, fire, water. I'm most adept with fire."

"So you can call lightning bolts down from the sky? Should I call you Zeus?"

"No, lightning is not in my repertoire. Electricity and I don't get along. At all."

"Good to know," she said. "I won't ask you to rewire my floor lamps."

He smiled at her, and she smiled back, and for a moment, despite the absurdity of the story he was telling, they were just a guy and a girl.

Then he continued, and the illusion of normalcy faded.

"I couldn't control it, though. The fire. Not back then. I was so young. So weak." He closed his eyes, and she watched as the memories caught up to him. "The entire town burned, and there was nothing we could do. Fifty-seven people died. My mother wailed and cried and said that she'd given birth to the devil himself. And then she killed herself," he said flatly.

"Doyle, my God, Doyle." She moved around the table

and knelt on the floor beside him, taking his hand in hers. "You're not. You know that, right? Because I've seen the devil, and you are not him."

"I thought I was. And I hated myself. Hated my father, my mother. And so I gave in. I quit fighting. And all that darkness rose up and spilled out." His laugh was raw, grating, and he looked hard at her. "You say I'm not like Creevey because I fight it? I didn't fight it then. I let it suck me under. Let it? No, I wanted it to happen. I wanted to drown in it."

She licked her lips, wanting to say something, but everything that came to mind sounded hollow.

"I went wild for a century. Did horrible things I don't want to think about. Things I don't even remember. And things I sure as hell don't want to tell you about."

"But you stopped." It wasn't a question. She knew him —dammit, she did—and at his core, he wasn't evil. He might have been lost, afraid and alone. Might have wanted the darkness to destroy him. But at his heart he was good. More than that, he was a fighter. A warrior.

He was the man she saw now. "You stopped," she repeated. "Tell me how. Because I see the man you are today, and nothing you did back then erases him. The deeper you fell, the more impressed I'll be, because that just means you had to claw and fight harder to change yourself."

He reached out and stroked her hair. "If you believe in them half as much as you believe in me, the teens at that center are lucky to have you."

"I believe in what I see. Will you tell me what happened? How you found your way back?"

He nodded. "I sank low—horribly low—and I set out across Europe. Those were dark years, and I met many others who were like me. Other Shadowers—vampires, werewolves, jinns. Some were wild—they had no moral code and they hunted humans. I clung to them, sinking deeper and deeper, letting myself truly be the man my mother had always believed me to be."

"Eventually you stopped."

"I met a group of vampires who had learned to control the serpent."

"Serpent?"

He nodded. "When a human changes into a vampire, it releases a dark malevolence. *Azag Mahru*. It's similar to what's buried inside of me—a dark force that needs to be controlled. It's sinister, like a snake. The vampires I met had gone a little wild, too. But they'd reined it in, and though their serpents still fought for release, they were winning the battle to keep the darkness suppressed. They helped me. We helped each other, and together we learned to control our darker urges. For years, they were my closest friends."

She expected him to go on, and when he didn't, she remembered what CeeCee had told her about how he and Luke had had a falling-out. "Was one of them Luke Dragos?"

He looked at her, startled. "Good guess."

"I'm a kick-ass reporter, remember?"

"You truly are amazing. Yes," he said, "Luke was one of them. For many years, he was my closest friend."

"CeeCee said you two had a fight. Actually, she said that was an understatement. So what happened? I mean, unless you'd rather not tell me."

"No," he said. "I want to tell you everything." He stood up and held his hand out for her. He led her to the couch and pulled her against him, so that she was tucked in under his shoulder. It felt so natural to be sitting curled up like that, even though everything they were talking about was completely unnatural.

"There was a woman," he said. "Kathryn. When I first

saw you, I thought of her. Your eyes are similar. Pale and beautiful. I loved her, and no, I didn't feed off of her. But I wanted to. I wanted to share it with her. I wanted to share everything with her."

"What happened?"

"It was during the French Revolution. Luke and Sergius and I were living in Paris. Despite the bloodshed, it was an exciting place to be. And for vampires and para-demons it wasn't nearly as dangerous as it was for mortals. While we were there, I met Kathryn. She lived outside the city but she had come into town to have a dress made. I saw her and I was smitten.

"I hadn't ever dated a human woman, but I decided to court her. She was flattered and flirtatious and I was swept up by the romance of it. Looking back, I think it was more the situation than it was the woman. At her core, she was a shallow girl. But that was a different time, and I was completely under her spell."

"What happened?"

"I urged Luke to go with me to her chateau one day. I was determined that Kathryn would need to learn the truth about me if we were to have a life together, and I wanted my friend to be there for moral support. It was a mistake. Those were hard years for Luke. His serpent has always lived close to the surface, and being around the revolution only stirred the beast up."

She dreaded the question she had to ask. "Did he kill Kathryn?"

"No," Doyle said, his words laced with cold amusement. "Though I blamed him for it for centuries."

"I don't understand."

"While I was in another part of the chateau, Luke lost control of his serpent. He fed upon one of the housemaids, and Kathryn saw him do it."

Andy shifted on the couch so she could face him. She

didn't know where the story was going, but she knew it wasn't over, and she stayed silent, letting Doyle finish in his own time.

"She was horrified. She believed the devil himself had entered her house—that she'd invited him in by having impure thoughts about me. By letting me touch her outside of wedlock. She set fire to the house, hoping to burn out the demons."

"Oh my God."

"When I realized the chateau was on fire, I searched frantically for her. I finally found her upstairs, behind a wall of flames. I was able to get to her, but I had to reveal my nature in order to manipulate the flames. She realized what I was—another demon that had invaded her house —and threw herself from the window, taking her own life to escape from me."

"Doyle." She clutched her necklace, her heart twisting for him and for that poor, confused woman. "It wasn't your fault."

He made a snorting sound. "For years, I've blamed Luke for Kathryn's death. It destroyed our friendship. I let it destroy our friendship."

"You were distraught."

"I was," he agreed. "I was also an idiot."

"Have you told Luke?"

A hint of a smile touched Doyle's lips. "No."

"You should."

"I know. I was young then—relatively speaking— whereas he'd already been walking the earth for millennia. I think I expected him to be stronger. And when he lost his grip on himself—despite knowing how important it was to me that our time at the chateau go smoothly—it reminded me of how fragile my own self-control was. I knew how much I owed him for helping me, but I didn't want a reconciliation because then I'd be living with that reminder every moment of every day."

"That's quite a feat of psychoanalysis."

His mouth pulled down in a considering frown. "Well, I could be wrong. It's possible I was just being an ass."

She laughed, relieved that he'd dispelled some of the tension. "What did you owe him for?"

"I have a true gift," he said. "And I discovered it because of Luke."

"What is it?"

"When I touch a body, I can see into the mind of the dead person or Shadower."

"What?" Never in a million years would she have expected him to say that.

"That's how I felt when I first realized what I'm capable of."

"How did you realize that? Does it work on any body?"

"Only the newly dead," he said. "The images fade quickly. As for how I discovered it, like I said, I have Luke to thank."

"I'm listening."

"This was before Kathryn's death. He was helping a woman who'd been abandoned by her husband and was raising her young daughter alone. There was nothing romantic between them, but he cared for her and the girl. He'd bring them food, check on their needs. Almost as if he were their patron. At the time, I didn't understand his motivations. I later realized that he saw his own wife and daughter—the family that had been destroyed when he turned into a vampire—reflected in them."

"Something horrible happened to them, didn't it?" She could feel the dread twisting in her stomach.

"They were murdered."

"Oh, God."

"Luke was devastated, of course. It was summer, and

we knew the bodies would begin to stink quickly. He asked me to help move them—to give them a proper burial. I agreed, and as I bent to pick up the little girl, I touched her head. There was so much fear in her that the images almost reached out and sucked me in. I thought it was a fluke, but I tried it on the mother and I was able to gain access to her thoughts, too."

"Did you see who killed them?"

"That was the beauty of it," he said. "In those days, the authorities paid little attention to the deaths of poor people. They weren't even going to investigate. But I saw everything, and I told Luke. We found the killers—and Luke meted out his own brand of justice."

"Good," she said. "And you?"

He shrugged. "I started to explore my gift, using it to help people. Just in my own travels at first, but eventually I joined the PEC."

"The PEC?"

"The Preternatural Enforcement Commission. It's an ancient organization, and it's changed over the centuries."

"So you're not really a part of Homeland."

"No, actually I am. Right now, in the United States, the PEC operates as a secret branch of Homeland Security called Division Six."

"So you're saying that the government really does know about all of this? Vampires and werewolves and demons like you?"

"Not everyone in the government, but certain highly placed individuals, yes."

"Okay, but what do you do? The PEC, I mean. What's its purpose?"

"We police our own," he said. "Investigate, apprehend, adjudicate. We're law enforcement for Shadowers. We have detectives, attorneys, judges, secretaries, medical examiners, forensics."

"Prosecutors," she said, as another piece snapped into place. "Sara Constantine."

"You know Sara?"

"From press conferences. All of a sudden she went to work for Homeland. Because she'd been changed." She met his eyes. "By Luke."

His brows rose. "You really are one hell of a reporter."

"Oh, totally. I'm amazing."

They shared a grin.

"It's not that different from the human world, is it?"

He shook his head. "It's not."

"So is that where Kevin is? Protective custody at Division 6?"

Doyle nodded. "I understand he's been having a fascinating time. One of the staff attorneys is a poltergeist, and apparently they're getting along famously."

"Really?" A couple of days ago, her cousin was all about killing werewolves. Now he was befriending ghosts. Things were changing so fast around her it was hard to keep up. "But this means that Paul's looking for Division Six, right? That's the centralized location that he thinks is the Holy Grail."

Doyle nodded. "And eventually he'll find it. My job is to stop him and as many of his lieutenants as possible. Bryce. Travis."

"My father?"

"I'm sorry, Andy."

She pressed her lips together. "He doesn't understand."

"What?"

"Evil," she said. "He thinks he understands evil, but he doesn't."

He took her hand and squeezed it. "Whatever happens, I'll try to help him."

"Why? That's more than he'd do for you." She blinked, and felt hot tears in her eyes.

"Because you love him."

She felt her chin quiver and knew that she'd start to cry if she wasn't careful. "Thank you."

"I haven't done anything yet."

"Thank you for telling me about all of this." She held both of his hands and looked into his face, into those dark eyes that held centuries worth of secrets. Secrets he'd shared with her. "Doyle," she said, and heard the need in her voice.

His eyes flashed with heat, and she felt a hot wire of desire that curled all the way through her and made her feel more alive than she ever had.

"Doyle," she repeated before she could chicken out. "Kiss me."

TWENTY-FOUR

"Kiss me."

Her words seemed to hang in the air like a cartoon bubble, and for a moment she feared that he'd just sit there, and she'd either have to repeat herself or beg or force herself on him.

Thank God he saved her from all of that.

"Andy…" He said her name like a prayer, and then—in an instant—his lips were pressed against hers.

She hooked her arms around his neck and pressed her body close to his as she deepened their kiss. Everything seemed to be spinning out of control—it was like she was living in some sort of surrealist painting where everything was beautiful, yet not quite what it seemed.

Doyle's touch was perfect, though. It grounded her. Made her feel alive. And right then, that was what she wanted more than anything.

She shifted so that she was lying down on the couch, the hard, strong length of him pressed against her. Her T-shirt had ridden up a bit, and he pressed his hand to the bare skin above the waist of her jeans. That simple touch was almost more than she could stand, and pleasure swirled through her like a demanding tide until all she could think about was how she wanted more. Just more.

"Do you have any idea how beautiful you are?" he asked.

"Feel free to tell me in extreme detail. Better yet, just show me."

"Close your eyes," he ordered, before taking the hem of her T-shirt and pulling it gently over her head.

Cool air stroked her body, and she sighed, then gasped as his fingertips stroked her bare stomach. The touch was feather light, and yet it sent an explosion of sensation rocketing through her, and she arched up, her body craving more.

She had on a thin lace bra and her nipples were painfully tight against it, getting more so as his palms pressed and stroked, fingertips sliding up and under the material—teasing, but never quite touching.

She squirmed, silently demanding, and he complied, slipping his hand under the cup of her bra, pushing it up so that he could palm the curve of her breast, then making her jump as he stroked her very hard, very aroused nipple.

She moaned with delight, the pleasure from his touch shooting through her like starlight. He unclipped the bra from the front and let it fall open, and the sensation of the cool air against her skin aroused her even more.

"Tilt your head back," he whispered, and when she did, he drew his lips over her neck, delivering soft kisses as his hands slid down to cup her waist. His kisses trailed lower, down her cleavage, over her breasts, and then down and down until he stopped just above the waist of her jeans.

"Andy," he whispered. Just her name, and then his fingers released the button on her jeans and eased the zipper down. She shifted her hips, feeling greedy, but not willing to back off from what she wanted—his touch. He slid his hand down and cupped her through the silk of her panties, and it was as if gravity had ceased to apply to her and she was floating on a current of pleasure.

She let the pleasure take her, but soon it wasn't enough. She wanted to see him, and so she opened her eyes and saw him smiling down at her, his eyes crinkling at the corners. Eyes that seemed capable of seeing all the way through her, to what she wanted and what she needed.

Slowly, his hands slid under the waist of her jeans. "Lift your hips," he said, and as she complied, he slid her jeans down and off. Her feet were bare, so there was no awkward tangle of clothes and shoes. She took his hand and tugged him back to her.

"What do you want?"

"You," she said without hesitation. "Duh."

He laughed, then raised himself up for long enough to kiss her, deeply and boldly. Then he trailed a line of kisses from her breasts down her stomach, his tongue teasing her navel as he eased lower and lower, his thumbs stroking the inside of her thighs as he gently eased her legs apart.

She closed her eyes, his hot breath making her almost as crazy as the feel of his beard stubble on the soft skin of her thighs. He pressed the pads of his thumbs lightly into her inner thighs, and she squirmed with delighted anticipation. A moment later, he tugged her panties down and started kissing her intimately, making her body quiver and her breath come in slow, shallow gasps.

She reached down, her fingers lost in his hair, and the pleasure built and built until, just as she was afraid she couldn't stand it any longer, she shattered, crying out with intense, mind-blowing pleasure that sent earth-quake-like tremors through her body.

When they slowed—when she could think and be human again—she pulled him up, gentle, but demanding. "More," she said, because despite the satisfaction she felt, she hadn't yet felt him, and she wanted to. Needed to. "Doyle, please."

His smile was pure guy. "If you insist."

He stripped out of his jeans, and she couldn't help but admire the lean lines of his legs, and his tight, sexy butt. It was the kind of butt that looked better out of jeans than in them, and it gave her a secret thrill to know just how amazing the total package was. He grinned at her. "What are you thinking?"

"About your ass."

"Really. What a coincidence. I'm thinking about yours."

She hooked her arms around his neck, pulled herself up, and kissed him. "No more talking."

He opened his mouth to reply, but she pressed a firm finger over it. "No. More. Talking."

He got the message and proceeded to show her just how much he could communicate without saying a single word. His hands stroking against her skin said he thought she was beautiful. His tongue tracing around her ear, that she was delicious. And his cock, hard and ready and demanding, that he wanted her. That she was his. And as he thrust inside of her—sliding in easily because she was so damn wet—her body agreed with him and answered back. He was hers, too.

They moved in a rhythm, their passion growing, their bodies slick with sweat. She never wanted this to end, and yet she knew that she couldn't stand it if it lasted much longer. She'd burn out, go supernova.

And then, that's exactly what she did. Her body

erupting into flashes of fire and color, her fingers digging into his back, the thrill of the moment growing when he reached his own climax and clung just as tightly to her.

The moment passed too quickly, even though it felt like it went on for an eternity. She fell back against the couch cushions, feeling warm and relaxed, not wanting this to end. Wanting more—wanting that sweet sensation of twining with him again. And she boldly twisted, easing around so that she was the one straddling him.

"Kiss me," she whispered. "Taste me. Take me."

His eyes widened just enough to let her know that he understood her request.

"Doyle, please, just—"

And then his mouth was on hers, and she felt it—that sweet tug, that sensual pull. Like sex, but not. A joining. A twining and twisting. Her energy, her essence, her soul.

For a moment, the thought hung there, drenched in pleasure.

But then she cracked, a finger of fear trickling down her back, and she broke away, ashamed.

"I'm sorry—I'm sorry—I didn't think I was ... I thought... Oh, God, Doyle. It does scare me."

But he wasn't listening. He'd turned away from her. He was sitting up, as if he was about to stand. As if he was about to leave.

She tugged his hand. "Doyle?"

"Don't worry," he said, and when he turned to face her, she saw that his eyes were filled with pain. "I'm leaving."

"Leaving?" She echoed his words back to him as she clutched his hand. "You're leaving?" she repeated as she grabbed the afghan off the couch and stood, wrapping it around herself. "What the hell happened to talking?"

"You're human," he said. "I'm not."

She stared at him. "And?"

His face seemed colored by regret and sadness. "And I should go."

"Wait," she said, as understanding grew. "Is this about her? Is this about Kathryn?"

Kathryn.

Her name seemed to hang on Andy's lips. He wanted to lie, but he couldn't. Not to her. "Yes," he said.

"Then you damn well better stay," she said. "If you're going to leave because some other woman with eyes like mine was too stupid to see what she had in you, then you'd better stay and talk to me about it."

He ought to just leave. Ought to simply walk past her and not look back. It would be simpler that way.

He couldn't do it. "She saw what I really was. Saw it, and couldn't bear it." He looked at her. "Kathryn chose death over me."

"And she was a fool."

He swallowed. If only that were true. "I'm not saying you would choose the same. You're stronger than Kathryn ever was." It was, he realized, that core of strength in Andy that attracted him the most. And why her fear of him had twisted like a knife. "You're strong and you're brave," he repeated, "but in the end you're both afraid of the same thing."

"No." She spoke the word firmly and shook her head. "No, she was afraid of you. I was afraid of losing a part of me." She took his hand. "Dammit, but you're being thick. There is nothing—nothing—about you that scares me. But my soul—that's heady stuff. And I believe it," she added, squeezing his fingers and looking deep into his eyes. "I believe everything Lissa said about it not hurting me, about how it would make my soul grow and flourish. I really do believe it all in theory."

Her throat moved as she swallowed. "In practice, though, it's going to take me some time. I've grown up in my father's church. I've grown up believing a soul is a thing to be protected. That it's easily stained. 'Now I lay me down to sleep.' "

" 'I pray the Lord my soul to keep,' " he finished. "Yes. I understand."

She closed her eyes in obvious relief, then clung to him. "I just need some time to get used to it. But I think—I think I want to get used to it. I got a taste of what it felt like, sharing that with you, and it felt sensual and erotic and sweet and wonderful."

She brushed a kiss over his lips. "Hell, Doyle, we're new to each other. But you have to believe me when I say I want to see where this leads." She pressed her lips together and offered him a small smile. "I've never felt this way about another man. I feel like we're connected, even without that whole soul-sharing thing. I look at you and I just get lost in you."

"I feel the same way," he admitted.

"I'm glad."

He put an arm around her and drew her close, then buried his face in her hair, the relief—no, the joy—that she still wanted him filling him like light. He didn't know what he'd done to deserve her—no, he knew that he'd done nothing to deserve her—but by God he was going to cling tightly to her now that he had her.

"Maybe that was all Kathryn needed," she said, her breath warm against his chest.

"What do you mean?"

"You said she chose death. But maybe if she hadn't been so rash—if she'd just given it time..."

The thought sat heavily with him, and he closed his eyes, remembering Kathryn's foolhardy leap through the window. "We'll never know," he said.

"I'm sorry, though. It must have hurt to lose her."

"It did," he said. "But it was a long time ago." *And now I've found you.*

He pulled her close, caressing her skin, telling her with every touch how much he craved her. How glad he was that she wasn't running. That she was there in his arms, and that her lips were turned up to his, just begging to be kissed.

How could he deny that? He lost himself in her kiss, in her touch. In the feeling of her body pressed against his. With a moan, he pushed her blanket away, then stroked her, touching and exploring until he wasn't sure where he ended and where Andy began.

Then she was on top of him, her hands pressed against his chest, the ends of her hair brushing his face. She danced kisses across his skin, then captured his mouth with a passionate demand. The kiss, long and deep, shot through him like lava, ratcheting up his need, making him crave more than kisses. He wanted to be with her, part of her, he wanted to get lost inside of her.

She looked at his face and gave him a slow smile. "Yes," she whispered, as if she knew exactly what he was thinking. Then she shifted and kissed him down, down, down, and he realized that she damn well did know. He closed his eyes and let her take him, groaning when her kisses turned into small bites, and when her hand encircled his cock, making him come close to exploding with her long, even strokes.

And then, when he didn't think he could take it any more without his sanity spilling out of his ears, she shifted again, straddled him, and lowered herself slowly —oh, God, so slowly—onto him. She moved in a mind-blowing rhythm, and when he opened his eyes to look at her, it was only Andy he saw—the ghosts of his past had finally been banished. As if reading his mind, she smiled at him, her movements taking him up and up and up, their bodies a perfect union until the explosion came, and he trembled beneath her and she melted back into his arms, her chest rising and falling as he held her, stroked her, loved her.

They lay together, his arms tight around her, until the shrill ring of his phone broke the silence. He cursed, and she laughed, then rolled off of him. She rummaged through the clothes on the floor, found the phone, and glanced at the readout.

"Paul," she said, and passed it to him.

Doyle took it, wishing the world couldn't interrupt what he and Andy were sharing, but knowing that it was inevitable. "Paul," he said. "What's up?"

"We're going on a little mission before sunrise. I was hoping you could join us."

He got the details, then hung up the phone and looked silently at Andy.

"A mission?"

"Apparently so."

"I'm terrified he's going to find out about you. Doyle, if he does—"

"There's no reason he would."

She nodded, her smile tremulous. "I know. But I can't help it, I—I just can't help it." She reached up and unfastened her necklace. "Would you wear this? The chain's long enough—no one will see it under your shirt. And I ... well, I know it's silly but I want you to have it. To keep you safe."

He couldn't speak as he held out his hand for the necklace. She was giving him her mother's—and her God's—protection. He already knew that she didn't think of him as evil—that to her, he was just Doyle, and he was a good man. He knew that ... but this gesture cemented it, and he found himself blinking to clear his moist eyes.

"I'll wear it," he said. "And I promise I'll come back to you."

TWENTY-FIVE

"What's going down?" Doyle asked as he climbed into Paul's Mercedes. They'd agreed to meet at a grocery store on the West Side, and Doyle had hurried to get there, leaving his Pontiac parked in the lot. Despite the fact that the store was open twenty-four hours, only four other cars were scattered across the lot.

He slammed the passenger side door, and Paul pulled out into traffic. "We have a lead on a location. But first we have to meet with a source."

Doyle turned to look more closely at Paul. "A source?"

Paul grinned. "Trust me. You'll find it interesting."

"Just you and me?"

Paul shook his head. "Bryce and some of the men are already on site, along with one of our newer assets." He tapped the brakes at a light and turned to grin at Doyle. "We're going vampire hunting. Thought that your particular skill in that area might come in handy."

Doyle forced himself to keep his expression bland. "Do you think that's smart? This close to a large operation, you don't want to risk revealing yourself to the creatures."

"Can't be helped. We have intel that this particular vampire can identify our target location. In other words it's worth the risk. And it should be one hell of a lot of fun."

"Shit yeah," Doyle said, feeling slightly sick. "Got a name?"

"Vamp's name is Millicent. According to our source, she was taken to someplace called Division Six, which is apparently where those fuckers congregate. It's all falling together."

"Division Six. Sounds spurious. Are you sure this source isn't pulling your chain?"

"I think it's solid," Paul said. "But even if it turns out to be bullshit, the worst that happens is we take out one more vampire."

"Can't argue with that," Doyle said. "Where are we going now?"

"Some place called the Club Rouge." He glanced at his watch. "And we should be right on time."

Doyle forced himself not to react. He wasn't worried about being recognized—the club had been cleared out before his arrival. But Millicent was the eyewitness who had been interrogated at Division headquarters. In other words, Paul's plan was pretty fucking feasible.

Shit.

They left the car a block away and then walked to the rendezvous site—a retaining wall above an alley at the back of the club. Bryce gave him a curt nod, then told Paul that the other men were set up on the roof. Doyle tilted his head back so that he could get a better look at the roof, but the men were positioned out of his line of sight—the only sign that they were there was the gleam of their sniper rifles.

As Paul and Bryce talked, Doyle ran through his options. The fact that Paul now knew that the Shadowers operated under the guise of Division 6 meant that it wouldn't be long before he figured out their location, with or without Millicent. Because Division 6 was, in fact, an on-the-books arm of Homeland Security, albeit one that engaged entirely in secret operations.

Once he made the connection between Division 6 and Homeland, he'd undoubtedly make the connection to Doyle. It meant that Doyle's days inside were numbered. And although they'd all been hoping that the PEC could shut Paul down on the eve of an operation—thus casting the widest net and capturing the most players—now it looked like the better plan was to move in as soon as possible, while Doyle still had access. This morning, even —after this operation, when the men were still celebrating their victory.

Yes, their victory. Because there was no way that he could thwart the mission without risking his cover. And he needed to keep that cover at least until the PEC could move in.

Antsy, he watched the back door of the club, taking small comfort in the fact that Paul had made it clear that he didn't intend to kill Millicent. Not yet, anyway.

Beside him, Bryce and another man were getting into position. "I need a weapon," Doyle said.

"We're using tranq guns," Bryce said, "with Tasers for backup. I'll get one of each for you." He started to turn, then tapped his ear. "Hang on. Go ahead?" Doyle watched Bryce's brow furrow as he listened. He glanced once at Doyle, then at Paul. Then he nodded. "Affirmative," he said, ending the communication.

"Well?" Paul said.

"We have confirmation," Bryce said. "She's in there."

"Weapons?" Doyle reminded him.

"Right," Bryce said. A black duffel was lying open

beside him, and he pulled out a Taser. "Here you go," he said—and fired it.

A web of electrical tendrils encircled Doyle, and he fell backward, shaking, trying to fight the debilitating effect of the high voltage that was racing through him.

"What the hell are you doing?" Paul rushed forward, trying to knock the Taser from Bryce's hand, but Bryce shifted, keeping the charge on full and on Doyle.

"He's one of them." His voice was low and urgent. "That was Creevey on the comm. He's got a clear view of us from his position on the roof. And he says that Doyle is one of them."

Paul slammed his fist on the antique desk that filled his private study in the safe house.

"What the hell is he?" Paul demanded, looking hard at both Bryce and Creevey. "What the hell is that thing that wormed its way into my operation?"

His fury was hot and palpable. It took a lot to fool Paul Vassalo, and goddammit, Doyle had managed to do it. He'd played his little mind games with Travis, he'd put on a fancy show with the vampire, and Paul had swallowed it all. He'd been made to look like a fool, and that wasn't acceptable. That wasn't acceptable at all.

"Well?" he demanded of the two men who still hadn't spoken.

"I don't know," Creevey said. "He can go out in the daylight, so he's not a vamp."

"And the electricity hasn't caused the eruption of hair or any bone changes," Bryce said, "so he's not a werewolf. I'm not going to risk getting too close, but his skin's taken on an orange hue, and his eyes—well, they're not normal. But what that adds up to—I haven't a clue."

"They just keep propagating," Paul said. "Like goddamned cockroaches. You step on one, and a dozen more come scrambling out of the garbage." He rounded on Bryce. "He's under control? You're sure the bastard isn't going to bust out anytime soon?"

"I've got him locked up in the weapons vault off of the garage."

"Without the weapons, I hope."

"We moved them out, but it was the best cell I could rig up for him. I don't know what Doyle is, but electricity rips him a new one. The floor in there's metal, and the walls are conductive. I've got it rigged to run a constant current. He touches the floor or the walls, and he's slammed with electricity."

"Hard not to touch the floor or walls."

"Not unless he can fly," Bryce said, then shrugged. "Hell, for all I know, maybe he can."

Paul ignored that disturbing possibility. "It's locked?"

"The door is shut and locked up tight."

"Even if he can fly, the ride will be over once he reaches one of the walls." He nodded, satisfied. "For now, that'll do. We'll deal with him more thoroughly after we move against Division Six."

"Just kill the son-of-a-bitch now," Creevey said.

Paul shook his head. "No, he made this personal. I intend to make Mr. Doyle pay for his transgressions, and I need sufficient time to properly extract that payment."

"My kind of guy," Creevey said. He stretched out his arms and sighed. "And thanks mightily for that antidote. I feel better already."

Paul bit back the retort that formed on his lips. "You earned it. You delivered the location, not to mention valuable information about the infiltration of my organization." He nodded toward Bryce. "Take our guest to his quarters. We'll return him to the wilds of Los Angeles tomorrow. Blindfolded, of course. I have no intention of letting a son-of-a-bitch like him know where our safe house is located."

Creevey snorted. "Fair enough."

Paul caught Bryce's eyes, saw the quick nod as he led Creevey away. Little fucker thought he'd gotten away with something? Not damn likely. A man like that—a human who actually wanted to be a vampire?—Paul had no use for such a man. He'd paid the price; he'd administered the antidote. But he'd never once promised that the bastard would be kept safe afterward.

Still, he had to admit that Creevey had been useful. Without the sociopath, they wouldn't have captured Millicent. And it had taken only one injection of hematite for the bitch vampire to reveal everything she knew. That Division 6 was a secret preternatural organization. That highly placed humans actually knew about it, and it was hidden within Homeland Security. That news had disgusted Paul—important men, men who were supposed to be protecting this country, not only knew about these creatures, but actively supported their insinuation into the human world.

The only good bit of information had been the location. That, at last, had been nailed down. The Criminal Justice Building in downtown Los Angeles was their target. And at this very moment, Travis was putting Phase I into place.

"Who would have thought these creatures would be holed up in the Criminal Justice Building?" Bryce said. "But at least we've got Travis."

"And his ID badge and parking pass," Paul agreed. All in all, it had worked out very well. Travis's access to the building eradicated at least a dozen security issues. "We move in tomorrow," he said, then looked at Bryce. "Your men will be ready?"

"Of course."

"Good. There will be human casualties."

"With that target, it's inevitable."

Paul nodded. "Call Andrew Tarrant. I'd like to speak to him in his official capacity before we move out. He can pray for the souls of the martyrs. And ask him to bring Andrea. I have a job for her, too."

The doorbell rang, and Andy threw it open, relieved to see Tucker standing on the stoop.

"Thank you for coming. I feel like an idiot for calling, but I've been so worried."

"What time did he leave?"

"About four A.M.," she said, shutting the door and following him inside. "He got a call from Paul about something going down, and he went. He said he'd come right back. I didn't necessarily expect him to, but I thought he'd at least phone. Or text. Something."

Tucker tossed himself down on her couch, his long legs stretched out in front of him. "We haven't heard anything, either."

"You're worried. Oh, shit. You're worried."

"Doyle can take care of himself," Tucker said. "Believe me."

"I know."

He cocked his head and looked at her. "What do you know?"

"Everything," she said. "At least I think so. That he's a para-demon. That he feeds on souls. That he and Luke had one hell of a falling-out. And that you play mind games."

"He did tell you everything." The surprise in Tucker's voice was unmistakable.

"He's probably okay, right? I mean, how would they have found out about him?"

"I don't know. But I think the best thing to do is assume that the mission is under control. If they're moving in soon, maybe he just doesn't have his phone with him. They could be doing weapons tech, keeping anything with an RF signal away from the detonators. We don't know what's happening."

She nodded, slightly appeased. "But you're still worried?"

"Paul's a brutal son-of-a-bitch. We've had a team investigating the werewolves who butchered Stu—"

"Were they the ones who attacked us at Wes's house?"

"They were. But that's not my point. It's about one of Paul's men—that guy Aaron?"

"Paul said he died in the attack."

"Oh, he died. He was bitten. But when we went to recover his body, we saw that his throat had been slashed, too."

"What? Why?"

"Guess Paul didn't want to risk his little soldier turning into a werewolf."

"You're not making me feel any better."

He sat up and ran a hand through his hair. "Sorry. I really do think he'll be fine. He's been my partner for years, and if there's one thing I've learned, it's that he's got a few tricks up his sleeve." He looked at her. "You really care for him."

It wasn't a question, but she answered anyway. "Yes, I do."

"Good. He's fucking head over heels for you."

She couldn't hide her smile. "Really?"

"Cross my heart."

She sighed. "And hope to die?"

"It'll be okay." He stood. "I'm going to go back in. See if anything new comes up. You'll be okay by yourself?"

The phone rang, and she signaled for him to hold that thought while she answered. "Daddy, hi."

"I just got a call," her father said. "Paul wants us to come by. Are you free?"

"Yeah, of course. Sure."

"He's at one of his ranch houses; he gave me the address. I'll pick you up in ten minutes," he said, then hung up.

Andy looked up at Tucker. "Looks like I'm heading over to Paul's."

"Are you up for it? With Doyle MIA, you're our only asset."

She nodded, suddenly a bit overwhelmed by the weight of the responsibility on her shoulders.

Tucker moved beside her and set a hand on her shoulder. "You'll be fine. Here, give me your cellphone."

She did, and he programmed in his number. "Text me, call me, whatever you need. Just be discreet."

"Right."

"And stay safe," he added with a grin. "Doyle will kill me if something happens to you."

TWENTY-SIX

"You're quiet," Andrew Tarrant said, looking sideways at his daughter. "Is something on your mind? The young man you told me about?"

"He hasn't called me recently. I'm feeling a little like he's gone missing."

Andrew chuckled. "Boys have a way of turning up again. Ah, here we are." The long dirt driveway was marked by a single battered mailbox. Paul owned several properties around the Los Angeles area, and this was one Andrew hadn't seen before. The driveway was long and bumpy, and he and Andy rode in silence until they reached the nondescript home, significantly less ostentatious than Andrew would have expected of his friend.

"Come in, come in." Paul stood in the doorway and ushered them inside. To his left and right, flowers shriveled under the sun, the lack of care obvious. Not a second home, Andrew realized. A place of work.

"You have news?" he asked as soon as they reached the living area. Bryce and Travis were already inside settled in on a hideous plaid sofa.

"Amazing news," Paul said. "This is an historic day."

The interior walls were dark wood, as was the furniture—shelves, desk, and a table. The only light emanated from a single desk lamp and the vague hint of sunlight that was sneaking in around the corners of the heavy, velvet drapes. "But first, I want to talk to you." He pointed at Andrew.

"Paul," Travis said. "You're going to keep us waiting?"

Paul laughed. "Yes, I know. I have a flair for the dramatic. But I promise it's important that Andrew and I speak, and we won't keep you waiting for long." He smiled at Andy and the two other men. "If you'll excuse us."

Since he apparently didn't have a choice, Andrew followed his friend into the adjoining room.

"What's going on?" he asked, noticing Paul's grave expression.

"I wanted to speak to you alone, because I don't want to scare Andy. I know she spent some time talking to him, and I don't want her to think that he was, perhaps, targeting her."

"I don't know what you're talking about," Andrew said. "But if Andy's in danger—"

"No," Paul said quickly. "She's not. And if she was, she's not anymore. We caught him."

"Who?"

"Ryan Doyle. He was at the party. Said he was with Homeland Security—apparently he got in through Travis."

Homeland? Andrew remembered the man in the rumpled suit who had been talking to Andy. He thought also of her recent confession that she was attracted to a cop. Andrew might not be the smartest man on the planet, but he could put two and two together as far as his daughter was concerned. "Caught him?" he repeated. "What has he done?"

"He's one of them," Paul said flatly, and Andrew felt

such a rush of fear on Andy's behalf that he physically flinched.

"Are you sure?"

"I've seen the proof with my own eyes. I don't know what he is, but he's not human. He's a threat, Andrew. And I intend to deal with him appropriately."

"Where is he?"

"In the vault off of the garage."

"Is—is that safe? What if he gets out?" The very idea of that creature escaping and going after Andy gave him chills.

"He won't." Paul clapped him on the shoulder. "I thought you should know, but there's no need for you to worry. But come on. I have news to share with the group, and we don't want to keep them waiting any longer than necessary."

Back in the living room, Bryce and Travis broke apart, interrupting their conversation to turn their attention to Paul, who seemed positively giddy. Andrew couldn't remember seeing his friend this pleased about anything, and while he wanted to share his happiness, his mind kept returning to Doyle—and Andy.

That creature was Andy's cop. He'd sucked her in, tainted her. Did she know? Of course she didn't know; she'd never knowingly allow an evil being to touch her.

"Daddy?" She looked sideways at him, her brows lifted in question.

"I'm fine." He nodded toward Paul, who was beginning to speak.

"The Criminal Justice Building," Paul said. "That is our target."

"But that's a government building," Andy said. "You can't really think that there are vampires and werewolves hiding in there."

Her hands, Andrew noticed, were knotted in her lap, a classic tell that she was nervous.

"That was exactly my reaction," Travis said. "But I've been convinced otherwise."

"Our intelligence is sound," Paul said. "Honestly, it surprised me, too. The building's structure includes a number of subterranean levels, and those are occupied by the dark creatures."

"What is it you intend to do?" Andrew asked.

"We're going to level the place," Bryce said, but he had to be joking. Andrew kept his eyes trained on Paul, expecting to see him chuckle. Instead, his old friend only smiled.

"We're going to teach them a lesson they won't soon forget," Paul said.

"Now, wait a minute," Andrew said. "Even if you're right and the basement levels are filled with these creatures, most of the building is occupied by humans."

"Humans who are catering to the dark ones' needs."

"Not most of them," Travis said. "I certainly never knew they were there."

"You see?" Andrew said. "If you destroy the building, you're going to be taking innocent lives with you."

"And they will go down as martyrs," Paul said, without hesitating. "Andrew, I'm surprised at you. We're making this attack in the name of all that is holy."

"And you—us—all of the Dark Warriors will be branded as terrorists."

"That is inevitable. Eventually, though, the tide will turn and we'll be able to spread our influence. Once humans realize the threat that we've acted against, the world will band with us, and the Dark Warriors won't be blamed for the deaths of the innocent humans, the blame will rest where it belongs—with these creatures of the night. The humans who die today will be martyrs to the cause. Andrew, I asked you here for your blessing."

"You won't get it," Andrew said, and beside him, his daughter took his hand and squeezed it.

"I'm disappointed," Paul said. "But of course I respect your position even though you won't change mine. I trust that I have your discretion, though? We've been friends for too long for me to worry about you doing something like contacting the authorities."

"You know I wouldn't do that," Andrew said, wondering how he was going to surreptitiously leave the room so he could make a phone call to do that very thing.

"I'm glad to hear it. Well," Paul said, and a muscle in his cheek twitched. "The truth is that the location isn't the only interesting information I acquired recently, but I have to admit you took the wind out of my sails, Andrew. You'll have to forgive me if I need a moment to regroup." He crossed the room and poured himself a drink at the bar. After a second's hesitation, Andrew stood and crossed to the opposite side of the room, gesturing for Andy to follow him.

"I'm proud of you, Daddy," she whispered.

He brushed it off. "Sweetheart, I want you to be careful."

"Don't worry. I'm with you. I wouldn't do anything to hurt—"

"No. Not that. Doyle."

He saw her flinch, and he instantly realized the mistake he'd made. "Dear God, girl, you know? You know what he is?"

"Where is he?" she asked urgently. "Did Paul—oh, God, Daddy, what did Paul do to him?"

Shock, fear, anger, regret. They all washed over him, making his knees weak and his stomach queasy. He took a single step backward. "You're no daughter of mine."

"He's not the evil one in this equation, Daddy. That would be Paul. Doyle's trying to save lives, he's trying to help people. Daddy, please—"

But he wasn't listening. He turned away and walked across the room to join Paul. "I'll leave now," he said. "You have my complete discretion."

"I appreciate that. Let me walk you out." They stepped out onto the front steps together. "I realize this is difficult for a man of your calling to accept, but I know that my mission is a holy one."

"I understand," Andrew said. If he could just get in his car, he could make it far enough down the drive to place the cell call without Paul noticing... He opened the door and slipped inside, then tried to pull it shut, but Paul had a grip on it and he was still talking.

"It's my calling, you see. And I have to protect it. I'm sorry, Andrew," he said as he pulled out a pistol with a silencer screwed on. "I'm very sorry," he repeated, and pulled the trigger.

Andy sat in the living room, hoping she looked calmer than she felt. Her skin was clammy and the staccato beat of her pulse sounded like tribal drums in her ears. *Be calm. Be calm.*

But how could she be calm?

Doyle ... dear God, Doyle...

If her father knew, that meant Paul knew, too.

And if Paul knew, that meant that he'd somehow managed to capture Doyle. Or worse, kill him.

When Paul stepped back inside, she forced a smile and

tried to look normal. It took all of her strength not to betray herself.

"I'm sorry your father and I aren't seeing eye to eye."

"You don't have to apologize," she said. "I'm not my father." She pulled out her phone. "I should text him," she lied. "Let him know that I respect his position even though I agree with yours." One text. A simple text to Tucker, and he'd rally the troops, evacuate the building, help her find Doyle...

Paul walked over and perched himself on the armrest of the sofa where she was sitting. "You can use the land-line in a minute," he said, plucking the cellphone from her hands and tossing it onto the coffee table. "Not to make you nervous, but Bryce's men have the equipment for the job packed in the next room. I'd hate for your cellphone to accidentally trigger an explosion."

"Oh." She glanced at the phone and felt a little bit of her hope slip away. "Sure. I could call him now?"

"Absolutely. Just as soon as we finish here. The fact is, Andy, I need to know if you want to participate in today's mission. You're not a soldier, but I know how passionate you are about our cause, and if you're up for it, I have a role for you to play."

"Of course I'll do it," she said, her mind churning.

"I was hoping you'd say that. Bryce, show Andy what we have in mind for her."

Bryce lifted his hand, gesturing for her to join him—he was standing over a table that was spread with a map of downtown Los Angeles. "That's it," Paul said, pressing his index finger down on the map. "This is our target."

"All right," she said, as Bryce grabbed up a pen, scribbled a note, and then stepped behind her as he headed to the other side of the table. "But what am I supposed to do?"

"It's easy," Bryce said from behind her, as he twisted her arms together and jerked her toward him. "You die."

Pain ripped through Doyle. Brutal, horrible, biting pain brought on by tendrils of electricity that shot upward from the floor and outward from the walls, propelled by thin, dangerous wires. It curled through him, the electricity like a sharp-fanged serpent that was biting and tearing and ripping him up from the inside. Pain so great it brought him to his knees, collapsed him, and ripped away his control over his powers.

But there was something even worse than the pain—his fear for Andy.

She was here, in this place, and she was afraid.

He'd caught the scent of her terror, and it had filled him, overcoming even the smell of his own burning flesh.

Let her be safe. Please, please let her be safe.

But he knew she wasn't. If Creevey had exposed him, then odds were he'd exposed Andy, too, telling Paul that she was a reporter. And he might even know that she and Doyle were together.

Would Paul kill her? The thought made him writhe with a fear even more potent than the electricity that was draining him.

He had to get out somehow. Had to get away from this cell that had been rigged for only one purpose: torture.

Another whack of electricity shot through him, and he convulsed, dropping to his knees, his limbs shaking, his body no longer under his control.

He wouldn't last long like this. The electricity wouldn't kill him, but it would sap him. Drain him so far that when they returned there would be no fight in him. No strength to protect him through the final indignity when Paul stood in front of him and with one swift swing from an ax, beheaded him.

Or maybe he'd burn him. Or rip out his heart.

Doyle didn't know how—didn't care how—but he knew that the end was coming. That he was alive now only because Paul wanted to play with him or use him for a bargaining chip.

No. He had to think. Think and act and get himself free.

Andy.

He pulled her image close to him, using it to anchor his wildly spinning thoughts.

Another tremor rocked his body, and he focused on breathing. He sucked in air through his teeth and told himself he could stand it. But that, of course, was a goddamned lie. The Tasers they'd used to capture him had more power than the standard devices that were available on the open market. These were serious shit—a good shot would have killed a human. As it was, it had taken down a para-demon. He hated to admit it, but his enemies were formidable. And they had Andy.

Conjuring all his strength, he forced himself to look around, to focus on the room. Any little details that might help him escape this room and the violent attack of electricity.

There was nothing. A door. Walls. Metal all around. Not even a keypad. Just the small holes from which the Tasers shot. Just the door through which they'd drag his body once the energy had done its work and reduced him to rubble.

Think, dammit, think.

He lifted his hand, determined to find the strength to conjure a wormhole, and the movement was met with a lightning storm of currents. Movement, apparently, increased the storm. He tried again, hand thrust out, mind focused. But of course nothing happened. He'd known it wouldn't. He needed strength to call a wormhole, and the electricity was steadily sapping his strength.

The only way out was through that door. If he could gather enough energy—if he could pound against it hard enough—maybe he could blow it open.

A quick surge of excitement shot through him, and he focused on the door, sucked in air through his nose, and rushed forward. His scream of pain seemed to shake the walls as the electrical currents—the strongest so far—curled around him and through him. Too much. Too much...

And yet the current skittered over the door, too, ripples of sparking electricity scurrying across the polished metal like tiny spiders.

Maybe ... just maybe.

He backed up. One step, then another. Wincing with each movement as the currents shot from the walls, trying to snare him in their grip.

One, two, three.

Another leap forward and he tossed himself at the door. More skittering spiders. On the door. In his head. His hands buzzing and his feet tingling as the dancing currents swarmed over and through him. Over and over through the metal of the door.

It worked—it had to have worked.

But when he thrust himself against it again, the door stayed firmly closed, and Doyle had to accept the simple truth: He was trapped. Trapped and alone and helpless.

And terribly afraid for Andy.

TWENTY-SEVEN

Andrew peeled open his eyes and realized his cheek was pressed into something warm and sticky. Blood. His own blood.

He blinked, trying to remember, then gasped when it all came back in a flash. The gun. The bullet.

The pain.

He was on the floorboard of his car, and it was dark. Night?

No.

It took him a second, but when he could finally see through the driver's side window, he realized that he was in a garage. Someone had moved his car, then left him here.

Experimentally, he moved his fingers, and when they complied, he slowly lifted his hand to his head. He felt the warm and sticky injury, and when he brought his hand down he saw blood mixed with crushed bone and little bits of gray matter.

They'd left him for dead. They'd left him for dead because that's what he was. Or would be soon.

He didn't fear death, but for some reason he wasn't

ready for it. Why? What was he waiting for? Why couldn't he just let go and drift away to his reward?

Andy.

Fear, sharp and brutal, cut through him.

He remembered—his daughter was in danger.

He didn't understand everything that had happened, but he knew enough to know that Paul was dangerous— and that Andy was with him. Except she wasn't. She'd aligned herself with that creature. With Doyle. And if Paul knew about Doyle, then he surely knew about Andy.

And that meant Paul would hurt her. He'd hurt her the way he was hurting Doyle.

He gasped, his body convulsing as death edged near.

No. He pushed it back, determined to cling to life. Determined to think of a way to help his daughter.

But he was locked in a garage with a hole in his head. There was no way.

The vault.

The monster was in the vault.

If he released the monster...

But no, he couldn't do that. Doyle was evil. Inhuman. A demon cut from the fabric of hell.

Except Andy trusted him.

His daughter was a fool. But if Andrew didn't do something, then soon she'd be a dead fool.

With incredible effort, he gathered his strength, then reached up and grabbed the passenger door handle. He tugged, and the door clicked open. He pushed it ajar.

But he couldn't sit up.

Clawing at anything he could get purchase on, he tugged himself across the floorboard toward the door. And then, with one final push, he fell in a lump onto the concrete.

He lay there for a moment in a pained heap, telling

himself that he couldn't die. Not yet. He still had a job to do.

He looked around, searching for a way into Paul's house, then realized how much God was looking after him when he saw a door leading to the vault instead. It was on the far side of the room.

Why did it have to be on the far side?

He inched in that direction, making small moaning noises as he moved, leaving bits of blood and brain in his wake. He wouldn't even be a person by the time he got there, but he would get there. He'd get there, he'd free the monster, and then, dammit, he'd pray.

Just a few more feet, just a few more inches.

Yes.

He was there.

The latch, however, was too high. He'd need to get on his knees. But how? He didn't have the energy. There wasn't enough blood pumping through his veins. Do it.

He burst up, knowing this would be his only shot, and grabbed the metal handle before collapsing back onto the floor, his heart beating so hard it would surely explode.

The door clicked, then sagged open a single centimeter.

"Doyle," he whispered. But there was no reply.

"Doyle," he said again. *No, the monster couldn't be dead. Please, please don't let the monster be dead.*

"Doyle."

And then the door burst open and Doyle fell out, his skin mottled and burned, his eyes blazing.

He looked hard at Andrew, his expression confused.

"They have Andy," Andrew said. "Save her. Please. I'm trusting you to take care of my daughter."

For a moment, he wasn't sure the monster understood. Then his face softened, and Doyle nodded. "I will," he said, and Andrew believed him.

It was enough. It was all he could do.

Andrew let go, and let death take him away.

Andy.

From his prostrate position on the floor, Doyle looked at the body of Andrew Tarrant and said a silent thank-you. He'd given Doyle a chance. Given Andy a chance.

Now Doyle had to make sure he didn't waste it.

Exhausted, drained, he forced himself onto his feet, then shuffled, hunched over, to the far side of the garage and the door that he assumed led into the house. He had a vague, pain-tinged memory of being brought through here, Bryce holding him tight, the electricity coursing through him all the while.

Overcome, he stopped, then vomited on the concrete floor.

Weakness enveloped him. How the hell was he going to be of any use to anyone?

He reached the door, his hand resting on the knob. He turned it, and when nothing happened, he feared that it was locked. Then he realized he was so damn weak that he hadn't turned the knob forcefully enough.

Once he put all of his strength behind it, he managed to get the door open. He stepped over the threshold into a small kitchen. Not the kind of food that was going to give him strength.

He heard a noise from the next room, though. Foot-steps coming toward him. He looked around, knowing that he needed a place to hide. He didn't have the strength for a full-on attack. His only chance at survival was if he had the element of surprise.

Just in time, he slipped in behind the door. It swung open, then closed, and Travis Sullivan walked in. They'd left Travis here alone? Why?

And then the answer dawned on him—they'd used Sullivan's ID and parking card to access the building. Travis wouldn't want to incriminate himself, and Paul would agree—Travis's political position was too useful to compromise. So he'd say that he was kidnapped. His cards stolen. He was an innocent, drawn into something horrible.

Fuck.

With his back to Doyle, Travis started to walk toward a full pot of coffee on the far counter. Once he got to it, he'd turn around and see Doyle. Travis would have plenty of opportunity to grab a weapon because Doyle would be across the room from him.

Doyle wished he wasn't so weak, but he had to move now, and he lunged, grabbing the back of Travis's shirt and sending both of them tumbling to the floor.

"You!" Travis shouted, as he tried to push Doyle off of him.

"Me," Doyle said. "Need ... your ... help." Doyle bent closer, and he could smell the man's soul, could practically taste the essence of him, dark and rotting and tattered. But it was there. By the gods, it was right there.

And although Doyle reviled the direct taking of a soul —although he'd spent his life cursing himself and what he needed to do to survive—this time there were no curses. There was only joy in the knowledge that what he needed had come so willingly to him. And that by taking the soul of this putrid creature, he could gain the strength to stop Paul and, he hoped, save the woman he loved.

Power.

Doyle had never been so thrilled to feel the thrum of his demon half as he was when he broke the connection between him and Travis, who now lay in a heap on the floor. He wasn't dead, but he'd have one hell of a headache when he woke up, and Doyle had used a couple of extension cords to truss him up nice and tight.

He grabbed the politician's cellphone, only to discover that the goddamn thing didn't have a signal.

Fuck.

He saw a handset that was connected to the landline on the counter and he snatched it up. Dead.

He groaned.

Outside—he'd get a signal outside.

He was racing toward the door when he caught the scent of another human. He stiffened, fearing a trap, then realized that he knew that scent. *Creevey.*

Goddammit, the fucker was in the house.

He followed the scent, hurrying toward it until he found the bastard in a locked room.

Doyle ripped the door open.

"Shit, man, it's about time! They're about to nail your Shadower asses to the wall."

"They?" Doyle repeated. "I thought you were in tight with Paul. I thought you were the asshole who betrayed me."

"That fucker double-crossed me. You planning to bring him down? I'm the guy who can help you. Just get me the fuck out of here." He lifted his arm, and Doyle saw that he was handcuffed to a chair.

Doyle took one step toward him, then another. Then

he reached down, tugged on the handcuffs, and ripped the metal chain in two.

Creevey shook out his arm. "Nice trick, partner."

The little worm stood, and in one quick motion, Doyle had him around the neck, the murdering slimeball's body pressed up against his. He tilted his head and whispered in Creevey's ear. "I should suck your soul out, but I don't want to taint my own. But this is for what you did to Andy," he added, and then he grabbed Creevey's head and ripped the damn thing right off his body.

He shoved the body away and stepped back, avoiding the spray of blood. Then he left the room, left the house, and dialed Tucker's number from the sun-bleached yard.

"Now," he said. "The goddamn thing's going down now."

"Shit, Doyle, thank God." He heard Tucker call out to someone, telling them to put a stop to the search.

"Tucker!" Doyle yelled through the line. "Dammit, Tucker, Andy's with them. They're coming to blow up the building now, and Andy's with them."

"Doyle."

His partner's voice was low and serious, and dread writhed inside Doyle.

"You need to get your ass over here. Right now. Because I'm—"

Doyle didn't waste any time listening to what Tucker had left to say. He thrust out his hand, concentrating on his partner's voice. With more force than he'd ever used before, he drew energy in and through himself, spitting it back out in a long, spinning wormhole, a void that stretched through time and space, leading to the one place he wanted to be. Near Andy.

He leaped in, and tumbled out the other end, landing next to Tucker. "Where is she?" he demanded.

A tight-faced Tucker stood in front of a bank of video

monitors surrounded by a half-dozen other agents. Doyle followed his partner's gaze, his throat tightening at the sight displayed on the monitors. A dozen different camera angles focused on one single image: Andy, standing terrified on the plaza in front of the Criminal Justice Building, a vest filled with C4 explosives strapped tight to her body.

"How long?" Doyle asked, amazed his voice worked.

"Three minutes and forty-eight seconds ago, a black Cadillac paused in front of the building just long enough to let two people out. One stayed, the other got back in the car."

"Andy. And Paul."

"I'm so sorry."

"Have they made any demands?" Doyle knew the answer would be no. Paul didn't want anything except for the Shadowers to die.

"Not a goddamn thing," Tucker said.

Doyle clutched his hands at his sides, alternately forming and relaxing fists. He sucked in air, trying to stay calm. He wasn't any good to her if he couldn't think.

For the first time, he realized he didn't recognize the room into which the vortex had spit him. "Where are we?"

"Mobilization unit," Tucker said, referring to the tricked-out RV that Division 6 used for larger operations. "Core group moved in as soon as we became aware of the situation," he added, gesturing to the high-level RAC team commanders who shared the tight space with them.

"And the civilians? The humans?"

"We've started evac, but it's two in the afternoon. Everyone's back from lunch. The building is full up. And we haven't heard a word from Paul." Tucker's eyes met Doyle's. His expression was more serious than Doyle had ever seen it. "We don't know when he's planning to detonate the—"

Doyle was already at the door before Tucker finished

his sentence. Tucker might be a human, but he moved with preternatural speed to block him. "Don't," he said, grabbing Doyle's shoulder. "I know what you're going through—dammit, I do—but you rush in there without a plan, and you know she's dead."

Doyle slammed Tucker up against the wall, crossing his arm over his partner's throat. "Don't say that. Don't even think it."

"What I'm saying," Tucker said, "is be smart."

Doyle sucked in air and released his grip. Tucker was right. Dammit all, Tucker was right, and Andy was running out of time.

"What's the unit location?" he asked, referring to the RV they were in.

"Two blocks north of the building. Any farther and the video signal weakens. Local police and FBI have cleared the area, and we're now in a no-fly zone. No helicopters, no news cameras."

"And no word from Paul," Doyle said. "You already said as much. But do we have a lead on his location?"

"Nothing concrete," Tucker said.

"But?"

"But take a closer look at that vest," he said, tapping the screen. The RAC agents around them spoke into their microphones, communicating with one another and creating a constant buzz, like the drone of bees. Doyle tuned everything out except his focus on the screen.

"You see?" Tucker asked.

"No timing device."

"It's remote operated."

Doyle tilted his head up to look at his partner. "Then the son-of-a-bitch is nearby."

"The question is where."

"We do a search, it'll take too long." Tucker's expression was hard. "And he'll see us coming. Andy won't—"

Doyle lifted his hand. "Don't say it. Get Luke."

"Luke? Doyle, it's daylight. And he's with Leviathan in the command—"

The thin thread holding Doyle's temper in check snapped. "Goddammit, get Luke. I need him here. I need him here now."

TWENTY-EIGHT

Andy stood frozen, terrified her knees would lock up. That she'd fall. That Paul—who was, somehow, watching her—would see and think she was defying him. And then he'd push down the plunger.

She would almost welcome the end. At least then the fear would be over.

But she couldn't think like that. She needed to remember all the people who'd be dead. And Doyle—her heart ripped at the thought of never seeing him again.

Paul had told her that Doyle was still alive, but that he was being tortured, electricity ripping through him. Tearing him up from the inside. Frying him like a goddamned fast-food meal.

She'd wanted to punch the bastard in his face, so smug when he'd said those words to her. But the damned fear had stopped her. Fear, but mingled with hope.

Because Doyle could survive that. Doyle was smart and strong, and a lowlife like Paul was no match for him. They might think that they'd battled him down, but Andy didn't believe it. And she was determined to hold on until she knew the truth. So, dammit, she was staying alive, and Paul could just take his explosives and shove them, because she wasn't dying just because he wanted her dead.

She sucked in air, then let it out again slowly. In the middle of this hellish nightmare, it felt good to be defiant, even if it was only in her head. Her thoughts were the only refuge she had left.

Slowly, she shifted her legs, trying to keep her knees loose without looking like she was getting ready to run. Oh, how she wanted to run.

Was there something she could have done differently? Bryce had surprised her by grabbing her arms, pinning them tightly behind her back.

He'd wrestled her out the door and she'd found herself inside of a Cadillac with him and Paul, who'd grinned at her. "So glad you're on the team, Andy. It's a shame your father won't see your moment of triumph since he's dead. But you'll be joining him soon enough."

She shivered at the memory and squeezed her eyes shut, determined not to cry.

She remembered crying out for Doyle, his name echoing from her lips and seeming to hang in the overly thick air. She hadn't cared about concealing their relation-ship anymore—Paul obviously knew the truth. And although she knew that her cry wouldn't summon him, she drew courage from the sound of his name filling the air around her.

Once she was in the car, Bryce had pinned her to the huge bench seat in the back and forced her into the vest. She'd immediately known what it was. Not that she'd ever worn an explosive vest before, but she'd watched a lot of movies. It wasn't hard to figure it out.

The Cadillac slowed to a stop in front of the Criminal

Justice Building. "Stand there," Bryce had said. "Stand on the plaza and wait."

"Why the hell should I?"

"Let me explain this in words that you can understand," Paul said, leaning closer. "If you don't do as I say, your boyfriend will pay. Oh, yes. Doyle's still alive. But he won't be if you refuse to cooperate. I'm afraid the two of you are star-crossed lovers. You can sacrifice yourself willingly and I give you my word that he will live. Or you can both die. I confess I don't really care which way you choose."

She'd started to tremble at the mention of Doyle's name, and it had taken all of her concentration to keep her body under control. To make sure he couldn't see. She'd failed, and he'd smiled, smug in his certainty that he'd correctly identified her weakness.

But he'd also pushed her too far. She'd come to know Doyle. To really see him. And she knew damn well that he would sacrifice himself to save others. "I'm not getting out of this car," she'd said.

Maybe her defiance couldn't save the people in that building any more than it could save Doyle, but at least she was buying them time.

Paul was right about one thing—they were star-crossed lovers.

He'd just stared into her defiant eyes, his nostrils flaring as if he were breathing in the stench of her decision. "Bitch," he'd finally said, and then he'd grabbed her arm, yanked her out of the car, and forced her to the middle of the plaza.

"Stand still and be a good girl, and you'll buy yourself some time—and you can fantasize about your boyfriend saving you. But try to run, try to be clever, and I'll press the plunger that detonates your wardrobe."

"You'll do that anyway," she'd said.

"True. But this way you can have your fantasy. You can stand here and dream that your Doyle will swoop in and save you. That the FBI will rescue you. That your fairy godmother will wave her magic wand and send you to Never-Never Land. I'm doing you a favor. I'm giving you hope."

And as much as she hated Paul—as much as she wanted him dead—at that very moment, standing there with her knees aching and her body sagging under the weight of the vest, Andy had to admit that he was right. Because as she looked around the plaza and thought of the cameras hidden there, she really could believe that Doyle was looking back at her.

She believed ... and she clung gently to that fragile thing called hope.

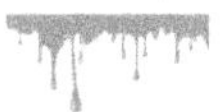

The door to the RV opened, and Luke burst in, swaddled from head to toe in a dark cloak. The team members, crowded tightly into the small space, parted like the Red Sea, opening a path from the door to Doyle.

Doyle moved forward to meet Luke as the vampire tossed the cloak aside.

"I need help," Doyle said. It had been years—centuries—since he'd said those words to Luke, and they rolled awkwardly off of his tongue.

"I'm sorry," Luke said. "I don't know how—"

"Dammit, Luke," Doyle spat, "don't you see what's going to happen to her? She's going to burn, she's going to die." He drew a breath. "For years I've been blaming you for what happened in France, for Kathryn's death. But it wasn't your fault. It was mine. It was mine, and it was

Kathryn's, because she wasn't willing to look past what I am to see me. But Andy is willing to do that. She does do that, and goddammit, I want a chance with her. Please, if there was ever a time when you were my friend, then don't deny me now."

"The fault for the past rests with both of us," Luke said. "And Ryan, I am your friend." He rested a hand on Doyle's shoulder, and Doyle closed his eyes, forcing himself not to shrug it off out of habit and frustration. "You helped me when Sara was in danger. Do you think I've forgotten that? There is nothing in my power that I wouldn't do to help you—and Andy. But it's daylight, Agent Doyle. You know as well as I do that my utility is severely limited." He waved his hand, indicating the RAC team. "These are good men. Use them."

"I intend to," Doyle said. "Blowing up Andy isn't Paul's primary objective. He wants to bring the whole building down, and an explosion on the plaza would only do minor damage. I've already sent a team into the parking garage and utility crawl spaces. These men are reviewing the surveillance footage from the last eighteen hours, hoping to find out where Travis or someone working with him planted explosives."

"She's a diversion," Luke said, his eyes focusing on the image of Andy in the monitor.

"She's the woman I love. And I need to find the man who holds her fate at the touch of a button…" He drew in a breath. "For that I need your help. I trust your abilities. Dammit all, I trust you."

Luke's expression didn't shift, but something dark seemed to fade from his eyes. "What exactly do you have in mind?"

"Mist," Doyle said. "If you transform into mist you can cover a broader area. You can find him, and you can keep him from detonating the explosives for long enough for me to get Andy out of that goddamned jacket."

"Not a bad plan," Luke said. "Unless he happens to be watching from a rooftop. I won't do you any good if I burst into flames."

"Your cloak will transform with you," Doyle said, knowing full well that the cloak would be a significant hindrance during the fight. "Look, it's your eyes I need. As mist, you have a better perspective. You can get into places that our satellite surveillance can't. The team hasn't found him yet. I think you can." He sure as hell hoped he could.

Luke nodded toward the monitors. "Have the team track me as well. If I find him, I'll maneuver in a circular pattern before descending. That can be your signal to move in on Andy, too—to get her out of that vest while I get the plunger from Paul. I won't be able to send any other signal." He indicated his clothes. "No weapons, no tech. You know how it works. I change into mist, and this is what I've got to work with."

"You'll do it, though?"

"For you? For Andy? Yes," Luke said. "Of course."

Luke moved as sentient mist over the heart of downtown Los Angeles. He tried to stay in the shadows—though the sun wouldn't destroy him as mist, it did sap his strength in much the same way as hematite. And although Paul was human, Luke was sure he would be well armed for battle against a vampire, and Luke was hardly going to be at his best.

He saw the RAC team tracking him from below,

watching the glimmer of mist in the sky, waiting to report back to Doyle when he found the target and moved in. Luke only hoped their plan would work. Paul could choose to set off the detonator whenever he felt like it. At any second, they could lose not only Andy but the building, and all the people who were still in the midst of evacuating.

He thought of Doyle—of the friendship they'd once shared. He had no illusions that they could rebuild what had been lost over so many years. But perhaps they could build something new. If this mission failed, though ... if Andy died ... Luke wasn't sure that Doyle would recover. He'd heard the tone of Doyle's voice—the need there.

No, not need. *Love.*

Losing her now would destroy Doyle in a much deeper way than he'd been destroyed before. And not only would Luke lose the potential to rebuild a friendship—the PEC would lose one of its best agents.

He pushed the thoughts from his mind. He wasn't going to fail, so there was no point in running scenarios through his head. Instead, he focused all of his attention on the ground, searching for the man whose visage he'd become so familiar with over the past few days. It was an exercise in futility. Paul could be inside a building. In a car. Hidden in the subway tunnels underneath the streets. If he was somehow tapping into the building's exterior video feed, he'd be able to tell what was happening on the plaza even without a direct visual. All he'd need to do was stay in range so that he could detonate with the hand trigger and—

What was that?

His eyes were drawn to the crowd that had gathered beyond the police blockade. Some were standing, necks craning as they tried to see what was happening at the Criminal Justice Building. Others were moving about, taking care of their own business. And then there was one man who was making his way through a small open area, distinct from the other businessmen because of his bulky overcoat and hat. The weather was mild, so the coat seemed out of place. Swirling in closer, Luke could see it was filthy. The hat, too. Homeless, he thought, and almost dismissed him. But then he saw the man's shoes. Perfectly polished. So shiny they practically reflected the sun.

And he saw the small handheld television that peeked out of one of the man's coat pockets.

This man wasn't homeless. He wasn't homeless at all.

Luke rose into the sky and circled, hopefully catching the attention of the lookouts. Then he hurtled toward the man, a rocket of mist that transformed right in front of the man's eyes. A handful of humans stumbled backward, confused and scared by Luke's sudden materialization. Luke ignored them. He was only interested in the man in front of him. The one who wasn't scared or surprised. The one who knew exactly what was happening.

Paul.

"Hello, vampire," Paul said, and as he spoke, some of those supposedly confused humans rushed forward. Paul's team. Well, shit.

Luke rushed forward, too, pulling Paul to him, then yanking the human's hands out of his pockets.

No detonator.

Paul began to laugh. "You're chasing the wrong person, vampire," he said. "And now for my second act," he added, as five humans rushed forward, grabbed Luke's black cloak, and yanked it off of him even as Paul put on a burst of speed and fled the area.

Luke's face and arms immediately started to burn. There was an oleander bush nearby, and he dove for it, protecting his body in the shade even as the RAC team swooped in. They managed to snatch three of Paul's men, but he was long gone.

"Go!" Luke ordered the team as one of the RAC members draped a blanket over him. "Contact Doyle. Tell him Paul did not—repeat, not—have the plunger. The vest is still hot. Tell him to stand down. Tell him to stand the fuck down before the entire building blows—and him and Andy along with it."

TWENTY-NINE

Only a few minutes had passed—Andy knew that—and yet it felt like it had been hours. Maybe she should run? At least then she'd be trying. And if she headed toward the street, away from the building's entrance, it might dilute the brunt of the impact when Paul pushed the button and turned her into a human mushroom cloud.

Oh God, oh God, oh God.

Should she? Could she?

She thought of Doyle's strength. And she wished desperately that he was beside her. She wanted him to tell her what to do. Wanted him to tell her it would be all right. Because even though Andy had always prided herself on her independence, right now the last thing she wanted was to be alone.

Better this way. No sense taking anyone else into the abyss.

Of course. Of course. God, her mind was in a muddle. She craved him, yet she also wanted him far away and safe.

The air seemed to shimmer in front of her. Fear was

messing with her mind. Making her vision go wonky. No, not that. Making her imagination fly. What had Paul said about fairy godmothers? Well, that wasn't what she was imagining. But she was fantasizing that Doyle was somehow going to come for her. That he would materialize in front of her and then, poof, they'd both fly off into the sunset.

It was a lovely fantasy, and so clear in her mind that she could picture him stepping right out of the air, her name on his lips. His face was pulled into harsh lines of fear, but his eyes were shining with love.

And then his lips were on hers and he was unbuckling the vest and—

"Doyle!" He was real. Dear God, he was real. "How did you—?"

"Wormhole," he said, which made no sense, but now wasn't the time to ask.

"The vest! They're watching. Don't—"

He kissed her, silencing her, and all her fears evaporated. "Luke has him. You're safe. Let's get you out of this and out of here."

"Yes," she said. "Yes, let's do that now."

He was on the last buckle when he cocked his head sideways and tapped his ear.

"What?" she asked.

His face crumbled and his already quick fingers shifted to frantic, dancing over the last strap that was securing the vest to her.

"What?" she repeated. "Doyle, talk to me."

"That was Tucker. Luke found Paul, but he didn't have the detonator."

For a moment, she didn't understand. Then she gasped. "Bryce. But that means—" Her gaze cut to the front of the building, where she knew the cameras were looking down on them. "If they can see us."

"I know … I know…"

He got the strap off.

"Doyle!"

"It's off!"

"Doyle!"

A silver disc that she'd assumed was some sort of rivet holding the explosives in place had turned red.

"Fuck!" he cried. He hurled the vest straight up into the air, all of his strength sending it flying at an incredible speed. "Get down!" he yelled, shoving her to the ground, and covering her body with his own even as he thrust his hand out, and, as she watched, the air around them started spinning into a vortex—a vortex that just happened to be right in the vest's trajectory.

In it went, into a dark, curving tube that looked like the inside of a garden hose. And then, just as the blackness filled with the noise and spark of the vest bursting into a million pieces, exploding with so much force it seemed to rock everything around them, the vortex snapped shut and—poof—there was nothing in front of them but air.

He pulled her into his arms and kissed her as she clung to him, so overcome with relief that she had to fight to form words once he pushed away, his hands stroking her face as if he couldn't quite believe she was real. "What was—I mean, where—? Where is it?"

"Space," he said. "I sent it into outer space."

She held him close, unable to stop smiling. "You really are the most amazing man."

"Don't you forget it."

They clung to each other again, then Doyle pushed her away. "I want you to get into the control van with Tucker." He nodded at one of the uniformed RAC officers who was running toward them. "Bryce is still out there somewhere. I want you safe."

"And you? You're going to go looking for him?"

"I'm going into the building," he said, his expression hard. "You were a diversion. We're certain he's wired the building to blow."

She clutched his hand. "Be careful," she said as a thin mist, like a haze above a swamp in winter, shimmered in front of them, transforming as she watched into the large form of Luke Dragos, who was wrapped in a heavy cloak. "Paul's a wild card," he said.

Doyle's eyes cut immediately to Andy. "What are you talking about?"

"He was ready for us. He had a team with him—they yanked my cloak and Paul pulled a disappearing trick. The RAC team managed to snag three of Paul's men, but Paul himself got away."

Doyle cursed. "We can't worry about him right now. We need to lock down the rest of the explosives."

Andy wanted to tell the RAC officer who was escorting her that she could make it to the control van on her own, except she knew damn well that Doyle would be furious if she did. Not only that, but as much as she wanted to be independent and strong, she also knew that she was no match for Paul and Bryce.

Better to keep the escort.

"You're not a vamp," Andy said. "Werewolf?"

The officer nodded once. And that was the end of that conversation.

They walked a few more yards in silence, but then Andy couldn't stand it any longer. She needed to talk with someone. Needed that activity to keep her fears at bay.

Because no matter how confident Doyle seemed, the basic fact was that he was heading into the bowels of the building to look for explosives, and that really didn't sound like much of a safe plan.

"How much farther?"

"Not far," her guard said. "The van's parked around that corner. Just down these stairs," he said, as he led her down into the architectural plaza of the building next door. "Then we veer to the right and—"

She never learned what they were going to do after they veered right, because her escort stumbled, then slumped to the ground, a single silver bullet pierced through his heart. She saw him as he flinched, right at the point of impact, and instead of running or dropping to the ground, she went for his weapon, grabbing it and aiming it in the direction of the sound that had rung out the instant before the werewolf had fallen.

She got off three rounds, then heard a thud at the top of the shallow flight of marble stairs. Quickly, she rushed in that direction, and found that one of her three bullets had gotten Bryce square in the chest.

He wasn't dead yet, though, and he swung his gun arm up and around, his movements slow but full of dark purpose.

She fired twice more, and his hand dropped limp to his side. She kicked the gun out of his hand and stood there, sucking in air and trying very hard not to hyperventilate.

"An excellent display," Paul said from the shadows near the front entrance of the office building.

She spun and fired—but this time the gun only clicked.

"It's a specially designed gun," he said, stepping to her side and taking it out of her hand. His own gun was aimed at her, and because of it, she chose not to run. "I have a supplier who sells them to me, and apparently he also sells them to Division Six. They shoot bullets that are a combination of wood and silver. Protection against both vampires and werewolves. But because of the unorthodox nature of the ammunition, the chamber holds only five rounds."

"You'll never get away with it."

"I think you're wrong." He flashed a wide smile. "Won't it be interesting to see which of us is right. And which of us is dead."

"You need to feed," Doyle told Luke as they plodded through the building's huge, multileveled parking structure. "You're weak. I can see it in your face."

"Mist. Daylight. Not an extraordinary combination." He faced Doyle. "The place has been rigged. We'll find the charges—but you know as well as I do that our bad guys are long gone by now. They're kicking back in a hotel somewhere with the television tuned to CNN so they can watch the coverage of the Los Angeles Criminal Justice Building getting taken down by an unnamed group of terrorists."

"They won't stay unnamed for long. Paul's going to want credit, even if he only announces himself to the Shadowers."

Ahead of them, RAC team members spread out, some led by bomb-sniffing dogs, others by werens who'd also been trained in bomb detection.

"How far along is the evac?" Doyle called to one of the men.

"Fifty-seven percent, sir."

Doyle nodded. It seemed like such a small amount

considering that it felt like this entire ordeal had taken forever. On the clock, though, it hadn't even been ten minutes since Andy had been dragged out onto the plaza.

"Got something, sirs!" A young ordnance officer called out to Doyle and Luke, and they hurried forward. Sure enough, one of the support columns was packed with C4 —and the timer was only two minutes away from zero. "Wouldn't take the whole building down," the officer said, "but if he put similar wads in the other support beams…"

"On it," Doyle said. He raced in one direction, and Luke shot off in the other. Sure enough, another wad of C4 had been packed in the northeast support beam. Doyle disarmed it and continued racing against time. No way to be sure, but it was a rectangular building. Four in the corners, one in the middle. If Luke and the officer got the other two corners, that left the center beam. It was possible there were charges more deeply hidden within the building, but he doubted it. The explosives had undoubtedly been planted by Travis or one of his lackeys. They'd want to stay in places that were normally accessible by the building's personnel. A parking garage was easy—and since the team had already checked the other floors, Doyle hoped that meant that they were on the trail of the last of the C4.

He sprinted toward the final support column, knowing that only seconds were left.

He didn't make it.

He was still yards away when the charge exploded, sending great chunks of concrete and rebar flying through the air.

Doyle ducked, then crawled forward, trying to see through the dust.

What he saw made his stomach twist.

The building hadn't collapsed—one column crumbling wasn't enough to do that. For that matter, he doubted it had even been noticeable enough from the outside to catch the attention of the press. But it had caused one hell of a mess. And—he saw as he looked around—right there, in the mess, was Luke.

Doyle hurried to his side. "Good job," he deadpanned, masking his fear. "You found the last one."

His friend didn't answer.

No. Oh, please, no.

"Luke? Dammit, Luke—"

The vampire's eyes opened, and Doyle could see his pain. Hell, he could smell it.

"My leg," Luke said, and Doyle peered through the dust to see that at least three tons of concrete and steel had smashed down on Luke's leg.

"Shit. Can you move it?"

Luke's smile was thin. "Even on my best day, I doubt it. Weak like I am..." He trailed off.

"You need strength." He rolled up his sleeve. "Drink." But Luke only shook his head.

"Dammit, Luke. Drink."

Doyle's earpiece buzzed. It was Tucker, wanting a report.

"What the hell happened?"

Doyle told him, ending with the news about Luke and a request that a medical team be sent in, along with several bags of blood. "Tell Andy I'm fine and I'll be there as soon as I'm sure Luke's okay."

"Andy? I thought she stayed with you."

Doyle's blood ran cold. "She didn't go back to command? She's not with you?"

"Oh, shit," Tucker said. "I'll start pulling up video feeds. Maybe we can find her."

"Go," Luke said, the moment Doyle dropped his hand away from his earpiece.

"You heard?"

"Enough. I said go. Go now."

Doyle stood, ready to run away to do just that. Then he paused and looked back at Luke. "I love her."

"All the more reason to run to her."

THIRTY

"Anything?" Doyle spoke into the headset as he rushed, dust-covered, out of the garage. The immediate area was clear; beyond that, a huge crowd had gathered, currently held at bay by the human police department. For a moment, he wondered where the more exotic Shadowers were, but then he realized that he honestly didn't give a damn. Right now the only thing he cared about was Andy.

"Got them on the north camera. They crossed the plaza and were heading around the building next door en route to the RV."

"After that?"

"We're scouring traffic cameras and ATM footage. So far, nothing."

"Fuck."

"I'll mobilize the werens on the team. We'll find the scent, Doyle. We'll find Andy."

"I'm coming in. I want to see all the footage. Maybe I'll catch something you missed."

"I'll have it ready for you."

Doyle tapped the earpiece, shutting down their

conversation. He didn't want Tucker in his head. Not when Andy was with Paul. Paul, the son-of-a-bitch who Doyle wished was shut up in a hotel room watching CNN like Luke had said, because then—

Wait a minute. Wait one goddamn minute.

He pulled out his phone and did a search for nearby hotels. The closest was the Warford, just down the hill. Obvious, considering that's where Paul had thrown his party for Kevin and the boys. But Paul thought he was smarter than everyone else. And he certainly never thought he'd be caught.

He was there. Doyle was certain of it.

He was there, and now that his operation had taken a right turn toward failure, he was pissed. And that couldn't be good for Andy.

He turned his earpiece back on and conveyed his suspicions to Tucker. "Check the register for me."

"Not registered," Tucker reported back. "But there's a Dirk Warfield in the penthouse. D.W. Dark Warrior. Might be a coincidence, or—"

"It's not," Doyle said. "He's there. I'm going in."

"I'm sending backup."

"Do not engage," Doyle ordered. "Not without my authorization. I don't want a team bursting in. Paul's got an itchy trigger finger. We've contained the threat at the building; I don't want to increase the risk to Andy."

"Understood. We won't move until you say so."

At the hotel front desk, he flashed his badge to a twenty-something girl who looked awestruck that someone from Homeland Security was interested in one of their guests. "I need to know if there's another way into the penthouse. Staff elevator?"

"Nothing that's, well, real," she said.

"What's that supposed to mean?"

She gnawed on her lower lip. "No one's supposed to

know about it—I mean, we worked really hard to keep it out of the papers—but last year some frat boys from UCLA broke into the penthouse suite by shimmying down a pipe that runs from the roof to the balcony."

"Did they? And the pipe's still there?"

"It would be a huge deal to move it. Something to do with plumbing and codes and the fact that the building is so old."

"You've been very helpful." He paused before walking away. "And how exactly do I get to the roof?"

When he first dragged her into the penthouse, Paul was positively cheerful.

"Almost time for the show," he said as he clicked on the television. He sank into one of the leather chairs and lit a cigar, then gestured toward the sofa. "Sit," he said. "I insist."

She sat, her eyes on the television and the exterior shot of the Criminal Justice Building that took up the whole screen.

"Now, don't be so nervous." Paul poured a glass of wine from a carafe on the coffee table, then passed it to her. "Sit. Watch. I'm not going to kill you. Not yet, anyway," he said, then laughed as if he'd just said the funniest thing ever.

"How long until you blow it up?" she asked. She didn't want to give him the satisfaction, but she had to know.

Paul glanced down at his watch. "Just over a minute." He stood up then, and moved around the room, adjusting wires and cables—all presumably related to some elaborate security system—then dropped back into his armchair. He left his cigar in the ashtray, and as it burned down, the sickly sweet scent set her stomach on edge.

Andy sat and pretended to sip her wine as she tried to think what she could do to get out of this mess.

Then the timer on his watch beeped, and Andy jumped in her chair. Paul, however, leaned forward, his grin wide. But that grin soon faded.

"No," he whispered, the word coming out like a curse. "No, goddammit, no!"

Then he launched himself out of his chair, sending his glass of Scotch flying across the room to shatter against the far wall.

Andy tried to disappear into the couch, and for a while it seemed to work. Paul had apparently forgotten she was there.

But she now had to shift—the leg she'd tucked up under her had gone completely numb—and when she did he stalked up to her, lashed out, and smacked her hard across the cheek. "Bitch," he cried. "Do you have any idea what you've cost me? What those filthy demonic creatures you've sidled up to have cost me?"

She didn't answer. Nothing she could say would be right. Better to say nothing at all.

He slapped her again, so hard her head whipped to the side.

When it did, she saw Doyle.

He was on the patio, and he indicated the door handle, then pressed a finger to his lips, and she looked away, staring hard into Paul's eyes. Trying to hold them tight with her hate.

A sharp cracking sound rang out from near the balcony door, and Paul shifted to look in that direction. She expected an expression of shock or fear—Doyle was here after all. Instead, Paul just looked amused.

Not a good sign, and when Andy shifted to see what

was amusing him, her stomach twisted with dread. The cracking was the sound of electricity. Paul had wired the doorframe, and now Doyle was caught in an electric web, shaking violently where he'd fallen in the doorway.

"I thought you might escape from the vault. And if you did, I was certain you'd eventually drop in on us. Rude not to knock, Doyle. Very rude indeed."

"What can I say?" Doyle replied, his voice rough and scratchy. "I like to make an entrance."

"Hmm." Paul's mouth curved into a frown, and he walked toward a small metal box on the floor near the patio door. "I thought I set this high enough that I wouldn't have to listen to idle chitchat." He twisted a knob, and Doyle writhed in agony on the floor.

"Stop!" Andy cried. "Please, please stop!"

But Paul didn't stop. He just kept twisting the knob higher and higher. And Doyle kept writhing and twisting, moaning and screaming.

"Please," she whispered, tears streaming down her face. "Please. You're going to kill him." She said it flatly, but inside she was filled with grief and impotence. What could she do? What the hell could she do?

"Kill him? Of course I'm going to kill him." He twisted the knob and reduced the voltage. "But first I'm going to play with him."

"Dammit, no!" Andy screamed and launched herself at him, but he backhanded her and sent her flying.

"Do not fuck with me."

She looked at Doyle, and she could see some of the awareness return to his eyes. But if he had any ideas about what they could do to get out of this mess, he wasn't sharing them.

"Please," she said. "Can I say goodbye?"

"You ask that as if you think I'm a monster. I'm not.

That's your problem, Andy. You've forgotten which side you should be on."

It would be so easy to lie and say that she was on his side. But she couldn't do it. He probably wouldn't believe her anyway, but she couldn't even force herself to try.

Instead, all she said was, "Please. Can I kiss him? One kiss before you take everything away from me. Dammit, Paul, you killed my father. You owe me that."

"Owe you?" he repeated.

"He was your friend," she said, the words low. "Please. If that meant anything to you at all."

He stared at her, and she was certain he was going to refuse. But then, to her relief, he gave her one quick nod. "But I'm keeping the power low. You're gonna get a buzz. And if you try anything, I'll fry you both. Understand?"

"I don't think he's in any condition to try anything," she said, trying to keep her face bland. Trying to hide her fear that he would stop her before she could do the only thing she could think of that might save them.

Doyle was dreaming.

Andy was there, her lips brushing over his. "Take," she whispered, so low that only his preternatural hearing could catch it. "Take, get strong. There's a cigar in the ashtray on the table. It's lit."

Such a pleasant dream. Her lips on his. Her tongue urging his mouth to open wider. Her soul, so sweet and strong. He could hear her voice again. "Take, take, take."

And he realized with mild confusion that this wasn't a dream. It was real and it was wonderful and Andy was here and here was...

Where was here?

And then he remembered.

"Now, Doyle. Take now."

He heard the urgency in her voice. Saw Paul standing so smug a few yards away. His mind was slow—it took him a second. But then he got it.

And because she had offered—and because he needed it—he closed his mouth over hers and let her warm, vibrant, beautiful soul flow in.

As it did, his mind became clearer and his muscles instantly became stronger.

He took and took, until he gently pushed her away. She collapsed onto the ground beside him, a smile of smug satisfaction on her lips.

Paul cursed in confusion, but he didn't wait to figure out what was going on. He started to turn the dial on the box that controlled the electricity—and Doyle realized that Andy was now lying right on top of the primary wires. And the wires were hot.

Screw that.

Doyle thrust out his hand toward the cigar, then pulled it back in, urging the flame to grow. A huge flame shot up on the table, scorching the ceiling before settling down to a more manageable two feet in height. It leaped off the table, caught on a wind of Doyle's making, which spun Paul around and around, right into the dancing flames.

The son-of-a-bitch screamed and then dropped to the floor. He banged wildly at his legs, trying to put them out, his stream of curses filling the air.

Doyle pulled Andy into his arms. "Are you okay?"

"I'm perfect now. Are you going to shoot him into space, too?"

"Not a bad idea. But I have another destination in mind." With one hand, he held her tightly to him. With the other, he reached into the air and drew forth the void. It whipped around, then it grabbed on to Paul, and sucked him inside.

"If not space, then where?"

"Division Six. Detention. As much as I'd like to see him dead, I think my satisfaction will be just as great when he's executed after trial."

Andy got up on her knees, leaned over, and kissed him.

"What was that for?"

"What do you think? Because I love you."

And since that answer couldn't be beat, he leaned over and kissed her back.

And then again and again and again.

"Is it really over?" she asked, after about a dozen kisses.

"It's over." He pulled her into his arms. "Andy—your father."

She closed her eyes. "I know. Paul killed him."

"Paul shot him, yes. But he didn't die instantly."

He saw her head tilt up and the question flash in her eyes. "What happened?"

"Your father rescued me. If it weren't for him, I'd still be trapped in that vault."

Her hand reached for his neck and the cross that still hung under his shirt. He took her hand and pressed it against the cross, covering it with his own hand.

"He told me he was trusting me to protect you."

The corner of her lips curved up, and a single tear spilled down her cheek. "He said that?"

"He did. I promised him I would. Andy," he said, tilting her chin up, "I'll never stop."

"I know," she said, leaning into his embrace. "I never want you to."

They sat like that until Doyle remembered Tucker and

the rest of the team. "Come on," he said, standing up and holding out his hand for her. "Time to go. It's been one hell of a long day."

They met up with Tucker in the hotel lobby and walked back to the Criminal Justice Building together, as Tucker filled them in on the progress of the cleanup and the final sweep for any potentially missed explosives. Then Andy told Tucker about what had happened in the penthouse. She didn't finish, though. As soon as she crested the hill and the plaza came into sight she went quiet and stopped on the sidewalk, holding tight to Doyle's hand.

"We won," she said.

"We disabled most of the explosives," Doyle said. "But one section of the garage is a mess."

"Doesn't matter," she said. "In the end, we won and the bad guys lost." Her smile was as bright as the sun. "Score one for the good guys," she said. "And evil can just go take a hike."

Doyle laughed, then twined his fingers through hers as they stood there, looking at the building he knew so well. After a moment, he turned and met Tucker's eyes. "It's a whole new ballgame now, isn't it?" Tucker asked.

Doyle thought of the humans who knew that the Shadowers existed. Men like Paul's mercenaries, who'd apparently survived the assault. Men like Paul himself, who might even be able to spur others to action from his cell.

"Yeah," Doyle said to Tucker. "It is."

But that was okay, he thought, hooking his arm around Andy's waist and pulling her close. The future might be new, but he was going into it with the woman he loved.

THIRTY-ONE

Andy grabbed the package off the front step of the house and then raced inside to find Doyle.

"It's here!" she called. "Look, it's here!"

He came in from the kitchen, trailed by Luke and Tucker and Sara, who'd come over for dinner. CeeCee was already on the couch plugged into an iPod, but she looked up at the sound of the commotion and yanked out her headphones.

"What is it?" Tucker asked.

"My book." She ripped off the tape from the box and pulled out the packing. A stack of paperbacks were inside, the title shining out at her: In the Shadows.

"I got into all of this because I wanted to write a book about Paul and all his crazy beliefs. But once I found out that the world he believed in wasn't so crazy, I knew I was out of luck."

"You'd look as crazy as he did," Sara said, smiling.

"So I called it fiction." She handed them each a copy. "Don't worry. I changed all the key details."

Luke took it and laughed. "I can't wait to read it."

Doyle pulled her close and kissed her, and she leaned

against him, happier than she could remember being. "Some people will know it's not fiction," he said. "Paul's wasn't the only cell."

"Let them know," Tucker said. "They'll know we fight back."

"And not all humans think the Shadowers are evil," CeeCee added.

"No," Andy agreed, as Doyle squeezed her hand. "A lot of us know better."

She twisted in his arms and pressed her lips to his, joining him for a celebratory kiss. And when she did, she felt a bit of her soul break free. But it wasn't frightening— it was beautiful, and her soul twined with his, melding and joining.

Forever.

I hope you enjoyed Hurt Me Sweetly! This is the end of the series, but there might be more later (or other series or from me!) So be sure to sign up for my newsletter so you don't miss anything!

I would love it if you would spread the word and post a review at Amazon and Goodreads, along with sharing on your social media! As you know, reviews help authors tremendously!

And, of course, be sure to follow me! You can find me at Amazon, Bookbub, Goodreads, Facebook, and, of course, at my website!

ABOUT THE AUTHOR

Kira James is the semi-secret paranormal pen name of a *New York Times* bestselling author. As such, she lives mostly in someone else's head. Which, frankly, isn't such a bad deal, and definitely saves on rent.

You can find her at:
https://www.kirajamesauthor.com

Be sure to sign up for Kira's Elite Reader Group so you don't miss any news about this or other series! (Not to mention bonus scenes, character tidbits, and more!)